散文欣賞學英語

編著者 / 何高大

萬人出版社

前　言

　　喜歡散文的讀者有福了，本書收集經典散文３５篇，以中英文對照，並配上了文章欣賞，使你更能去體會、更有興趣，去學習本書，除了能提昇你寫作能力、閱讀能力，並對欣賞散文能力益助良多。

　　在文章翻譯的過程中，筆者既遵循「忠實原文」的原則，又儘可能使之美化，而欣賞部份，筆者費時多載精心完成，希望讀者好好利用它、珍惜它！

作者　謹識

目　錄

1.Of Praise

Francis Bacon

Praise is the reflection of virtue; but it is as the glass or body which gives the reflection. If it is from the common people, it is commonly false and naught, and rather follows vain persons than virtuous. For the common people understand not many excellent virtues. The lowest virtue draw praise from them; the middle virtues work in them astonishment or admiration; but of the highest virtues they have no sense or perceiving at all. But shows, and species virtutibus similes, serve best with them. Certainly fame is like a river that bears up things light and swollen and drowns things weighty and solid. But of persons of quality and judgement concur, then it is: (as the Scripture says,) A good man is like a fragrant of ointment; not fills all round about, and will not easily away. For the odours of ointments are more durable than those flowers. There are so many false points of praise, that a man may justly hold it a suspect. Some praise proceed merely of flattery; and if he is an

1. 論 讚 揚

弗朗西斯·培根

讚揚是品德才能的反映，但它具有如鏡子或其它反映影像的物體般的特徵。如果讚揚來自平常的人，那麼這種讚揚往往是虛假的、毫無價值的，但正中虛偽者的下懷，因為平常之人對才德了解不深刻。他們讚揚的是末流的才德；對中等的才德是驚訝或者羨慕；但對於最上品的才德，他們毫無辨別和察覺的能力。他們酷愛的是賣弄、炫耀以及"貌似德才的東西"。聲譽的確猶如江河，浮載輕飄鼓脹之物，質量之體則穩沉江底。然而，倘若身份高貴的人和有識之士交口稱讚，那麼，這便猶如《聖經》所說"美名賽過名貴的香膏"，香氣四溢，經久不散。因為香膏的香氣比花卉的香氣更加持久不衰。虛情假意的讚揚錯處雜多。人們完全有理由對它置疑。有些讚揚純粹出於逢迎；如果這是個普通的吹捧者，那麼這人就只會幾套

ordinary flatter, he will have certain common at-
tributes which may serve every man; if he is
cunning flatter, he will follow the arch-flatter,
which is a man's self, and wherein a man
thinks best of himself, therein the flatter, will
uphold him most; but if he is an impudent flat-
terer, look wherein a man is conscious to himself that he is most defective and is most out of
countenance in himself, that will the flatter en-
title him to perforce, spreta conscientia. Some
praise come of good wishes and respects, which
is a form due in civility to kings and great persons, to teach by praising, when by telling men
what they are, they represent to them what they
should be. Some men are praised maliciously to
their hurt, thereby to stir envy and jealously towards them; The worst class of enemies are men
who praise you, insomuch as it was a proverb a-
mong the Grecians, that he that was praised to
his hurt should have a push rise upon his nose,
as we say, that a blister will rise upon one's
tongue that tells a lie. Certainly moderate
praise, used with opportunity, and not vulgar,
is that which does the good. Solomon says, He
that praises his friend aloud, siring early, it is

普通的諛辭,這些諛辭對誰都可以適用;如果這是
個奸詐的馬屁精,他會模仿頭號吹捧者———即一
個人的自我。一個人自認哪方面最強,奸詐的馬
屁精就會在哪方面拼命抬高他;如果這是個無恥
的諂媚之徒,那麼他就會尋覓一個人在哪方面有
缺陷和在哪方面自己最感羞愧,然後便千方百計
使人覺得在哪方面是盡善盡美的,也就是說促使
那人"藐視自己的感覺"。有些讚美出於善意和敬
意,這類讚美往往是對帝王和偉人們表示的一種
應有的禮貌方式,所謂"寓規誠於讚美";即當他們
說是如何如何的時候,實際上是向他們指出應該
如何如何。有些人受到讚揚,實質卻是受到惡意
的傷害,因為讚揚的用意在於挑起別人對他們的
嫉羨妒恨;"那吹捧你的人就是你最危險的敵人。"
所以希臘人流傳這樣一句成語:"受到惡意讚揚,
鼻上要生小瘡。"英國人也有一句成語:"說謊自有
惡報,舌上長起水泡。"適宜的讚揚,使用得當,且
不鄙俗,是確有好處的。所羅門說:"清早讚揚朋

to him no better than a curse. Too much magnifying if man or matter does irritate contradiction, and procure envy and scorn.

友,無異對他詛咒。"過分誇大其人,過分誇大其事,必然激起矛盾、產生嫉妒、引起蔑視。

欣賞

　　讀了此篇散文,我們不禁會想到這麼一個事實:幾乎每一個成功者,幾乎每一個偉大的政治家,每一個腰纏萬貫的富豪都是憑借別人的讚美獲得成功的。從人際關係角度看,在人與人的相處中,每個人都想得到對方的讚美,假如得不到的話,就表明自己在對方的心目中缺乏地位。因此,他的人際關係便是失敗的。不錯,成功的人都會獲得別人由衷的讚美,正如培根所說"讚美是品德才能的反映。"但現實的生活告訴我們,並不是所有的讚美都是美意。培根指出"有些讚美出於假意或逢迎,這號人就是'馬屁精',是'無恥之徒'。"培根的觀點反映了當時英國社會人際關係的複雜性。

　　在藝術表現手法上,作者細膩的分析,夾敍夾議,雖無驚人之筆,卻不講乏味的理論,只談實感,只引實例。且娓娓動聽,明白透徹。文章中那信手拈來的引用,那貼切生動的比喻,無不讓人動情,無不令人叫絕。

2.Of Beauty

Francis Bacon

Virtue (elsewhere Bacon notes that 'virtue is nothing but inward beauty' and 'beauty nothing but outward virtue' (Works, IV.473).) is like a rich stone, best plain set: and surely virtue is best in a body that is comely, though not of delicate features, and that has rather dignity of presence than beauty of aspect. Neither is it generally seen, that very beautiful persons are otherwise of great virtue, as if nature were rather busy not to err, than in labour to produce excellency. And therefore they prove accomplished, but not of great spirit, and study rather behaviour than virtue. But this holds not always; for Augustus Caesar, Titus Vespasianus, Philip the Faur, King of France, Edward the Fourth of England, Alcibiades of athens, Ismael the sophy of Persia, were all high and great spirits, and yet the most beautiful men of their times. In beauty, that of favour is more than that of colour, and that of decent and gracious motion more than that of favour. That is the best

2．論　　美

弗朗西斯·培根

　　美德猶如一塊瑰麗的寶石，在素樸襯托下最美。當然美德如果是在一個容貌雖不姣美，但卻形體較好，氣質高貴的身體裡，那是再好不過了。不過一般說來，很美的人在其他方面不見得有什麼大的美德；好像造物主在其繁忙的工作中只求平淡無過，並不刻意創造完美的事物似的。所以，那些很美的人雖然看上去頗有敎養，但卻胸無大志；他們講究的是儀表舉止，而不是美的品德。但這種觀點並不永遠是對的，因爲奧古斯都·凱撒、提圖斯·韋斯巴薌、法國"俊美的"菲利普、英國的愛德華四世、雅典的亞爾西巴德、波斯的伊斯邁爾都是高尙而又偉大的人物，然而也是他們那個時代最美的男子。就美而言，容貌之美勝於服飾形態之美，端莊優雅舉止之美又勝於容貌之美。美

part of beauty, which a picture cannot express;
no, nor the first sight of the life. There is no
excellent beauty that has not some strangeness
in the proportion. A man cannot tell whether
Apelles or Albert Durer were the more trifler;
where of the one would make a personage by ge-
ometrical proportions, the other, by taking the
best parts out of divers faces to make one excellent. Such personages, I think, would please
nobody but the painter that made them. Not but
I think a painter may make a better face than
ever was, but he must do it by a kind of felicity
(as a musician that makes an excellent air in
music), and not by rule. A man shall see faces
that, if you examine them part by part, you
shall find never a good; and yet all together do
well. If it is true that the principal part of beauty is in decent motion, certainly it is no marvel
though persons in years seem many times more
amiable: The autumn of the beautiful is beautiful; for no youth can be comely but by pardon,
and considering the youth as to make up the
comeliness. Beauty is as summer fruits, which
are easy to corrupt, and cannot last; and for the
most part it makes a dissolute youth, and an age

的最好的那一部分，是既不能用圖畫來表達，也不是一眼就能看到的。任何絕妙的美，無不在比例上有某種奇妙之處。誰也說不出阿佩勒斯和阿爾伯特·丟勒究竟哪一位是更大的戲謔者：其中一位是根據幾何學的比例來畫人，另一位則從幾個不同的面孔中選取最好的部分不定期創造一張完美的面孔。我想，這樣畫出來的人，除了畫家本人之外誰也不會喜歡。並不是說我認為一個畫家不可以創造一張比以前更美的面孔，而是說他應當靠一種靈感去創造（像一個音樂家創造優美的樂曲一樣），不應當根據某種規則去描繪。誰都會看到一些面孔，如果你把它們一部分一部分地加以審察，你就會覺得哪一部分都不好；但是如果把各個部分合在一起，你們就會覺得那些面孔很好看了。如果美的主要部分真的就在端莊的舉止之中，那麼上了年紀的人常常看上去更加和藹可親當然就不足為奇了。"美人的秋天也是美的。"因為我們如不加以寬恕，不把青春看作是對美的補充的話，他們誰也說不上美。美猶如夏天的水果，很容易腐爛，不能久存。美往往使人年輕時放蕩不羈，到

a little out of countenance; but yet certainly a-
gain, if it alights on a worthy person, it makes
virtues shine, and vices blush.

了老年就有點難堪。但如果美落在人身上得當的
話，當然它也可以使美德生輝，使邪惡汗顏。

▬欣賞▬

　　談到美，這應當是一個哲學與美學的問題。從培根
的人生來看，他並不擅長哲學和美學的理論。但讀了這
篇散文，我們會覺得作者的立意之美是它的特色。美是
一個普遍的意義。他立意對比品德美與形體美，就此展
開討論，其用意並不是對美進行廣泛的哲學、美學兩大問
題的宏論，而是引經據典，巧妙地借它山之石，來陳述自
己的觀點。讚揚的是男子的陽剛之美。因此，他認為，動
態之美與靜態之美是和諧的美；形體之美勝於容顏之美。
舉止優雅之美勝於形體之美。美應有其獨特的靈性，“無
不在比例上有某種奇妙之處”。在我國古詩中富有傷感
的詞語“美人遲暮”與培根引用的拉丁諺語“美人的秋天
也是美的”迥然不同，因為他認為年長者之美未必遜於年
輕人的美；因為美人的秋天標誌著美的成熟，而不是美的
凋謝。文章起筆不凡，開門見山，直接入題，這也是散文
的一大特點。

3. Of Love

Francis Bacon

The stage is more indebted to love than the life of man. For as to the stage, love is ever in matter of comedies and now and then of tragedies; but in life it does much mischief, sometimes like a siren, sometimes like a fury. You may observe that among all the great and worthy persons (whereof the memory-remained, either ancient or recent), there is not one that has been transported to the mad degree of love; which shows that great spirits and great business do keep out this weak passion. You must except, nevertheless, Marcus Antonius, the half-partner of the empire of Rome, and Appis Claudius, the decemvir and lawgiver: whereof the former was indeed a voluptuous man and inordinate, but the latter was an austere and wise man. And therefore it seems, (though rarely) that love can find entrance not only into an open heart, but also into a heart well fortified, if watch is not well kept.

It is a saying of Epicurus, Satis magnum

3. 論 情 愛

弗朗西斯·培根

　　舞臺上的愛情比人生中的愛情要多得多。因
爲在舞臺上，愛情總是喜劇的題材，有時也是悲劇
的題材，但是在人生中，它幾乎總是帶來災禍，有
時像海上的女妖，有時像復仇的女神。我們可以
看到，在一些偉大的、可敬的人物中（無論是古人
還是今人，大凡還能記得的），沒有一個是被愛情
搞得神魂顛倒而達到瘋狂程度的。這表明，偉大
的心靈和偉大的事業能排除這種柔弱的感情。但
是，你必須把統治羅馬帝國半壁江山的馬可·安東
尼和執政官及立法者的阿庇烏斯·克勞狄烏斯除
外。這兩個人中，前者確實是一個淫逸無度的人，
但後者卻是嚴謹而聰慧的人。所以看起來，（雖然
這是很少見的）如若其守備不嚴的話，愛情不但能
進入開放的心靈，而且也能進入壁壘森嚴的心靈。
　　伊壁鳩魯說：“我們每人在他人看來都是一個

alter Each of us is enough of an audience for the other (Seneca, Epistles, VII.11). as if man, made for the contemplation of heaven and all noble objects, should do nothing but kneel before a little idol, and make himself subject, though not of the mouth (as beasts are), yet of the eye, which was given him for higher purposes. It is a strange thing to note the excess of this passion and how it braves the nature and value of things, by this: that the speaking in a perpetual hyperbole is comely in nothing but in love. Neither is it merely in the phrase; for whereas it has been well said that the arch-flatterer, with whom all the petty flatterers have intelligence, is a man's self, certainly the lover is more. For there was never proud man thought so absurdly well of himself as the lover does of the person loved: and therefore it was well said. That it is impossible to love and to be wise. Neither does this weakness appear to others only, and not to the party loved, but to the loved most of all, except the love be mutual. For it is a true rule that love is ever rewarded either with the reciprocal feeling or with an inward and secret contempt. By how much the

相當大的劇場。"這話說得不怎麼樣,好像人類只是應當跪在一個小小的偶像前,使自己成為奴隸,雖然不是嘴巴的奴隸(像禽獸那樣)卻是眼睛的奴隸,而上帝賜與人類的眼睛有其更崇高的用途。奇怪的是,人們可以通過下述事實而目睹這種情欲的無度,以及它是如何置事物的本性和價值於不顧的,這一事實就是:那種永久不變的誇張之辭只適宜於愛情,而不適宜於其他任何事情。這種情慾也不僅僅表現在言語中。有人說得好:最大的諂媚者(一切小的諂媚者都是與他互通聲氣的)乃是一個人的自我,而情人肯定有過之而無不及。因為不管一個人怎麼驕傲,怎麼自以為是,他對自己的評價無論如何也不會達到情人將其所愛的人捧上天的那種荒謬程度。所以有人說得好:"人在戀愛中是不可能明智的。"這種弱點也不是只有旁人才能看得出來,而被愛者看不出來的;相反,被愛者看得最清楚,除非這種愛情是交互的。因為,自古以來愛情的報酬只有兩種,不是得到對方的回愛,就是遭受其內心的蔑視,這確實是一條規律。

more men ought to beware of this passion, which loses not only other things, but itself. As for the other losses, the poet's relation does well figure them: that he that preferred Helena quitted the gifts of Juno and Pallas. For whosoever esteems too much of amorous affection quits both riches and wisdom.

This passion has his floods in the very times of weakness, which are great prosperity and great adversity (though this latter has been less observed); both which times kindle love and make it more fervent, and therefore show it to be the child of folly. They do best who, if they cannot but admit love, yet make it keep its proper place, and sever it wholly from their serious affairs and actions of life; for if it checks once with business, it troubles men's fortunes, and makes men that they can no ways be true to their own ends. I know not how, but martial men are given to love: I think it is but as they are given to wine; for perils commonly ask to be paid in pleasures. There is in man's nature a secret inclination and motion towards love of others, which, if it is not spent upon some one or a few, does naturally spread itself towards

因此，人們應當十分小心地防範這種情慾，因爲它不僅會使人失去其他東西，而且連它自己也保不住。關於會使人失去其他的東西這一點，詩人的故事描寫得非常形象：他（帕裡斯）寧願要海倫，而寧願捨棄朱諾和帕拉斯的賞賜。因爲不管什麼人，若他過於重視愛情，就會喪失財富和智慧。

　　人在心力脆弱的時候，即在最得意和最困難的時候，這種情慾最容易泛濫成災，儘管在最困厄時這種情慾的泛濫不太爲人所注意。這兩種境遇都會點燃愛情之火，並使之越燒越烈。由此可見，“愛情”是“愚蠢”之子。倘若有人不得不戀愛的話，那最好也要有所節制，並且把它與人生的其他大事務必完全分開，因爲愛情一旦參與正事，它就會給人們帶來不幸，使人們無法始終如一地追求自己的目標。我不知道勇武的人爲什麼這麼容易墮入愛情。我想，這只是和他們喜歡喝酒一樣，因爲危險往往需要在快樂中得到補償。在人的天性中有一種神秘的愛他人的意向和動機，這種愛心若不只是給一個人或少數幾個人，那就會很自然

many, and makes men become humane and charitable; as it is seen sometime in friars. Nuptial love makes mankind; friendly love perfects it; but want to love corrupts and embarrasses it.

地普施予人世間，就會使人變得仁慈和寬厚，例如
在僧侶中有時就可以看到這種情形。夫婦之愛使
人繁衍；朋友之愛使人類完善；但淫逸之愛則使人
腐化墮落。

欣賞

　　培根生活在伊麗莎白時期，理想化愛情和牧歌情調
十分流行。因此，他說舞臺上的愛情比人生中的愛情故
事要多得多。"人間沒有愛，太陽也會滅"（雨果），"沒有
一點愛，人是活不下去的，人天生有個靈魂，就是爲了使
他能夠愛…"（高爾基）。如果世界上沒有愛，那就沒有光
明，只有黑暗；沒有溫暖，只有寒冷；沒有生命，只有死亡；
沒有社會和人生。正是因爲世界充滿了愛，才使它生機
勃勃，氣象萬千。正因爲"愛情不但能進入開放的心靈，
而且也能進入壁壘森嚴的心靈"。培根借他山之石，論述
了"愛的力量是無窮的"。這是第二層意思。在散文的結
尾處，培根強調愛要有所節制。否則，"這種情慾最容易
泛濫成災"；否則，"淫逸之愛則使人腐化墮落"。培根對
愛情的觀點飽含哲理，對愛情細膩分析，對情人間相互誇
張的見解尤爲鋒利。他的體驗是深刻的，這些體驗與培
根本人的兩次婚姻有密切關係。也正是這些體驗反映出
培根的愛情觀和人生觀。

4. Of Marriage and Single Life

Francis Bacon

He that wife and children has given hostages to fortune, for they are impediments to great enterprises, either of virtue or mischief. Certainly the best works, and of greatest merit for the public, have proceeded from the unmarried or childless men, which both in affect on and means have married and endowed the public. Yet it was great reason that those that have children should have greatest care of future times, unto which they know they must transmit their dearest pledges. Some there are who, though they lead a single life, yet their thoughts do end with themselves, and account future times impertinences. Nay, there ate some other that account wife and children but as bills of charges. Nay more, there are some foolish rich covetous men that take a pride in having no children, because they may be thought so much the richer. For perhaps they have heard some talk, Such an one is a great rich man, and another except to it, Yea, but he has a great charge of children, as if it were an abatement to

4. 論獨身與婚嫁

弗朗西斯·培根

　　凡有妻室兒女者,都把命運作了抵押品。因為有了他們,不論是善舉還是惡行,往往都難成器。毫無疑問,最有益於公衆的好事是由未婚或沒有子女的人們辦成的。因爲他們和公益事業在情感上相通,把財產饋贈給予了公益事業。可是按理說,有子女的人應當最關心未來,他們知道,他們必須將他們最寶貴的抵押品交托給未來。有些人,雖然過著獨身生活,而他們考慮的確實也只限於自身,把未來看得漠不關心。不僅如此,還有另外一些人,他們把妻室兒女只看作是累贅。什至還有一些愚民蠢才竟以沒有子女而自豪,認爲這樣他們在別人眼中就會顯得更爲富有。他們可能聽到過這樣的對話:"此人是個富豪"。另一人卻表示不同意地說:"是啊,可是他受子女的牽累太大"。彷彿這樣就意味著削減了他的財富。

his riches. But the most ordinary cause of a single life is liberty, especially in certain self-pleasing and humorous minds, which are so sensible of every restraint as they will go near to think their girdles and garters to be bonds and shackles. Unmarried men are best friends, best masters, best servants; but not always best subjects, for they are light to run away; and almost all fugitives are of that condition. A single life does well with churchmen, for charity will hardly water the ground where it must first fill a pool. It is unimportant either way for judges and magistrates, for if they are easily manipulated and corrupted, you shall have a servant five times put men in mind of their wives and children; and I think the despising of marriage amongst the Turks makes the vulgar soldier more base. Certainly wife and children are a kind of discipline of humanity; and single men, though they are many times more charitable, because their means are less exhausted, yet, on the other side, they are more cruel and hard-hearted (good to make severe inquisitors), because their tenderness is not so often called upon. Grave natures, led by custom, and therefore constant, are commonly loving husbands, as was said of Ulysses, *Vetulam suam praetulit im-*

　　不過,獨身生活最常見的原因是爲了自由,尤其是那些自得其樂性情怪僻的人,他們對於各種約束都極爲敏感,甚至把腰帶和吊襪帶都看作鐐銬。

　　未婚者是最好的朋友、最好的主人、最好的僕人,但往往並非最好的臣民,因爲他們很容易逃跑;幾乎所有的逃亡者都是這類人。獨身生活適宜於僧侶,因爲愛的施捨猶如水,若先須注滿一池,就難於普澆大地。獨身對於法官和地方官員來說無關緊要,因爲如果他們沒有主見,貪贓枉法,一個僕人所造成的危害比不好的妻室兒女還多五倍。我認爲,土耳其人對婚姻的輕視使得那些粗俗的士兵變得更爲卑劣。無疑,妻子兒女是做人的一種準則。至於單身漢,雖然他們手頭寬裕,往往比較慷慨大方,但在另一方面,他們也比較冷酷狠心(最好去當正兒八經的審問官),因爲他們難得產生同情。性情莊重的人受風俗習慣的薰陶,因而不易被打動,他們大都是多情的丈夫,正如人們所說的尤利西斯"他寧要他的老妻也不

mortalitati. Chaste women are often proud and forward, as presuming upon the merit of their chastity. It is one of the best bonds both of chastity and obedience in the wife if she thinks her husband wise, which she will never do if she finds him jealous. Wives are young men's mistresses, companions for middle age, and old men's nurses. So as a man may have a quarrel to marry when he will. But yet he was reputed one that made answer to the questions, when a man should marry: A young man not yet, an elder man not at all. It is often seen that bad husbands have very good wives; whether it is that it raises the price of their husband's kindness when it comes, or that the wives take a pride in their patience. But this never fails if the bad husbands were of their own choosing, against their friends' consent; for then they will be sure to make good their own folly.

要淫蕩的仙女"。貞潔的婦女往往高傲專橫,彷彿在自我炫耀貞潔。如果妻子認爲她的丈夫聰明,這就是可使她保持貞潔溫順的最可靠的約束;如果她發現他妒忌多疑,那她就決不會那樣了。妻子是青年時的情人,中年時的伴侶,老年時的保姆。因此,一個男人只要他願意,任何時候都有理由要求結婚。然而,在回答人應當在什麼時候結婚這個問題時,有一個被稱爲智者的人卻說:"年輕人還不到結婚的年齡,年老的人根本不該結婚。"經常看到一些壞丈夫卻擁有賢慧的妻子,這也許是因爲,當他們的丈夫有時表示情愛時,就會顯得更爲寶貴;或者做妻子的以自己的耐心而自豪。但這一點是決不會錯的,即這些壞丈夫必是她們不顧親友的勸告自己挑中的。這婚姻就永遠不會失敗;因爲她們必然要以此證明自己並不愚昧。

欣賞

　　這是培根《論父母與子女》的姊妹篇。培根這篇散文的主題是婚姻與事業;婚姻家庭子女對自己的事業的影響與利弊。關於結婚,他引用他人的觀點"年輕人還不到結婚的年齡,年老的人根本不該結婚"這一引言,道出自己的觀點,其哲理深刻,觀點鮮明而突出。

5. Women and Men

S. R. Sanders

I was slow to understand the deep grievances of women. This was because, as a boy, I had envied them. Before college, the only people I had ever known who were interested in art or music or literature, the only ones who read books, the only ones who ever seemed to enjoy a sense of ease and grace were the mothers and daughters. Like the menfolk, they fretted about money, they scrimped and made. But when the pay stopped coming in, they were not the ones who had failed. Nor did they have to go to war, and that seemed to me a blessed fact. By comparision with the narrow, ironclad days of fathers, there was an expansiveness, I thought, in the days of mothers. They went to see neighbors, to shop in town, to run errands at school, at the library, at church. No doubt, had I looked harder at their lives, I would have envied them less. It was not my fate to become a woman, so it was easier for me to see the graces. Few of them held jobs outside the

5. 男人和女人

S·R·桑德斯

我很長時間才理解女人深處的憂怨。這是因爲當我還是男孩時，我羨慕她們。讀大學以前，我所結識的所有人當中，只有那些做母親和女兒的人才對藝術、音樂和文學發生興趣，因此，也只有她們讀書，享受著閑情的樂趣。她們像男人一樣，爲賺錢而煩惱，節衣縮食，得過且過。即使她們收入落空，她們也並不算是失敗者。她們也不必要上戰場，依我之見，這應算她們一大福氣。相形之下，父親們的日子過得艱難而毫無生氣，而母親們的日子過得舒暢。她們走訪鄰居，上街購物，上學校，進圖書館和去教堂忙個不停。毫無疑問，要是我更深入體察她們的生活，我對她們的羨慕就會少幾分。我無幸做一個女人，這樣我就更容易看到她們體面的方面。她們中極少數人在外面有活

home, and those who did fill thankless roles as clerks and waitresses. I didn't see, then, what a prison a house could be, since houses seemed to me brighter, handsomer places than any factory. I did not realize — because such things were never spoken of — how often women suffered from men's bullying. I did learn about the wretchedness of abandoned wives, single mothers, widows; but I also learned about the wretchedness of lone men. Even then I could see how exhausting it was for a mother to cater all day to the needs of young children. But if I had been asked, as a boy, to choose between tending a baby and tending a machine, I think I would have chosen the baby. (Having now tended both, I know I would choose the baby.)

So I was baffled when the women at college accused me and my sex of having cornered the world's pleasures. I think something like my bafflement has been felt by other boys (and by girls as well) who grew up in dirt — poor farm country, in mining country, in black ghettos, in Hispanic barrios, in the shadows of factories, in Third World nations — any place where the fate of men is as grim and bleak as the fate of wom-

幹。即使有做事的也只不過是當小職員和招待員
之類,對此她們還非常感激。我原來並不明白家
庭怎麼可能會是監獄,因為在我看來家庭比工廠
要明亮而漂亮。我沒有意識到這一點,是因為這
樣的事情很少被談起——女人常常受男人的無禮
的欺負之苦。雖然我了解男人們的不幸,但我也
的的確確明白那些被遺棄的妻子、單身母親和那
些寡婦們的凄苦。然而,我還是更能夠理解母親
們整日細心護理照料小孩那精疲力竭的苦差。如
果有人問我我願意護理嬰兒還是願意看著機器的
話,我想我會選擇前者。(如今我兩個都照料過了
之後,我明白我會選擇照料嬰兒)。

因此我受到了女大學生的責備,她們說我和
我的同性壟斷了人間的樂趣,為此我很感苦惱。
我想其他的一些男生(和女生一樣)也會有我一樣
苦惱的感覺。尤其是那些出身貧困的鄉村、礦區、
黑人居住區、西班牙移民居住區、在黑暗的工廠
裡,在第三世界國家——任何一個地方的男人,都

en. Toilers and warriors. I realize now how ancient these identities are, how deep the tug they exert on men, the undertow of a thousand generations. The miseries I saw, as a boy, in the lives of nearly all men I continue to see in the lives of many — the body-breaking toil, the tedium, the call to be tough, the humiliating powerlessness, the battle for a living and for territory.

When the women I met at college thought about the joys and privileges of men, they did not carry in their minds the sort of men I had known in my childhood. They thought of their fathers, who were bankers, physicians, architects, stockbrokers, the big wheels of the big cities. These fathers rode the train to work or drove cars that cost more than any of my childhood houses. They were attended from morning to night by female helpers, wives and nurses and secretaries. They were never laid off, never short of cash at month's end, never lined up for welfare. These ran the world.

The daughters of such men wanted to share in this power, this glory. So did I. They yearned for a say over their future, for jobs wor-

會有我一樣的苦惱。他們是苦力同時他們又是勇
士。我現在已意識到像他們這樣的身份是何等古
老它們往男人身上所施加的壓力是多大！就好似
千層的巨浪！孩提時所看到的差不多所有作男人
的苦難，如今在許多男人中還依然可見：他們累得
快倒下；生活枯燥乏味；聽從嚴格的命令；權利受
到屈辱；他們還在爲生存和領土而戰鬥。

　　當我讀大學遇到的這些女學生說到男人所有
的歡樂和特權時，她們根本沒有我孩提時在腦海
裡所熟識的那類男人的印象。她們想的是他們富
有的父親，他們那些銀行家、醫生、建築師、股票經
紀人、大都市的有權有勢的父親。這些父親乘火
車或汽車去上班。他們的汽車比我孩提時所住過
的所有住房還要貴。從早到晚，他們有好幾個女
人伺侯著，諸如妻子、護理員和秘書。她們從來也
不會被解雇，從來在月底也不缺錢花，從來也不用
排隊去領救濟金。這些男人所做出的決定至關重
要。他們主宰著這個世界。

　　這些男人的女人希望分享他們的權力和榮
耀，我也希望如此。她們渴望自己毫不受人煩擾，
完全決定自己的前途和未來。是的，我想，應當是

thy of their abilities, for the right to live at peace, unmolested, whole. Yes, I thought, yes yes. The difference between me and these daughters was that they saw me, because of my sex, as destined from birth to become like their fathers, and therefore as an enemy to their desires. But I knew better. I wasn't an enemy, in fact or in feeling. I was an ally. If I had known, then, how to tell them so, would they have believed me? Would they now?

這樣的。這些女人和我的差別是因爲她們所看到的我,因爲我的性別,注定天生下來就要成爲像她們父親一樣的人,所以也注定把我看成是她們所期望的敵人。但我更清楚,無論從事實上還是從感情上來講,我不是敵人,我是同盟者。如果當初我早就知道怎樣向她們說這些,想想看,他們會相信我嗎? 她們現在會相信我嗎?

欣賞

這是一篇討論兩性之間隔閡的散文。即使在當今文明程度較高的社會裡,如何清除男女之間的"敵意"和"不平等",依然是一個世界性的課題。作者"很長時間才理解女人深處的憂怨",這一觀察經歷了孩提時代、大學時代。正因爲通過這些不同的時代的觀察,他才覺得男女之間的敵意無處不在,男女相互的仇視無處不在,表現出作者對美國社會的不滿,對男女之間的平等感到迷茫。列寧曾說過"沒有廣大勞動婦女的積極參加,社會主義革命是不可能的"。作爲婦女,應當是"有志婦女,勝如男人"。

6.Of Suitors

Francis Bacon

Many ill matters and projects are undertaken, and private suits do putrefy the public good. Many good matters are undertaken with bad minds; I mean not only corrupt minds, but crafty minds that intend not performance. Some embrace suits which never mean to deal effectually in them, they will be content to win a thank, or take a second reward, or at least to make use in the meantime of the suitor's hopes. Some take hold of suits only for an occasion to cross some other; or to make an information whereof they could not otherwise have apt pretext, without care what is come of the suit when that turn is served; or generally to make other men's business a kind of entertainment to bring in their own. Nay, some undertake suits with a full purpose to let them fall, to the end to gratify the adverse party or competitor.

Surely there is in some sort a right in every suit; either a right of equity, if it is a suit of

6. 論求情者

弗朗西斯・培根

　　許多不良的事情和謀劃總是有人承擔——私人的求情確實起著敗壞公益的作用。許多事本來不錯,但承擔者存在有惡意:所謂"惡意",不但指不道德,而且也包括狡猾虛僞之意在內;那些口頭上答應下來,心裡卻不打算去實行的人。但是一旦發現這事經過別人的努力有成功的希望時,他們就急於贏得求情者的感謝,要使那人相信他們真替他辦過事,或取得另一份報酬,或者至少在事情尚未決定的期間,充分利用求情者抱有的希望。有些人接受別人的請託,只是爲了利用它來阻撓另一個人,或散佈不利於那人的言論(否則他們是找不到適合的藉口的),當這一目的達到之後,原來所請託的事成功與否,他們是毫不關心的。一般地說,他們不過是把別人請託的事當作自己從中獲利的事而已。甚至還有些人應承某人請托的事,卻滿心要這事辦不成,以取悅於那人的對手或競爭者。

　　無疑地,在請託之中免不了有是非曲直。爲爭訟的請託,其中必有正當與不正當之別;求職位

controversy, or a right of desert, if it is a suit of petition. If affection leads a man to favour the wrong side in justice, let him rather use his countenance to compound the matter than to carry it. If affection leads a man to favour the less worthy in desert, let him do it without depraving or disabling the better deserver. In suits which a man does not well understand, it is good to refer them to some friend of trust and judgement, that may report whether he may deal in them with honour; but let him choose well his referendaries, for else he may be led by the nose. Suitors are so distasted with delays and abuses, that plain dealing, in denying to deal in suits at first, and reporting the success barely, and in challenging no more thanks than one has deserved, is frown not only honourable, but also gracious. In suits of favour, the first coming ought to take little place. So far forth consideration may be had of his trust, that if intelligence of the matter could not otherwise have been but by him, advantage is not taken of the note but the party left to his other means, and in some sort recompensed for his discovery. To be ignorant of the value of a suit is simplicity; as well

的請託,其中必有應得與不應得之別。假如一個
人受感情的驅使,在訴訟中袒護不正當的一方,最
好是利用他的影響促成雙方的和解,而不要把事
做絕。假如一個人受感情的驅使,在謀職提升中
偏向不大應得的一方,他最好是不要爲了提拔不
夠條件的一方,而貶低或損害那理應提升的人。

　　遇到自己不太明白的說情,最好請教一位可
以信賴而有見解的朋友,這樣就可以得知承辦這
種說情之事是否體面,是否有損聲譽。但是要慎
重選擇對象,不然就等於讓人牽著鼻子走啊!

　　請託者最厭惡的是拖延和受誑騙。因此,如
果一開頭就告訴他們不願承辦所請託的事,要辦
也要把事情進展全部告訴對方,或者在事成之後
除應得的酬謝外不再非分索求,這種直來直去的
舉動現在變得不僅是值得尊敬而且是深可感激的
了。在請求特殊照顧的說情中,誰先誰後應當是
無足輕重的。不過先來者對我們的請託卻不可不
放在心上;就是說,假如這個人告訴我們一些除了
從他那裡我們不可能得到的消息,我們就不可白
白地利用人家的消息,而應當給他一定的報酬,而
且讓他自由地試試他所知道的其他門路。不知請
託的意義,那是眞正無知,而不知道請託的正確與
否,那就缺乏良知了。

as to be ignorant of the right thereof is want of-conscience.

Secrecy in suits is a great means of obtaining, for voicing them to be in forwardness may discourage some kind of suitors, but does quicken and awake others. But timing of the suit is the principal. Timing, I say, not only in respect of the person that should grant it, but in respect of those which are like to cross it. Let a man, in the choice of his mean, rather choose the fittest mean than the greatest mean , and rather them that deal in certain things than those that are general. The reparation of a denial is sometimes equal to the first grant, if a man shows himself neither dejected nor discontented. Ask for more than what is just, so that you may get your due (Quintilian, The Education of an Orator, IV.5.16) is a good rule where a man has strength of favour, but otherwise a man was better rise in his suit, for he 'that would have ventured at first to have lost the sutor, will not in the conclusion lose both the suitor and his own former favour.

Nothing is thought so easy a request to a great person as his letter, and yet if it is not in a good cause it is so much out of his reputation.

　　在承辦委託之事時保守秘密是成功的要訣，因為公開張揚這事辦得如何固然可以使某些說情者望而止步，但是也會刺激並喚醒另外一些說情者開始行動。求情說情要適得其時，這才是主要的。我所說的適時不但要考慮到將要成全你的請託的人物，而且要考慮到可能會阻撓你實現請託之事的那些人。在考慮求情的人時，寧可選擇那些最適於辦所託之事的人而不要倚仗誰勢利最大，寧可選擇專辦某些事的人，而不要選包攬一切的人。如果一個人初次的請託被拒絕了，而他既不灰心也不抱怨，那麼從這次拒絕所得到的補償將不亞於初次請託之被接受。拉丁諺語"求乎其上，得乎其中"，對於深受寵愛的人來說是金科玉律。否則，最好是逐步提高自己的請求；這是因為有地位的人失掉一個初次前來的求情者或許無所顧慮，但如果這個求情者已從他那裡多次得到好處，他就不願意在最後關節，既失去這個求情者的好感，又把自己過去給予的恩惠一筆勾銷了。

　　通常以為請一位大人物寫封推薦信，是實在容易不過的事。然而，假如寫這封信的理由是不正當的，則這樣做也將影響寫信人的聲譽。再沒

There are no worse instruments than these general fixers of suits; for they are but a kind of poison and infection to public proceedings.

有比當今那些替人奔走、包攬說情的中間人更爲
惡劣的了,因爲他們不過是一種妨礙公務進行的
毒藥和傳染病而已。

欣賞

　　人並非生活在眞空,人不可能不與人交際。從某種
意義上來說,人不可能不求人。人們常說,做人難,求人
更難。聯想這篇散文,培根認爲,請託之術在於適得其
時,適得其人。求人的機會不佳,好事可能辦成壞事;求
的人不佳,即使可望成功,也會弄到萬事不成。有時不一
定就倚仗權勢,憲官不如現管。這種現象在我們現實社
會中很普遍。由此也說明,求情不僅是現代社會才有,而
且古代社會也存在。培根還淸楚地認識到,有的是正當
的事求人說情,但也"免不了有是非曲直",對此不可不
視,還必須採用巧妙的策略,"最好促成雙方和解",這就
是我們所說的"吃了人家的嘴軟,拿了人家的手短",旣接
受一方之請託,要想主持公道,這幾乎不可能。培根生活
在說情和公然行賄之風極盛的時代,對於說情這一套了
如指掌。有了這些經歷和經驗,他把求情刻畫得絲絲入
扣,搔到癢處。

7.Of Followers and Friends

Francis Bacon

Costly followers are not to be liked, lest
while a man makes his train longer, he makes
his wings shorter. I reckon to be costly, not
them alone which charge the purse, but which
are wearisome and importunate in suits. Ordinary followers ought to challenge no higher conditions than countenance, recommendation, and
protection from wrongs. Factious followers are
worse to be liked, which follow not upon affection to him with whom they range themselves,
but upon discontentment conceived against some
other; whereupon commonly ensues that ill intelligence that we many times see between great
personages. Likewise glorious followers, who
make themselves as trumpets of the commendation of those they follow, are full of inconvenience, for they taint business through want of
secrecy, and they export honour from a man and
make him a return in envy. There is a kind of
followers likewise which are dangerous, being
indeed spies, which inquire the secrets of the

7. 論追隨者與友人

弗朗西斯‧培根

代價過高的追隨者並不可取，怕的是那些尾巴太長則羽翼就要短的人。

何謂代價過高，不是指成本大的僕人，而是指糾纏求情、糾纏不休、令人生厭的那一些傢伙。一般的追隨者通常所求不應超出對主人的幫助，推薦以及提供的安全保護，使其免受欺侮等。那些結黨營私的追隨者更得人心，因為他們歸附你的門下並非出於對你的愛戴，而是因為對別人心懷不滿。從而導致我們常見的大人物之間的誤會。同樣地，那些好炫耀的追隨者，到處宣揚其主人，這也會帶來很多麻煩：他們由於洩露機密而壞事，糟蹋一個人名聲，反而使他不得人心。還有一種險惡的侍從實際上可以說是密探。他們常常窺探

house, and bear tales of them to others. Yet such men, many times, are in great favour, for they are officious, and commonly exchange tales. The following by certain estates of men, answerable to that which a great person himself professes (as of soldiers to him that has been employed in the wars, and the like), has ever been a thing civil, and well taken even in monarchies; so it be without too much pomp or popularity. But the most honourable kind of following is to be followed as one that apprehends to advance virtue and desert in all sorts of persons. And yet, where there is no eminent odds in sufficiency it is better to take with the more passable than with the more able. And besides, to speak truth, in base times active men are of more use than virtuous. It is true that in government it is good to use men of one rank equally, for to countenance some extraordinarily is to make them insolent, and the rest discontent, because they may claim a due. But contrariwise, in favour, to use men with much difference and election is good, for it makes the persons preferred more thankful, and the rest more officious, because all is of favour. It is good

主人家中的秘密,胡編一通,誤傳於人。而這種人常常很受寵信,因為他們特別會殷勤逢迎,而且總喜歡與人說三道四,充當耳目。

　　一個大人物如果有與他所從事的事業、身份相宜的追隨者(例如,經歷過戰爭的人以武士為其追隨者及類似情況),那是無可非議的事。即使在君主國中,只要此舉不過於聲勢煊赫或受人擁戴,也不會受人猜忌的。但是最高的一種隨從是能使各種人施展才華和美德的追隨者。然而,在沒有很多才德特別出眾的人才時,寧可任用較平庸的人也比任用較有才能者為佳。老實說,在世風不正的時代,有活動能力者比有德才者更為受用。的確,在政府中用人最好是對同等資格者一視同仁。如果破格提拔任用,被提拔任用者難免變得驕橫,而其餘的人則將不滿。因為他們既然資格相同待遇也就應該相同。反之,在寵信方面,根據不同的情況有選擇地用人是可行的。因為,這種作法可使被重用者感恩更深,而其餘的人則更為殷勤,堅信升遷全在得寵。

discretion not to make too much of any man at the first, because one cannot hold out that proportion. To be governed (as we call it) by one, is not safe, for it shows softenness and gives a freedom to scandal and disreputation; for those that would not censure or speak ill of a man immediately, will talk more boldly of those that are so great with them, and thereby wound their honour. Yet to be distracted with many is worse, for it makes men to be of the last impression, and full of change. To take advice of some few friends is ever honourable, for lookers-on many times see more than gamesters; and the vale best discovers the hill. There is little friendship in the world, and least of all between equals, which was wont to be magnified. That is, between superior and inferior, whose fortunes may comprehend the one the other.

　　對於任何人一開始不要過分看重，審穩妥當
爲良策。否則以後對他怎樣厚待也難以爲繼。只
受一個人的支配(如我們常說的)是不妥當的。這
只能說明你的軟弱，這也反而易於醜聞惡名的流
傳。因爲那些在主人面前不敢直進諫或批評的
人，在主人背後樂於對那些得寵的人說長論短，這
樣一來主人的榮譽必將受到損害。

　　然而更壞的是爲衆人口若懸河的群言所左
右，只是聽信最後一個進言者的話，毫無主見，全
無定見，變來變去。採納少數朋友的忠告永遠是
值得敬重的。因爲當局者迷，旁觀者清；山之所以
顯得高是因爲有低谷。人世間眞正的友情是少見
的，在地位相同的人們之間更少。這種友情以往
常常被世人誇大了。現今稱得上友情的只在主人
與僕人、上級與下屬之間，因爲二者榮辱與共。

欣賞

　　這篇散文反映的是當時貴族奢侈無度，耽於享樂，並
姑養過多的隨從的一大社會弊病。在這篇散文中，培根
對幾種不同的隨從進行了細膩的分析和全面的剖析，是
這篇散文的最精彩之處。這種分析來自於他對社會的觀
察和自身的體驗。說到用人之策，與我國詩人唐琬的詩
句"世情薄，人情惡，雨送黃昏花易落"以及諺語"人情如
紙薄"很是類似，這的確值得思考。

8. The Big Secret of Dealing with People

Carnegie Dale

There is only one way under high heaven to get anybody to do anything. Did you ever stop to think of that? Yes, just one way. And that is by making the other person want to do it.

Remember, there is no other way. Of course, you can make someone want to give you his watch by sticking a revdver in his ribs. You can make your employees give you cooperation — until your back is turned — by threatening to fire them. You can make a child do what you want it to do by a whip or a threat. But these crude methods have sharply undesirable repercussions. The only way I can get you to do anything is by giving you what you want. What do you want?

Sigmund Freud said that everything you and I do springs from two motives: the sex urge and the desire to be great. John Dewey, one of America's most profound philosophers, phrased it a bit differently. Dr. Dewey said that the deepest urge in human nature is "the desire to

8. 待人處世秘訣

卡耐基・戴爾

普天之下要別人爲你做事，方法只有一個。你是否想過這一點？對。僅此一法：那就是設法使別人自己想去做。

記住！別無他法。

當然，你可以拿槍頂住某人的肋骨，讓他把手錶給你。你可以威脅要炒雇員的魷魚使他們與你合作。你可以用一根鞭子或一句威脅，使小孩對你言聽計從。但這些粗俗之舉只會招來極大的逆反心態。

我要讓你做事的唯一方法就是：把你想要的東西給你。你要什麼呢？

西格蒙德・弗洛伊德說過：你我做的每件事皆出於兩個動機：性衝動和做大人物的慾望。

美國造詣最深的哲學家之一約翰・迪威對此的定義稍有不同。迪威博士說：人類天性中最深的衝動是"做名人的慾望"。記住"做名人的慾望"

be important." Remember that phrase: "the desire to be important." It is significant. You are going to hear a lot about it in this book. What do you want? Not many things, but the few things that you do wish, you crave with an insistence that will not be denied. Some of the things most people want include:

1. Health and the preservation of life.
2. Food.
3. Sleep.
4. Money and the things money will buy.
5. Life in the hereafter.
6. Sexual gratification.
7. The well-being of our children.
8. A feeling of importance.

Almost all these wants are usually gratified — all except one. But there is one longing — almost as deep, almost as imperious, as the desire for food or sleep — which is seldom gratified. It is what Freud calls "the desire to be great." It is what Dewey calls the "desire to be important."

Lincoln once began a letter saying: "Everybody likes a compliment." William James said: "The deepest principle in human nature is

這句話，它意味深長。你將在此聽到更多有關這
方面的論述。

你想要什麼？其實，你希冀的並不多，只不過
幾樣東西。你懷著一種強迫之情渴望不會遭受否
決。大多數人想得到的東西包括：

1. 健康和生命安全
2. 食物
3. 睡眠
4. 金錢和錢能買到的東西
5. 來世的生命
6. 性滿足
7. 孩子幸福
8. 被人看重的感覺

除了一個，幾乎所有這些願望都會得到滿足。
但是有一個幾乎與渴求得到食物和睡眠一樣深
切，一樣迫切的願望是絕少得到滿足的。它就是
弗洛伊德說的"做大人物的慾望"，而迪威稱之為
"做名人的慾望"。

林肯曾在一封信中寫道：每個人都喜歡恭維。
威廉·詹姆斯說：人類天性的最深處是要別人感激

the craving to be appreciated." He didn't speak, mind you, of the "wish" or the "desire" or the "longing" to be appreciated. He said the "craving" to be appreciated.

Here is a gnawing and unfaltering human hunger, and the rare individual who honestly satisfies this heart hunger will hold people in the palm of his or her hand and "even the undertaker will be sorry when he dies."

The desire for a feeling of importance is one of the chief distinguishing differences between mankind and the animals. To illustrate: When I was a farm boy out in Missouri, my father bred fine Duroc-Jersey hogs and pedigreed white-faced cattle. We used to exhibit our hogs and white-faced cattle at the country fairs and livestock shows throughout the Middle West. We won first prizes by the score. My father pinned his blue ribbons on a sheet of white muslin, and when friends or visitors came to the house, he would get out the long sheet of muslin. He would hold one end and I would hold the other while he exhibited the blue ribbons.

The hogs didn't care about the ribbons they had won. But Father did. These prizes

的慾求。注意！他不是說"希望"或"慾望"甚至
"希求"得到別人的感激。他說的是"慾求"得到感
激。

　　這就是全人類忍受著撕咬般苦痛而又執迷不
悟的渴求。那些老老實實滿足於這一內心渴求的
鳳毛麟角者，才能將其他人玩弄於股掌之間。並
且"即使是實施者都將會抱恨而逝"。

　　對被人看重的感覺的慾望是人類與動物的主
要差別之一。在我還是個密蘇里州一個農場的男
孩時，父親養了些短頭紅豬和純正白臉小牛。我
們常去西部鄉村集市和牲畜展覽會展示我們養的
豬和牛。我們得分第一。父親將藍色錦帶別在白
棉布單上。一旦朋友或來訪者登門，他便拿出那
塊長長的白棉布單。他握住一頭，我握住另一頭，
把藍錦帶展開。

　　豬並不在意它們贏得的錦帶，但父親卻在意。

gave him a feeling of importance.

If our ancestors hadn't had this flaming urge for a feeling of importance, civilization would have been impossible. Without it, we should have been just about like animals.

It was this desire for a feeling of importance that led an uneducated, poverty-stricken grocery clerk to study some law books he found in the bottom of a barrel of household plunder that he had bought for fifty cents. You have probably heard of this grocery clerk. His name was Lincoln.

It was this desire for a feeling of importance that inspired Dickens to write his immortal novels. This desire inspired Sir Christoper Wren to design his symphonies in stone. This desire made Rockfeller amass millions that he never spent! And this same desire made the richest family in your town build a house far too large for its requirements.

This desire makes you want to wear the latest styles, drive the latest cars, and talk about your brilliant children.

It is this desire that lures many boys and girls into joining gangs and engaging in criminal

這些獎勵給他一種被人看重的感覺。

如果我們的祖先沒有對被看重這種感覺有火熱的渴求,文明就將無從談起。沒有它,我們可能和其他動物沒有兩樣。

也正是這種慾望導致一個沒有受過教育的、貧窮的雜貨鋪職員學習了一些法律書籍。這些書是他在一個日用品的桶底發現,並花十五美分買下的。你可能聽說過他,他的名字叫林肯。

也正是這種想被人看重的慾望,激勵狄更斯寫出了他的不朽作品。這種慾望激勵了克里斯朵夫·沃倫設計出他的"石頭交響樂"。這種慾望使洛克菲勒聚集了他永遠花不完的萬貫家財。正是這同一慾望使得你所在鎮的最富有的家庭,建起了一棟超過它的需求的大屋。

這種慾望使你想穿最新式樣的時裝,開最新潮的名車,談論你名聲顯赫的子女。

但也是這種慾望,誘惑許多少男少女加入幫

activities. The average young criminal, according to E.P. Mulrooney, onetime police commissioner of New York, is filled with ego, and his first request after arrest is for those lurid newspapers that make him out a hero. The disagreeable prospect of serving time seems remote so long as he can gloat over his likeness sharing space with pictures of sports figures, movie and TV stars and politicians.

If you tell me how you get your feeling of importance, I'll tell you what you are. That determines your character. That is the most significant thing about you. For example, John D. Rockefeller got his feeling of importance by giving money to erect a modern hospital in Peking, China, to care for millions of poor people whom he had never seen and never would see. Dillinger, on the other hand, got his feeling of importance by being a bandit, a bank robber and killer. When the FBI agents were hunting him, he dashed into a farmhouse up in Minnesota and said, "I'm Dillinger!" He was proud of the fact that he was Public Enemy Number One. "I'm not going to hurt you, but I'm Dillinger!" he said. Yes, the one signifi-

派,捲入犯罪活動。根據紐約的一位警官伊‧皮‧
穆爾羅尼的調查,通常這類年輕的罪犯都是趾高
氣揚,被捕後他的第一要求是看那些把他作為英
雄進行渲染性報導的報紙。當他得意洋洋於與運
動員、電影和電視明星們的照片共享報紙版面時,
服刑期令人討厭的前景看來遙遙無期。

　　如果你告訴我,你是如何獲得被人看重的感
覺的,我會告訴你它們是什麼。這取決於你的性
格。這對你而言最重要。例如,約翰‧狄‧洛克非
勒是通過捐資,在中國北京建立一座現代化醫院
而獲得這種感覺的。醫院是為治療那些他從未見
過,也將不會見到的百萬窮苦人而建的。另一方
面,狄林格是通過當歹徒、銀行搶劫犯和殺人越獄
獲得這種感覺的。當聯邦調查局特工追捕他時,
他衝進明尼蘇達州的一座農莊,並說:“我就是狄
林格!”他以自己成為“公共第一號敵人”這個事實
而感到驕傲。他說:“我不會傷害你,但我就是狄
林格!”所以,狄林格和洛克菲勒之間最主要的區

cant difference between Dillinger and Rockefeller is how they got their feeling of importance.

History sparkles with amusing examples of
famous people struggling for a feeling of importance. Even George Washington wanted to be
called "His Mightiness, the President of the U-
nited States"; and Columbus pleaded for the title "Admiral of the Ocean and Viceroy of
India." Catherine the Great refused to open letters that were not addressed to "Her Imperial
Majesty"; and Mrs. Lincoln, in the White
House, turned upon Mrs. Grant like a tigress
and shouted, "How dare you be seated in my
presence until I invite you!"

Our millionaires helped finance Admiral
Byrd's expedition to the Antarctic in 1928 with
the understanding that ranges of icy mountains
would be named after them; and Victor Hugo
aspired to have nothing less than the city of
Paris renamed in his honor. Even Shakespeare,
mightiest of the mighty, tried to add luster to his
name by procuring a coat of arms for his family.

People sometimes became invalids in order
to win sympathy and attention, and get a feeling
of importance. For example, take Mrs. McKin-

別就是看他們是如何獲得這種感覺的。

帶著名人的有趣的榜樣，歷史點燃了人們爲獲取被人看重的感覺而進行的努力。即使喬治·華盛頓也希望被稱爲"美國總統閣下"。哥倫布祈求得到"大洋統帥和印度總督"的頭銜。凱莎琳大帝拒絕拆信封上沒注上"呈皇後陛下親啓"的信。在白宮，林肯夫人像隻母老虎似地罵格蘭特夫人："沒我的邀請，你怎麼膽敢坐在我的面前?!"

1928年，百萬富翁出資幫助柏德元帥遠征南極洲，他們明白那塊冰山構成的地域將以他們命名；維克多·雨果立志只要以他的名義重新命名巴黎城，他可以犧牲一切。就連莎士比亞這位巨人中的巨人，也曾試圖通過爲其家族獲得一件戰袍而給自己的名聲增添榮譽。

爲了贏得同情和引人注意，並以此獲得被人看重的感覺，人們有時變得病態。以麥克琳爲例，

ley. She got a feeling of importance by forcing her husband, the President of the United States, to neglect important affairs of state while he reclined on the bed beside her for hours at a time, his arm about her, to sleep. She fed her gnawing desire for attention by insisting that he remained with her while she was having her teeth fixed, and once created a stormy scene when he had to leave her alone with the dentist while he kept an appointment with John Hay, his secretary of state.

The writer Mary Roberts Rinehart once told me of a bright, vigorous young woman who became an invalid in order to get a feeling of importance. "One day," said Mrs. Rinehart, "this woman had been obliged to face something, her age perhaps. The lonely years were stretching ahead and there was little left for her to anticipate".

"She took to her bed; and for ten years her old mother traveled to the third floor and back, carrying trays, nursing her. Then one day the old mother, weary with service, lay down and died. For some weeks, the invalid languished; then she got up, put on her clothing, and re-

她強迫她丈夫,也是美國一位總統,疏理國政,要
他靠在床邊,與她同臥幾個小時,還要用手臂抱著
她睡,以此來獲得被人看重的感覺。她堅持要他
在她鑲牙時留在身邊,以此滿足她那要引人注目
的慾望。一次,他因爲赴國務卿約翰·海依的預
約,而讓她與牙醫待在一起,竟引得她雷霆大發。

作家瑪麗·羅伯特·賴哈特曾告訴過我一個故
事:"一個聰明、富有活力的青年女子爲了獲得被
人看重的感覺而病入膏肓。賴哈特說:"某天,這
位女子被迫面對某種東西,也許是年齡問題。孤
獨的歲月正在眼前延伸,幾乎沒有給她留下任何
她期盼的。她躺在床上,有十年光景,她的老母親
來到三樓,再帶著盤子回來護理她。後來有一天,
老母親勞累過度,躺倒後就去世了。有幾個星期,
病人了無生氣。再後來,她起了床,穿上衣服,從

sumed living again."

Some authorities declare that people may actually go insane in order to find, in the dreamland of insanity, the feeling of importance that has been denied them in the harsh world of reality. There are more patients suffering from mental diseases in the United States than from all other diseases combined.

此開始新生。"

有些權威人士稱,爲了在夢幻裡找到被人看重的感覺,人們實際上已經變瘋了。被人看重的感覺在現實這個嚴酷的世界裡已被否定。在美國,遭受精神病折磨的病人比所有其他疾病患者相加還要多。

欣賞

人生在世,都是爲幸福而來,幸福究竟是什麼呢?這篇文章也許會給你一個答案。幸福的涵義其實就是"得到你渴望得到的東西"。幸福和痛苦就像人跟人的影子一樣,形影不離,相伴相隨。生命個體的一切幸福或痛苦的源泉都歸根結底爲一個字:"慾(desire)"。因爲人的感官越健全,越發達,人的慾望就越多。越多就越難以滿足,這樣,痛苦就越深。人生活在世界上就是不斷滿足各種慾望的過程。

卡耐基的這篇散文通篇沒有一句大道理。語言簡潔曉白,毫無晦澀拗口之處。遣詞到位,沒有任何專業性很強的生詞或難詞,全是日常生活中口語化很強的詞語。語法簡單。句子結構口語化。像我們的"大白話",充滿平民氣息,毫無故作深沉之舉。

9.A Good First Impression

Carnegie Dale

At a dinner party in New York, one of the guests, a woman who had inherited money, was eager to make a pleasing impression on everyone. She had squandered a modest fortune on sables, diamonds and pearls. But she hadn't done anything whatever about her face. It radiated sourness and selfishness. She didn't realize what everyone knows: namely, that the expression one wears on one's face is far more important than the clothes one wears on one's back.

Charles Schwab told me his smile had been worth a million dollars. And he was probably understating the truth. For Schwab's personality, his charm, his ability to make people like him, were almost wholly responsible for his extraordinary success; and one of the most delightful factors in his personality was his captivating smile.

Actions speak louder than words, and a smile says, "I like you. You make me happy. I

9. 良好印象術

卡耐基·戴爾

　　在紐約的一次晚宴上，一位繼承了一筆遺產的女賓，急於給每個人留下愉快的印象。她將有限的財產揮霍在黑貂皮衣、鑽石和珠寶上。但是她對自己的面容卻不做任何修飾，流露出一種酸腐和自私。她對人人自明的東西卻一無所知，即：一個人臉上的表情遠比一個人身上穿的衣服重要的多。

　　查爾斯·斯科威伯曾對我說過，他的微笑價值連城。也許他深諳此道。他的性格、風度、能力深受人們喜愛。這些促成了他的非凡成功。他性格中最令人快慰的因素之一就是他的迷人的微笑。

　　行動勝過語言。微笑的含義是："我喜歡你。你使我愉快。我很高興見到你。"

am glad to see you."

That is why dogs make such a hit. They are so glad to see us that they almost jump out of their skins. So, naturally, we are glad to see them. A baby's smile has the same effect.

Have you ever been in a doctor's waiting room and looked around at all the glum faces waiting impatiently to be seen? Dr. Stephen K. Sproul, a veterinarian in Raytown, Missouri, told of a typical spring day when his waiting room was full of clients waiting to have their pets inoculated. No one was talking to anyone else, and all were probably thinking of a dozen other things they would rather be doing than "wasting time" sitting in that office. He told one of our classes: "There six or seven clients waiting when a young woman came in with a nine-month-old baby and a kitten. As luck would have it. She sat down next to a gentleman who was more than a little distraught about the long wait for service. The next thing he knew, the baby just looked up at him with that great big smile that is so characteristic of babies. What did that gentleman do? Just what you and I would do, of course, he smiled back at the ba-

　　這就是爲何狗討人喜歡的原因。它們見到人總是那麼欣喜若狂。自然，人也會高興見到它。嬰兒的微笑具有同樣的效果。

　　你有沒有去過醫生的候診室，環顧過周圍耐心候診的每張陰鬱的臉？密蘇里州的洛伊塔鎮的獸醫斯狄芬‧凱‧斯浦羅醫生，說起過一個特別的春天，他的候診室擠滿了替自己寵物注射疫苗的顧客。相互間沒一個人交談。所有人可能都在想亂七八糟的其他事情。諸如寧可自己被注射疫苗也不願站在那裡"浪費時間"。他對他敎的班裡的一個人說："當一個年輕婦女抱著一個九個月大的嬰兒和一頭小貓進來時，已有六七個人在等候。碰巧，她坐在了一位紳士旁邊。這位男士因爲等得過久，已有點心神不安。他知道的接下來發生的事就是：嬰兒剛好看著他，臉上露出那種攝人心魄的微笑，是那種稚氣未褪天眞的孩子笑。那位男士有什麼反應呢？換了你我也會和他一樣，他對著孩子還以微笑。很快，他與孩子的母親談起

by. Soon he struck up a conversation with the woman about her baby and his grandchildren, and soon the entire reception room joined in, and the boredom and tension were converted into a pleasant and enjoyable experience."

An insincere grin? No. That doesn't fool anybody. We know it is mechanical and we resent it. I am talking about a real smile. A heartwarming smile, a smile that comes from within, the kind of smile that will bring a good price in the marketplace.

Professor James V. Mc Connell, a psychologist at the University of Michigan, expressed his feelings about a smile. "People who smile," he said, "tend to mange, teach and sell more effectively, and to raise happier children. There's far more information in a smile than a frown. That's why encouragement is a much more effective teaching device than punishment."

The employment manager of a large New York department store told me she would rather hire a sales clerk who hadn't finished grade school, if he or she has a pleasant smile, than to hire a doctor of philosophy with a somber

這個孩子以及自己的孫子。接著，全屋子的人都加入了他們的談話。厭煩和緊張隨之轉變成了一次愉快的興趣盎然的經歷。"

假意露齒而笑？不行。這騙不了任何人。人人都知道那是一種機械動作。人人都恨這種假笑。我談的是眞正的微笑，一種發自內心的熱情洋溢的微笑。這種微笑在市場上才能帶來好價錢。

密執安州大學心理學家詹姆斯・韋・麥克科尼爾教授表述過他對微笑的情感。他說："微笑的人更容易從事管理、教育和推銷，培養更幸福的孩子。微笑所蘊涵的意義遠勝過皺眉。這也是爲何鼓勵比懲罰是一種更有效的教育手段。

紐約一家大商場職業部經理告訴我，她寧願雇用一個小學沒有畢業的人做推銷員，只要他或她具有令人愉快的微笑，也不會雇用一個滿臉憂鬱的有哲學博士頭銜的人。

face.

The effect of a smile is powerful — even when it is unseen. Telephone companies throughout the United States unseen. Telephone companies throughout the United States have a program called "phone power" which is offered to employees who use the telephone for selling their services or products. In this program they suggest that you smile when talking on the phone. Your "smile" comes through in your voice.

Robert Cryer, manager of a computer department for a Cincinnati, Ohio, company, told how he had successfully found the right applicant for a hard-to-fill position: "I was desperately trying to recruit a Ph.D. in computer science for my department. I finally located a young man with ideal qualifications who was about to be graduated from Purdue University. After several phone conversations I learned that he had several offers from other companies, many of them larger and better known than mine. I was delighted when he accepted my offer. After he started on the job, I asked him why he had chosen us over the others. He

　　微笑的力量無窮——即使眼睛看不見時。全美電話公司的服務眼睛就看不見。全美電話公司有一個叫"電話力量"的項目。它是提供給那些用電話推銷產品和服務的雇員的。在這個項目中，他們建議雇員在電話交談時要微笑，這種微笑來自於聲音。

　　俄亥俄州辛辛納提一家電腦部門的經理羅伯特·科拉約說過他是如何成功地正確申請到一份難以填補的職位的："我正千方百計爲部門招募一個電腦學科方面的哲學博士。我最終敲定了一個即將從葡爾帝大學畢業的資格理想的年輕人。經過幾次電話交談，我了解到他還受到其他幾家公司的青睞，那幾家公司比我公司大得多，條件也優越的多。當他接受我的條件時，我大喜過望。他開始工作後，我問過他爲何選中我公司而放棄其

paused for a moment and then he said: 'I think it was because managers in the other companies spoke on the phone in a cold, businesslike man-ner, which made me feel like just another business transaction. Your voice sounded as if you were glad to hear from me...that you really wanted me to be part of your organization.' You can be assured, I am still answering my phone with a smile."

The chairman of the board of directors of one of the largest rubber companies in the United States told me that, according to his observations, people rarely succeed at anything unless they have fun doing it. This industrial leader doesn't put much faith in the old adage that hard work alone is the magic key that will unlock the door to our desires. "I have known people," he said, "who succeeded because they had a rip-roaring good time conducting their business. Later, I saw those people change as the fun became work. The business had grown dull. They lost all joy in it, and they failed. "You must have a good time meeting people if you expect them to have a good time meeting you."

他公司。他略停了一會兒,然後說:'我想大概是因爲其他幾家公司的經理,在電話交談中用的是一種淡漠、公事公辦的語氣的緣故吧。這種語氣使我覺得像是另外一場商業交易。而你的聲音聽起來讓人覺得你很高興與我交談──讓人感到你是眞誠地想使我成爲貴公司的一員。'毫無疑問,我現在仍然帶著微笑接每個電話。"

美國一家最大的橡膠公司董事會主席曾告訴我,根據他的觀察,人對某事如果沒有樂趣去做,那成功者將寥寥無幾。這位工業巨頭對"只有努力工作才是打開慾望之門的神奇鑰匙"這句古老格言並不是十分信奉。他說:"我認識那些成功的人,因爲他們有歡樂愉快的時光經營自己的事業。後來,當樂趣變成工作時,我發現那些人變了。事業變得沉悶單調,他們失去了事業中所有的樂趣。他們失敗了。"

如果你期望人們見到你時愉快,那你見到別人時也一定要愉快。

I have asked thousands of business people to smile at someone evey hour of the day for a week and then come to class and talk about the results. How did it work? Let's see...Here is a letter from William B. Steinhardt, a New York stockbroker. His case isn't isolated. In fact, it is typical of hundreds of cases. "I have been married for over eighteen years," Wrote Mr. Steinhardt, "and in all that time I seldom smiled at my wife or spoke two dozen words to her from the time I got up until I was ready to leave for business. I was one of the worst grouches who ever walked down Broadway."

"When you asked me to make a talk about my experience with smiles, I thought I would try it for a week. So the next morning, while combing my hair, I looked at my glum mug in the mirror and said to myself, 'Bill, you are going to wipe the scowl off that sour puss of yours today. You are going to smile. And you are going to begin right now.' As I sat down to breakfast, I greeted my wife with a 'Good morning, my dear,' and smiled as I said it."

"You warned me that she might be surprised. Well, you underestimated her reaction.

　　我要求幾千位生意人一個星期裡每天每一個小時對某人微笑，然後回到課堂來談論結果。結果如何呢？讓我們讀讀這封從一位紐約股票經紀人威廉‧彼‧斯戴漢特那兒來的信。他的情況不是孤立的。事實上，它在眾多事件中是很典型的。信中寫道：“我結婚已十八年多，在這段時間裡，從我起床直到上班離家，我很少對妻子笑一笑，或說上幾句話。我是個走在百老匯街上脾氣最壞的人之一。”

　　“當你要求我帶著微笑談論我的經歷時，我想，我只嘗試一週時間。所以，第二天上午，我梳頭時，看著鏡子中陰鬱的臉，對自己說：‘比爾，今天你要將一臉愁雲一掃而空。你要微笑。而且從現在開始。’當我坐下吃早餐時，我對妻子打招呼說：‘早上好，親愛的。’並且邊說邊微笑。

　　“你提醒過我她可能會感到吃驚。沒錯，可你低估了她的反應。她簡直是手足無措！她驚呆了

She was bewildered. She was shocked. I told her that in the future she could expect this as a regular occurrence, and I kept it up every morning."

"This changed attitude of mine brought more happiness into our home in the two months since I started than there was during the last year."As I leave for my office, I greet the elevator operator in the apartment house with a ' Good morning' and a smile. I greet the doorman with a smile. I smile at the cashier in the subway booth when I ask for change. As I stand on the floor of the Stock Exchange, I smile at people who until recently never saw me smile.

"I soon found that everybody was smiling back at me. I treat those who come to me with complaints or grievances in a cheerful manner. I smile as I listen to them and I find that adjustments are accomplished much easier. I find that smiles are bringing me dollars, many dollars every day."

"I share my office with another. One of his clerks is a likable young chap, and I was so e-lated about the results I was getting that I told him recently about my new philosophy of human

！我告訴她將來她會看到這是習以爲常的事，我從此每天早上都堅持下來了。

"我的態度的變化給我的家庭帶來了更多幸福，自從那以後兩個月裡我們得到的幸福比我們去年一年得到的還要多。

"當我去上班時，我對公寓開電梯服務員說了'早上好'並報以微笑。我用微笑同守門人打招呼。在地鐵電話間換零錢時，我對出納員微笑。站在股票交易所大廳時，我對那些直到最近從沒見過我微笑的人報以微笑。"

"我馬上發現每個人都對我還以微笑。我以一種歡迎的態度接待前來投訴或訴苦的人。我微笑著聽他們訴說，發現完成調解任務比起以往容易得多。我還發現微笑正每天給我帶來越來越多的金錢。"

"我與另一伙伴共用一個辦公室。他有個職員是個可愛的傢伙，我正陶醉於自己近來的收穫，於是將我最近對人際關係的心得告訴了他。他隨

relations. He then confessed that when I first came to share my office with his firm he thought me a terrible grouch — and only recently changed his mind. He said I was really human when I smiled."

"I have also eliminated criticism from my system. I give appreciation and praise now instead of condemnation. I have stopped talking about what I want. I am now trying to see the other person's viewpoint. And these things have literally revolutionized my life. I am a totally different man, a happier man, a richer man, richer in friendships and happiness — the only things that matter much after all."

You don't feel like smiling? Then what? Two things. First, force yourself to smile. If you are alone, force yourself to whistle or hum a tune or sing. Act as if you were already happy, and that will tend to make you happy. Here is the way the psychologist and philosopher William James put it: "Action seems to follow feeling, but really action and feeling go together; and by regulating the action, which is under the more direct control of the will, we can indirectly regulate the feeling, which is not." "Thus

即承認，當我最初與他的公司共用辦公室時，他認爲我是個脾氣壞、討厭的傢伙———最近才改變了這種觀點。他說我微笑時眞的很有人情味。"

我也排除了來自本系統的批評。我現在不再譴責，而是感謝或表揚。我不再談我要怎麼樣。我正試著看看其他人的觀點。這些事的確使我的生活方式發生了革命。我同過去判若兩人，我更快樂、更富有，無論在友情上還是幸福上———這才是最重要的事。"

"你不會覺得不喜歡微笑吧？怎麼辦？只要做兩件事。第一：逼迫自己微笑。如果你是一個人，強迫自己吹吹口哨或哼哼小調或者唱歌。就好像你已經很快樂，這樣一來，就會讓你快樂。以下是哲學家和心理學家威廉·詹姆斯提供的簡便法則：

"行爲伴隨情感，但眞正的行爲與情感是融合在一起的。通過調整行爲，這些行爲多半受意志的控制，我們就能間接地調整情感，而情感是不受意志控制的。"

the sovereign voluntary path to cheerfulness, if our cheerfulness is lost, is to sit up cheerfully and to act and speak as if cheerfulness were already there..."

"這樣,如果我們的快樂之本已喪失,那麼,去做吧,去說吧,通向快樂的自由之路就將愉快地鋪開,因爲快樂就在前面!"

欣賞

上蒼創造了萬物,卻唯獨給人賦予了笑神經,這不能不說是上蒼的恩惠。笑使人跟動物區分開來。既然如此,我們幹嗎還要吝嗇我們的笑呢? 甚至許多人可能已經忘掉了自己具有笑的功能。達·芬奇的《蒙娜麗莎》之所以流芳百世,價值連城,不就是因爲她那神秘的微笑嗎? "一笑泯千仇",那是笑能"化干戈爲玉帛"的神奇功力。但當今是以創造物質財富多寡來衡量一個人成功與否的時代。多少人都成了印證"天下熙熙,皆爲利來;天下攘攘,皆爲利往"這句古話的最好注解。一個"利"字使人們在物慾之海裡迷失。科技的高速發展,卻帶來了人與人之間交往空間的日益狹窄。在城市混凝土森林裡,人可以足不出戶而知天下,整天只面對冰冷的機器,敲打幾下鍵盤就可以安天下。人際交流已潛移默化爲"人機交流"。又到哪裡去尋找久違的微笑呢?

10. Welcome to the Real World

Wes Smith

Congratulations, Graduates. Welcome to the Real World, where there ain't no spring break and Christmas vocation starts the night of December 24 and ends shortly after the wrapping paper comes off.

It is a painful course that you are about to take. The lessons come unannounced. But to aid you upon your entry into the Real World, a few of your predecessors have compiled some sage advice. Heed the following words well. They will do you much more good than all those French adverbs.

In The Real World:

Never answer an advertisement seeking a "liberal roommate." You probably are not that liberal. Having a drink with the boys every night after work is a bad idea. Notice that the boss doesn't do it. That's why he's the boss and they're the boys. Instead of buying a new stereo for your city car, skip a step. Buy a window sticker that says, "It's already been stolen." Never play racquetball with an old guy

10. 歡迎踏上現實社會

韋斯·史密斯

　　祝賀你們，畢業生們，歡迎踏上社會。在這裡，沒有春假，也沒有聖誕結束的十二月二十四日夜晚打開禮物盒子時常有的感情。

　　你們要學的是一門苦惱的課程。沒有宣布，課程便開始了。但爲了幫助你更好地進入社會，你的一些先行者編輯了一些賢明的建議。好好留意下面的這些話，他們將比所有的法語副詞對你更有幫助。

　　在現實社會裡：

　　不要去應徵尋找"思想解放的同屋人"的廣告。你可能沒有那樣解放。每天下班後跟一群夥計去喝酒是個壞主意。你會注意到你的上司不會這樣做。這就是爲什麼他是上司而那些人是夥計的原因了。爲了不去爲你的汽車重新買立體聲收音機，你可超前一步，買一張貼在玻璃上的字條，上面寫著："它已被偷走了。"不要和已打了 40 年

who has played handball for 40 years. He will destroy you. Buy an alarm clock that works. They aren't kidding when they say, "Wash whites separately. Never date a woman whose father calls her "Princess." Chances are she believes it. Never date a man who still goes shopping with his mother. "Heat included" does not mean "Heat guaranteed." Life insurance is best for married people; otherwise, the chief beneficiary is the life-insurance company. Eat good meals. Greasy burgers take their toll. If you don't like your job, quit. Otherwise, shut up. If you get invited to a wedding, send a gift. Otherwise, don't expect a crowd when your turn comes. There is no such thing as a self-cleaning oven. Be nice to the little people. You're still one of them. Young women, just because a man looks like your father doesn't mean he thinks of you as a daughter. Young men learn which finger gets the ring. No one sells a car because it runs too well. Never chew red peppers during a job interview. At some point in your life, your family will be all you have. Treat them right. Decide now what you want on your tombstone. "He had a job that paid well but he hated it" or "He enjoyed his work."

Never get married simply because you fig-

網球的老傢伙打球，他會讓你慘敗的。買一隻性能良好的鬧鐘。當人們說：「把白色的衣物分開洗」時，他們並非在開玩笑。不要和被她的父親稱做「公主」的女孩子約會，很可能她真的相信自己是公主。不要和一個還在和他的母親一起上街買東西的男人約會。「包括暖氣」並不意味著「保證有暖氣」。人壽保險最合適於已婚者，否則，人壽保險公司是主要的受益者。吃有益於健康的飯菜。常買肥肉的人自會付出代價。如果你不喜歡你的工作，要麼辭職，要麼閉口不言。如果你被邀請去參加婚禮，送一份禮物。否則，不要期望在你結婚時會賓客盈門。世界上還沒有自己會乾淨的鍋子。對小人物要友善，因為你也是他們中的一員。對年青的姑娘來說，一個男人看起來有點像你的父親並不意味著他會把你看作是他的女兒。年青的小伙子應該知道哪個指頭戴戒指。沒有人會因為他的汽車跑得太好而把它賣掉的。決不要在求職面試時嚼紅辣椒。在你生命的某些時刻，你的家庭將是你所擁有的一切。好好對待家庭的成員。現在就決定在你的墓碑上是寫上「他曾有一分報酬豐厚但卻令人生厭的工作」，還是寫上「他喜歡他的工作。」

　　不要僅僅是因為覺得該是結婚的時候了便結

ure it is time to get married. Get married because you want to live with someone for the rest of your life, including days off and vacations. Everyone is lonely at times. Learning to deal with it is part of growing up. The only thing worse than asking people how much money they make is telling them how much you make. Get a credit card. Sales clerks are suspicious of cash. Nice people get roaches too. Face up to it, you must dust. A $ 15 haircut hardly ever lasts as long as a $ 5 haircut. Dirty laundry never goes away. Two of the largest groups of people in the world are those who almost went to law school and those who are going to write a book someday. Be aware that until your married friends get a few years of experience in the kitchen, spaghetti will be served. Never trust a landlord to make improvements after you have moved in. If you screw up, admit it. Hurry up and learn patience.

婚，你結婚是爲了想要和一個你願意與他白頭偕老的人共同生活，包括休息日和假期。每個人都有孤獨的時刻。學會怎樣對待它是成熟的一部分。唯一比問別人掙多少錢更壞的事是告訴別人你賺多少錢。力爭一張信用卡，營業員對用現金付款總存有戒心。好人也會碰上蟑螂。你必須正視它，你必須撣撣你身上的灰塵。我花15美元理的髮幾乎從不比花5美元理的髮保持得更長久些。禦衣服從不會自己跑掉。世界上最多的兩種人是那些幾乎考上了法律學院的人和那些準備在某一天寫一本書的人。應該心中有數，除非你的已婚朋友已經有了幾年在廚房裡的經驗，否則擺出來的主食會是通心麵。不要相信房主在你搬進去住以後還會做什麼修繕。如果把事情弄糟了，就承認弄糟了。行動要迅速，但要學會耐心。

欣賞

讀罷這篇散文，從結構上你會覺得兵散零亂，支離破碎，其實現實生活本來就如此。作者正是運用這零散的結構，紛亂的訊息，自然的語言，眞實的感情向畢業生致辭。致辭內容幽默而豐富，語言和語氣錯落有致，不是課堂教學的語言，而是閒談時的口吻，蘊涵著爲人處世、生活、工作等方面的哲理，能啓迪人生，鼓舞青年學生正視現實，正視現實生活中的周圍世界。這正是畢業致辭的一大特點。

11. Set off to a Fast Start in Your New Job

William Di Ellis

As a College Freshman Jay Layden landed a job parking cars in Houston. So did a lot of other young fellows, but Layden considered it a career and pushed off to a very fast start. Within months he was in charge of two parking lots for Allright Auto Parks. Inc. At age 36, he became president of the multimillion-dollar company, the world's largest autoparking firm.

After graduating from Vanderbilt University, Jane Evans went into the training program at Genesco Inc.'s I. Miller Shoe subsidiary. At 25, she was president of I. Miller, subsidiary. At 25, she was president of I. Miller. She became president of Butterick Fashion Marketing Co.. At 30, and at 36 was named executive vice president of General Mills Fashion Group, which grosses over $650 million annually.

There are many stories like these, which add up to an important lesson: a fast start on a new job can program your whole career for success — not just when you're starting out but

11. 下崗之後另求職

威廉姆·迪·艾裡斯

　　傑伊·萊登在大學一年級時，就在休斯敦的一個停車場找到了一份工作。這和很多其他年輕人的情況相同。但萊登把它看作是一種職業，並且努力在一開頭就表現不凡。在幾個月內，他就開始在奧爾賴特汽車停車場有限公司負責兩個停車場。在 36 歲時，他成了這個擁有幾百萬資產，世界上最大的汽車停車場公司的總裁。

　　簡·埃義斯從溫特比爾特大學畢業後，進入了吉尼斯科有限公司米勒製鞋分公司的一個培訓班。25 歲時，她成了米勒公司的總經理。在 30 歲時，她是巴特里克時裝銷售公司的總經理，36 歲時，她被任命為傑納勒爾·米爾斯時裝集團的執行副總裁，該集團的銷售額為 6.5 億美元。

　　類似的例子很多，合在一起就是一條重要的經驗："在新的工作中起步快會把你的整個事業帶向成功——這不僅適用於你剛剛踏上工作崗位，

anytime you change jobs. The faster you rise, the higher you aim. Conversely, a plodding start induces lower expectations.

In studying nine major organizations, management researchers Thomas P. Ference, James A. F. Stoner and E. Kirby Warren found, moreover, that sophisticated organizations make very early judgments about new people. "These judgments, whether accurate or not, become self-fulfilling prophecies," they concluded.

Here are six strategies used by successful business people that can help you get a fast start in a new position.

1. Make yourself visible early. Jack Albrecht found himself lost in a herd of competitive young advertising employees at a larger New York City ad agency. They were assigned to survey drugstore managers on sales of various products – but busy store managers regularly brushed them off. Albrecht decided on a radical tactic. He borrowed a Chesterfield coat and rented a chauffeur-driven car, instructing the driver to deliver him ostentatiously in front of each store visits. Albrecht came in with such an outstanding num-

也適用於你變換工作的時候。你上升得越快,你的目標也就會越高。反過來說,起步緩慢,你的期望就會降低。

在研究了 9 個大的組織機構後,管理研究員托馬斯·費倫斯,詹姆斯·斯托納和柯比·沃倫發現,成熟組織機構在很早就對新來的人作出了評價。他們得出結論說,這些評價,不管是否準確,都會變成一種會自動實現的預言。

下面是成功的工商企業界人士採取的六種戰略,它們會使你在新的崗位上很快升職。

1. 很早就使自己受人注意。傑克·阿爾布雷克特發現自己埋沒在紐約市一個大的廣告公司裡一大群年輕、很有競爭力的雇員中。他們被指派去向雜貨店經理了解各種產品的銷售情況。但忙碌的經理們往往把他們晾在一邊。阿爾布雷克特決定採取一種完全不同的策略。他借了一件切斯特菲爾德牌的上衣,租了一輛配有司機的汽車,讓司機開著車,很風光地送他到一家家雜貨店的門口。在絕大多數情況下,經理們對這種氣派十足的來

ber of store interviews that he was offered an excellent number of store interviews that he was offered an excellent staff job at the agency.

2. Overkill that first assignment. After Victor Kiam graduated from Harvard Business School, he accepted a job with Lever Brothers Co. Selling health and beauty aids to retail stores. He didn't know whether he was a great salesman or not, but he was determined. While the other salesmen put in 30-or 40-hour workweeks, Kiam called on potential customers 12 hours a day, six days a week. He overwhelmed his quota and climbed the marketing ladder at Lever Brothers. Today he is president of Remington Products, Inc.

3. Get the lay of the land. Making a mid-career shift from journalism, Lillian Graeff joined the Cleveland Trust Company. "Going in." Says Graeff, "I decided to use the first three months to learn more about that bank than anyone else knew."

In addition to doing her job, she explored a different corridor each day, noting the names and locations of the various departments. She also spoke with someone from a different opera-

訪顯得很是高興。由於阿爾雷克特和經理們會見的次數比別人多很多，因此，他在這家公司裡得到了一個極好的職位。

2. 把第一次任務完成得好上加好。維克托‧基埃姆在哈佛商學院畢業後，受聘於利弗兄弟公司，向零售店推銷保健化妝品。他不知道自己是否是一個偉大的推銷員，但他幹勁十足。當其他的推銷員每週工作 30 至 40 小時時，基埃姆用一天 12 小時、一週六天的時間去拜訪潛在的顧客，他大大超額完成了指標，創造了該公司最好的銷售記錄。今天，他已是雷明頓產品有限公司的總裁。

3. 熟悉所處的環境。莉蓮‧格拉夫從當記者轉到了克利夫蘭信託公司。她說：「進了這家公司後，我決定用頭三個月的時間去了解這家銀行，從而成為一個對它最為了解的人。」

除了完成自己的工作外，她每天去探索一條不同的走廊，記下各個不同部門的位置和名稱。

tion of the bank each day, asking, "What exactly do your guys do?" By the end of three months, many bank veterans were coming to depend upon her as a quick and authoritative information source. From that fast start, she quickly rose to the position of public-relations officer. The simplicity of the technique still amazes her. "Anybody can do that in any big institution," she says, "It isn't even hard, but the results are fantastic."

4. Say "sure" and figure out how later. Management values the new employee who grabs a challenge and runs with it. Howard Fowler, an experienced construction worker, landed a job in a manufacturing plant in Temple, Texas. He was assigned to general in – plant engineering work. One day the company president sent for him. "Howard, we need a device that will grab the paper strip off the last roller and then cut it into sheets and stack them up without stopping the rollers. Could you build us a thing that would do that?" After a long silence, Fowler said, "Sure." As he now explains, "I didn't have the faintest notion how to make such a thing. All I knew was that I wasn't about to say no." After

她還每天都和一個不同部門的人聊天，詢問“你們到底在做些什麼事?”三個月快結束時，很多銀行的高級職員都已把她當作一個快捷、牢靠的訊息來源。由於起步快她很快就得到了公關官員的職務。這一技巧之簡單依然使她覺得開心。她說：“在任何一個大的組織裡，任何一個人都能做到這一點，它甚至談不上難，但結果卻令人難以置信。

4. 先說“行”，過後再想怎麼辦。管理階層對那些敢於接受挑戰並敢做下去的雇員是會很器重的。霍化德·福勒是一個經驗豐富的板金工，他在得克薩斯州坦普爾的一家製造廠找到了一份工作。他被分配到廠裡的工程部門。有一天，公司經理把他叫去，對他說：“霍華德，我們需要一種裝置，它能把紙從最後的捲筒上取下來，切開，叠好，在這同時捲筒又不能停下來，你能不能為我們設計製作這樣一種裝置。”停了好長一會，福勒回答說：“好的。”他後來解釋說。“我當時對這樣一種設備一點概念都沒有，我所知道的就是當時不該說‘不

a lot of trial and error, he designed a device that solved the problem. Fowler quickly became plant engineer, and after that director of engineering.

5. Rev up your enthusiasm. An enthusiastic newcomer can spark a whole department. Yet some days your enthusiasm will run low. There is a remedy, however; If you want to be enthusiastic, act enthusiastic. Inner enthusiasm follows, and it will have an effect on colleagues and bosses. Even cynical old hands want to help an enthusiastic new person.

6. Dare to change an entrenched method. When Jerry Simpson stated the engineering trainee program at Empire Gas & Fuel Co. Okla, he was eager to make use of his engineering education. But his first trainee assignment found him stashed in a field warehouse counting nuts, bolts and other small parts. Then on to other field warehouses. "Hey," he thought, "I could be sidetracked on this for months!" So he figured out a system of weighing the parts in large hatches, then translating the weight into numbers of units. When the foreman discovered that simpson completed the warehouse inventory in a

'字。"經過很長一段時間的試驗和失敗,他試製成功了一個能解決這一難題的裝置。福勒很快就成爲工廠的工程師後來還成了工程總指揮。

5. 要有熱情。一個熱情的新來者可以點燃整個部門的熱情之火。你的熱情不久也許會冷下來,但還是有補救的辦法:如果你想成爲一個熱情的人,首先行動要熱情。內在的熱情自會產生,而這將會在同事和上司身上產生反響。甚至常嘲笑人的老手也會願意幫助一個熱情的新來者。

6. 敢於去改變舊習。萊里·辛普森從俄克拉何馬州的帝國天然氣和燃料公司的工程人員培訓班結業後,很希望把所有學到的東西用於實踐。但在第一次實習時他卻被分配到了一個倉庫裡去清點螺帽和其他小零件。爾後,他又被指派到另一個油田倉庫工作。"嗨,"他想道:"我可能會成年累月地埋在這裡了。"於是他想出了一個先乘個數的統計方法,當工長發現辛普森只用通常所需時間

fraction of the usual time, he told a supervisor about the young engineer's method. Immediately Simpson was moved into field engineering work. He went on to head a subsidiary. The greatest advantage of the fast start on a new job is the early creation of a winning mystique. But even if you were a little slow shoving off the starting blocks, nothing says you can't go to work tomorrow morning and act as if it was your first day on a new job.

的一小部分就完成了倉庫的清點工作後，他把這
個年輕工程師的方法向上級作了報告。辛普森馬
上被調到油田的工程部門工作，後來又成爲一個
子公司的領導。從新的崗位上很快就嶄露頭角的
最大的好處是在很早階段就建立了一種贏家的神
秘性。但是即使你在排除開頭難的障礙方面行動
較緩，並不等於說你不可以把明天早上起來後要
去幹的工作當作你的新工作。

▰▰▰欣賞▰▰▰

　　下崗是時髦的詞眼，是一個充滿著活力與憂愁的詞
眼。同時也是一個充滿著挑戰和機遇的詞眼。文章指出
下崗並不可怕，而是"在新的工作中起步快會把你的整個
事業帶向成功"，這是作者分析成功者的一個觀點。這一
觀點充滿著人生的哲理，是事實而不是推理。作者用了
大量的事實後，加以說明。在表現手法上，擅長以例證連
引，穿插舉例說明。在謀篇上前後呼應，一氣貫穿。

12. Getting along with Your Boss

George Berkley

From The Junior Clerk to the senior executive, from the newest volunteer to the head of a community fund-raising drive, virtually everyone has a boss who can affect his or her career, health and peace of mind. Maintaining a good relationship with your boss may be critical to your future. Here are ten guidelines for doing just that.

1. Listen. Much of the time we only pretend to listen. We are so busy looking for sign of approval or disapproval or framing our response that we fail to hear what is being said. Good listening means hearing not only what the boss says but also what he or she implies. It means being able to summarize and to respond intelligently. How? Forget any nervousness and concentrate on what your boss is saying. Create eye contact without staring. Take notes. When your boss has finished, pause to show that you are letting the words sink in. Ask a question or two to clarify a few points, or briefly summarize what has

12．與上司相處

喬治·伯克利

從小職員到經理人員，從最新的志願者到一個籌委會的負責人，幾乎每個人都會有一個頂頭上司，他會影響你的職業前途、健康和內心的安寧。和你的上司保持良好的關繫對你的未來可能是很關鍵的。下面是怎樣去做的十個要點：

1．傾聽。有很大一部分時間我們只是假裝著在傾聽別人。我們急於得到肯定或否定的指示或在構思應該怎樣回答，對上司正在講的是什麼反倒沒怎麼聽進去。很好地傾聽意味著不僅要聽上司在講些什麼，還要聽出他或她在暗示什麼。這就是說要能夠概括和恰到好處地作出反應。怎麼去聽呢？忘掉任何緊張的情緒，把注意力集中於你的上司在講些什麼。要有視線的接觸，但不要盯視。不妨作些筆記。當你的上司說完了，稍停一下表示你讓這些話進入了腦子裡。問一二個問題以澄清一些疑問，或者簡潔地復述一下上司所說

been said. Remember: bosses like people who don't have to be told things twice.

2. Be concise. Time is a manager's most precious resource, so brevity is essential. Being brief doesn't mean jamming a lot of information into a rapid-fire monologue. It means being selective, direct and clear. It's a good idea to limit memos to one page. If you must submit a detailed report, begin with a one-page summary. Effective prose reflects not so much an ability to write as an ability to think; make sure you have thought the matter through before you write.

3. Be diplomatic. If you wish to make a point, marshal the supporting facts and present them in a way that makes your idea become obvious. Try as much as possible to let your boss express the idea. A good approach is to offer your boss options. Instead of proposing a particular policy or course of action, present a list of possibilities, including all their merits and demerits, and allow your boss to choose. This was a favorite device of former Secretary of State Henry Kissinger. Such a presentation permits the boss to make the final decision, and it forces you to

的要點。記住：上司喜歡那些不必把一件事對他說兩遍的人。

2.要簡潔。時間是一個經理人員最寶貴的財富之一，所以簡潔是至關重要的。簡潔並不是指射機關槍似地說一大堆音美而無味的話，而是指講話要有選擇，明了和清晰。不妨把備忘錄限制在一頁紙的長度。如果你必須交一份詳細的報告，最好有一頁概要。好文章不光反應了寫作能力，更顯示了思維能力，在你寫東西前應把事情想透些。

3.要有外交手腕。如果你希望表明一個觀點，應列舉事實根據，並應使你的思想顯而易見的陳述出去。儘量讓你的上司表達他的意見。一個很好的辦法是向你的上司提供一些選擇方案，你不是只建議一種特定的政策或行動的方案，而是列舉一些可能性，包括它們所有有利和不利的方面，從而讓你的上司自己去選定。這是前國務卿亨利·基辛格喜歡的方法。這種建議方法能夠讓上司來作出最後的決定，並迫使你更全面，透徹地去想問

consider the problem in a more rounded and thorough manner. The result should benefit both of you. Never reject out of hand a proposal your boss mentions. He probably has seen some merit in it or he wouldn't bother to seek your reaction. If you end up disagreeing, present your objections as questions ("Can we make this change without much disruption?") or as objections others are likely to make ("Personnel might raise the roof on this"). If you can indicate that your objections are based on relevant data not available to him, so much the better. Don't be afraid to present — ever diplomatically — bad news to your supervisor. The employee who is willing to point out gently that the emperor isn't wearing any clothes will be better off in the long run than those who so flatter the boss that they allow him to make bad moves.

4. Solve your own problems. Nothing eats away at a manager's time — and influence — more than employees who can't solve their own problems. Handling you own difficulties will help you develop the skills and contacts you need to work effectively and will raise your value in your boss's eyes.

題,其結果是雙方都有利。絕不要馬上拒絕上司提到的一個建議。他可能看到了這一建議的一些有利的方面,或者他無意徵求你的意見。如果你最後還是不同意,你可以用提問的方式來表示反對意見。(我們是否能稍作一下這種不會引起什麼混亂的變動呢?)或者是提及一下可能有別的人會反對("職員們可能會爲這事鬧翻了天的")。如果你能說明一下你的異議是以你上司還不知道的情況爲依據的,那就更好。不要害怕對你的上司講出——儘管要注意用外交手腕——壞消息。從長而計,那些願意和善地講出皇帝什麼衣服也沒穿的下屬要比那些對上司過分奉承拍馬以至寧願讓他作出壞決定的人日子會好過得多。

4. 解決自己的難題。再也沒有什麼比一個不能解決自己難題的下屬會更多地吃掉一個經理人員時間——以及他的影響的了。解決你自己的難題將有助於你發展技能和擴大接觸面,從而提高工作效率,並會提高你在上司眼裡的價值。

5. Make your boss look good. This is the heart and soul of boss management. Point out his or her strengths to others. Keep him informed. Never offer new information in a meeting where your bosses present. Give him the facts in advance, and let him do the talking. In making your boss look good, you may have to let him take the credit for something you conceived. As long as he isn't chronically stealing your ideas, this will further your long-term interests. Someone once said, "A man can do a great deal of good in the world if he's willing to allow others to take the credit for it." When your boss looks good, you look good; when he's promoted, your chances for promotion improve.

6. Accent the positive. Successful executives are generally optimists who look for the same outlook in their subordinates. The positive approach isn't a mere tactic but an attitude. One skillful subordinate I know seldom uses terms such as "problem", "crisis" or "setback." He describes difficult situations as "challenges", and then makes plans to meet them. In speaking about colleagues to your boss, mention their good points rather than their bad ones. This will

5. 使你的上司有面子。這是處理和上司關係的核心。向別人提出他或她的長處。確保使他消息靈通。在你同上司一起出席的會議上不要提供新的情況。應提前告訴他事實，讓他來談。為了使你的上司有面子，有時候可能不得不把你想出來的主意歸功於他。但只要他不是慣常地剽竊你的思想，這將有助於你的長遠利益。有人說過："一個人如果願意讓別人拿走自己的功勞，他可以做很多的好事。"當你的上司顯得有面子時，你也有面子，當他得到提升時，你得到提升的機會也會增加了。

6. 樂觀。成功的經理人員一般來說都是樂觀的。他們希望下屬有同樣的樂觀精神。樂觀不僅僅是一種戰術，而是一種精神狀態。我認識一個能幹的下屬，他很少用"難題"、"危機"或"受挫"之類的詞。他把困難的形勢叫做"挑戰"，然後制定計劃去迎接挑戰。在同上司談起你的同事時，多提及他們的長處而不是他們的短處。這將有助於你建

help establish you as a team player and enhance your reputation as someone who can handle people.

7. Don't stay late; come in early. Hard work shows enthusiasm and dedication, inspires others and flatters your boss — after all, your're working for him. Put in extra hours at the beginning and not the end of the day. You'll be fresh, not tired. Plus, coming in early says, "I'm eager to get started," while staying late says, "I didn't get things done."

8. Keep your promises. Bosses adjust to their subordinates shortcomings as long as their strengths outweigh them. What they cannot adjust to is uncertainty. If you indicate that you can do an assignment, but fail to, you will make your boss doubt your reliability. When you find you cannot deliver, alert your boss as soon as possible. His annoyance will be far less than if he learns about it later . "It is better to be known for making honest mistakes ," writes management consultant William Delaney, "than as someone whose word cannot be relied upon."

9. Know you boss. "Knowledge is power,"Francis Bacon once said. Learn your boss's back-

立一種團結人的形象，從而增加你在善於和人打交道方面的信譽。

7. 上班早些，但不必推遲下班。努力工作顯示了熱情和奉獻，這能激勵別人，使上司臉上有光——歸根到底，你在爲他幹，把超時工作放在一天的開始，而不是在一天的結束。這樣你會顯得生氣勃勃，而不是疲倦不堪。再說，上班早似乎是在說："我渴望早點開始工作，"而下班晚則是在說："我還沒把事情做完。"

8. 守信用。上司一般能容忍下屬的短處，只要他們的長處超過其短處，他們不能適應的是猶豫不決。如果你表示說你能夠完成一項任務，結果卻沒能完成，這會使你的上司對你的可靠性產生懷疑。當你發現自己難以完成某項工作時，要盡早告知上司。這樣他不高興的程度要遠比到最後才知道低得多。管理顧問威謙·德萊尼寫道："因誠實犯錯誤而爲人所知遠比一個說話不牢靠的名聲來得好。"

9. 了解你的上司。弗朗西斯·培根曾經說過："知識就是力量。"了解你上司的背景、在公司的歷史，

ground, company his tory, work habits, career
goals, likes and dislikes. If your boss is a
sports fan, it's probably not wise to ask him to
solve a major problem the morning after his team
gets trounced. A savvy boss will appreciate the
subordinate who knows him well enough to anticipate his moods and wishes. Be careful not to
leap to conclusions. If your boss never went to
college, you may feel he's jealous of your M.
B. A. as a subordinate.

10. Don't get too close. Knowing your boss
should not reach the point get too close. Knowing your boss should not reach the point at
which you become closely involved with each
other's personal lives. You and your boss aren'
t equals in your organization. Intimate friendship has an equalizing — often perilous — effect. Confidences may be exchanged and later
regretted, inordinate demands may be placed on
you, and your freedom to think and act inde-
pendently may be curtailed. Being too close to
your boss might cause coworkers to distrust you
and to try to undermine your position. Anyone
who bases his standing in an organization solely
on his relationship with his boss has rooted him-

工作習慣，職業目標，喜歡什麼和不喜歡什麼。如果你上司是一個運動迷，那麼在他所在的隊被擊敗後的第二天早上你還去讓他解決一個重要的問題，就顯得有點不明智了。一個精明的上司欣賞那些了解自己，能預知自己的心情和希望的下屬。小心不要很快得出結論。如果你的上司從沒進過大學，你就可能會感到他忌妒你的管理學碩士學位。

10. 不要與人接觸過於密切。了解你的上司不要超過某種界線，也就是說不應密切到捲入對方私人生活中去。你和你的上司在你們的組織中是不平等的。而親密關係有種使雙方各自的秘密交換後又後悔不及的影響。上司可能會向你提出不適當的要求，你思想的獨立性和行動的自由可能會受到妨礙。和上司接觸過密還可能會引起同事對你的不信任，你的位置會因此而受到威脅。任何一個把自己在一個組織中的地位完全建築在他和上司的關係上的人就像是把自己根植在極易衝走

self in thin soil that can easily be washed away. Maintaining a good relationship with your boss should never be such an overwhelming consideration that interferes with creativity and productivity. The best thing you can do for your boss is to do your job well. Still, a good relationship should help both of you to be more effective, generating in the process blessings and benefits for all.

的薄土上一樣不安全。和上司保持良好的關係絕不應該成為一種妨礙你的創造性和工作效率的主要顧慮。你可能為上司做的最好的事便是把工作做好。不管怎麼說，一種良好的關係會使你們雙方的工作都更有效率，而這種過程中會給大家都帶來益處和幸福。

欣賞

　　與上司相處無不謹小慎微。聰明的人會把每一個細節，每一個言行都設計得完美無缺。難怪有人說下屬永遠都受氣，這說明當下屬的艱難是可想而知的。其實也不然。這關鍵取決於你與上司的關係。如果你有像散文中所說的幾種技巧，你肯定不會愁難與上司相處。與人相處，聰明的人的確會有犧牲精神，不僅是足智多謀，而且還要有綠葉襯托紅花的性格，切不可"志士幽人莫怨嗟，古來材大難為用。"

13. How to Be a Leader

Sherry Suib Cohen

Being Considered a leader in our society is the ultimate compliment. "Leadership has become the universal vitamin C pill," says psychologist David Campbell of the Center for Creative Leadership in Colorado Springs, Colo. "People seem to want millions."

No wonder. Leadership bestows power, commands respect and, most important, fosters achievement. Unlike vitamins, though, leadership skills can't be easily gulped down. They must be carefully cultivated.

Contrary to popular belief, most good leaders are made, not born. They hone their skills in their everyday lives. But which do they cultivate? How do they (and how can you) get others to follow?

Always give credit. Many leaders note that the most efficient way to get a good performance from others is to treat them like heroes. Giving public credit to someone who has earned it is the best leadership technique in the world. It is also

13. 怎樣做一個領導

雪利·蘇伯·科漢

被人認為是一個領導者在我們社會裡是一種非常高的讚譽。科羅拉多州的科羅拉多斯普林斯"創造性領導研究中心"的心理學家戴維·坎貝爾說："領導能力猶如常用的維他命 C 藥片,看起來人們想要成千上萬片的劑量。"

這毫不奇怪。領導能力帶來權力,贏得尊重,而最重要的是,它帶來成就。但與維他命不同的是,領導能力並不是輕易可吞下去的,它們需要仔細培養。

和一般的觀念相反,絕大多數出色的領導者是後天造就而不是先天生成的。他們在日常生活中鍊就了他們的技能。但是,他們培養的是哪些素質呢? 他們是怎樣贏得人心的呢?

經常讚揚別人。很多領導人物指出,讓別人出色工作最有效的辦法是像對待英雄似地對待他們。世界上最好的領導技巧是當有人取得成就時就當眾讚揚他們。這也是一種人們永遠不會忘記

an act of generosity that's never forgotten.

Giving credit is more effective than even the most constructive criticism, which often hurts rather than helps. Kenneth Blanchard, co-author of The One-Minute Manager, agrees. "Catch people doing something right!" he says. Then tell everyone about it. The loyalty you will generate is arguably the most important currency a leader has.

Take informed risks. "The best leaders know that taking a risk is not a thoughtless exercise," says management consultant Marilyn Machlowitz. "Sky divers don't go up in an airplane without checking the parachutes beforehand."

Because the idea of risk also carries with it the possibility of failure, many of us tend to wait for others to take charge. But if you want to be a leader you must learn to fail — and not die a thousand deaths. Pick yourself up and start all over again.

Show the way. In 1965, Lee Ducat was a Philadelphia homemaker with a child who had just been found to have diabetes. Ducat tried to reach out to other mothers of diabetic kids, but at first no one wanted to talk.

的慷慨行爲。

給予讚揚比即使是最有建設性的批評更有效。這種批評常常會傷害人，而不是幫助人。《一分鐘經理》一書的作者之一肯尼思·布蘭查德也這樣認爲："注意人們做得對的時候，然後把這告訴大家。這樣人所引發的忠誠很可能是一個領導者所能擁有的最重要的成功保證。

冒預料中的風險。"最好的領導者都知道冒風險並不是一種魯莽的行爲。"管理顧問瑪裡琳·馬克洛維茨這樣說，"跳傘者在沒有檢查降落傘是否準備好之前是不會上飛機的。"

由於冒風險也包含了失敗的可能性，我們中很多人就傾向於讓人們帶頭去冒險。但是，如果你想成爲一個領導者，你就必須學會失敗——但不是一受挫折就躺倒不幹，而是跌倒了再爬起來，一切從零開始。

以身作則。李·杜坎特是費城的一個家庭婦女，1965 年，她的一個孩子得了糖尿病。杜坎特特別想和其他有糖尿病孩子的母親交往。但一開始沒有人願意和她交談。

Finally Ducat managed to find three other mothers willing to share their experience, and from that beginning she went on to found and lead the Juvenile Diabetes foundation, which currently has 150 chapters worldwide. Ducat also formed and now heads the National Disease Research Interchange, which procures human tissues for vital research. Lee Ducat's secret? Being a role model.

"Have you ever noticed that if you smile at people, they smile back?" she asks. "Well, if you're giving, people want to give right back. If you're sure-footed, they want to follow in your footsteps, If your're confident about reaching a goal, others echo that confidence and try to achieve it for you." "The best thing you can do is get followers to mirror your actions by being what you wish them to be."

Keep the faith. Successful leaders often say that if you trust others to do well, they will. If, on the other hand, you believe your people will fail, they will probably meet your expectations as well. Businessman — philanthropist W. Clement Stone suggests that you express your faith in a letter. He says the executive who

後來，杜坎特終於設法找到了三個願意彼此分享經歷的母親，自此以後，她再接再勵，建立並領導了"靑少年糖尿病基金會。"現在該基金會在全世界已有 150 個分會。杜坎特還建立並領導了"全國疾病研究交流中心"，該中心設法獲得供生命研究用的人體組織。杜坎特成功的秘密是什麼？身體力行。

她這樣問道："你是否注意到，如果你向人們微笑。他們也會向你報以微笑嗎？"是的。如果你給予別人，別人也會給予你。如果你的步伐堅定，人們就會跟從你。如果你對達到一個目標充滿信心，其他人就會同樣具有信心並會試著和你一起去實現它。"你能做的最好的事情是得到這樣一些跟隨者，他們效仿你的行爲、成爲你所希望的那種人。"

堅持信念。成功的領導者常說，如果你相信別人能做好，他們就會做好。反之，如果你相信你的人會失敗，他們可能眞的會和你想像的一樣失敗了。信奉博愛主義的企業家克萊門特·斯通建議你以寫信的方式來表達你對別人能獲得成功的信念。他說，那些給推銷員寫信表示信任，給推銷

writes of faith in and commitment to his sales-people can motivate them to break records; the teacher who writes individual notes of encouragement to students can lead them to extraordinary heights. Having faith in someone gives him selfconfidence and pleasure. It may sound corny, but the experts agree it works.

Get a compass. People don't follow leaders who lack direction. Estee Lauder, founder of the cosmetics company, has led thousands of employees to great success. She claims that every business leader she knows puts a clear picture of what he wants to achieve in his mind and stays focused on the picture. "People want to follow those who promise — and deliver — success," she says.

Act the part. Good leaders have learned to sound and look like winners. They may sometimes doubt themselves, but they don't show it, says management consultant Paula Bern. They act as if they know where they're going.

Leaders also know that appearance and manners count. They are usually pleasant to be with; their speech is polished, their demeanor unruffled and assured.

員一定的自主權的領導者們,可以鼓勵推銷員打破他們原有的推銷記錄;那些給學生寫鼓勵性評語的教師能夠把他們的學生引向非凡的高度。對別人抱有信心能給予他自信和快樂。這聽起來似乎是陳腔濫調,但專家們認爲這確是有效的。

有明確的目標。人們不會跟從那些沒有方向感的領導。埃斯蒂·勞德———埃斯蒂·勞德化妝品公司的創始人引導了她的成千上萬的雇員走向巨大的成功。她說,她所知道的每一個商界領導人在心中都有一幅他想要達到的目標的清晰構想,並總是瞄著這一構想。她說:"人們願意跟從那些許諾成功和帶來成功的人。"

扮演角色。好的領導者都學會了怎樣聽起來和看起來像個勝利者。他們有時可能也會懷疑自己,但他們並不顯露出來,管理顧問葆拉·伯恩說。他們顯得好像很清楚自己在走向何方。

領導人物也知道外表和舉止很重要。他們常常是和藹可親,談吐文雅,舉止穩重,信心十足。

Be competent. Knowledge is power, the saying goes, and the best leaders know that their savvy and proficiency are part of their charisma. Competence impels people, and will make them look to you for guidance and direction.

Foster enthusiasm. "When people understand the importance of work, they lend their mental strengths," says Lee Ducat. "But, oh, when they get excited about the work, all their energy gets poured into the job. That's a massive force! The best way to generate excitement? Be enthusiastic yourself — it's contagious."

Delegate. Chris Alger, a young, divorced Forida mother, was too busy getting her own life together to think about leading anyone anywhere. But one day she noticed how many people were going hungry in downtown Miami. She returned that evening with a friend and 20 bologna sandwiches. The next night, she brought more sandwiches. She began preparing soup and coffee, and soon it became apparent that she and her friend couldn't handle everything. "I'd never mobilized people before, but I had no choice," says

要有競爭性。常言說，知識就是力量。而最出色的領導人物都知道他們的見多識廣和對專業精通是他們的非凡魅力的一部分。具有競爭性能促進人們向你尋求引導和方向。

激發熱情。"當人們理解了工作的重要性時，他們便會用心工作，"杜坎特說。當他們對工作充滿激情時，他們所有的活力都會激發出來，全身心地投入工作，這是一種巨大的力量。那麼，激發激情的最好辦法是什麼呢？你自己投入激情，而這種激情是會感染別人的。

授權。克里斯·阿爾杰，一個離了婚的年輕母親，曾一直忙於重新組織自己的生活而無心去想有關領導別人的事。但有一天她注意到在邁阿密市區有很多挨餓的人。那天傍晚她回來時帶了一個朋友和 20 個紅腸三明治。第二天晚上，她買了更多的三明治。她開始準備湯和咖啡，不久，她和她的朋友很明顯地忙不過來了。"我以前從來沒有動員別人，但我別無選擇。"阿爾杰說，"別人在

Alger. "Others were depending on me to act. I picked up phone."

She became so visible that a local newspaper and television station did stories on her. The power of the press produced other volunteers, among them a philanthropist who donated money, contacts and organizational skills. Now volunteers make and serve 500 sandwiches a day, as well as gallons of soup. "It's not just me doing all this," Alger stresses. "So many have become involved. I couldn't do it alone."

Exactly. Leadership.

等著我行動，於是我拿起了電話。”

　　她變得越來越引入注目，地方報紙和電視臺都來採訪她。這種輿論的力量引來了其他的義務人員，他們中有一個是慈善家，他捐獻了錢、介紹了關係和組織的技巧。現在義務人員每天製作和提供 500 份三明治，以及大量的湯。“所有這些，不是我一個人幹得了的。”阿爾杰強調說，“有這麼多人要來，我一個人肯定是不行的。”

　　這就是領導。

欣賞

　　領導應是眾人之傑，應具有非凡的智慧和能力。正因為如此，才會有“一種非常高尚的讚美。但作為一個有能力的領導，並不是輕易吞下去的，它們需要認真培養。”文章圍繞這一主題，精挑細選，事例蟬聯，引語豐富自然，說明了如何成為一名領導者。立意之處平凡而睿智，現實而有啟發。大凡讀了此文會覺得做下屬難，做領導更難。但要做一個傑出的領導，只有從每件事中鍛鍊自己，靠溜須拍馬即使混個官位，也會遭到世人的唾罵。並不會得到世人的承認和讚美。這篇文章的觀點字句真誠，其結構好似一席悠閒聊天，別樹一幟。

14. Learning English

Joan Waller

Many students have asked me what is the best way of learning English, as if there were some magical way by which they could wake up one morning able to write and speak English fluently. But a language is like any other skill; it has to be practiced regularly. If you want to be a pianist or to play volleyball well, you know that you need to play every day, and that you have to master the basic skills before you can become proficient. It is the same with learning a language: trying to read or speak a little every day is better than spending three hours on English one day, and then forgetting all about it for the rest of the week!

But there are other factors which will help you to be successful, and there are some methods by which you can help yourself to become more proficient.

Research has shown that motivation is very important in learning a language, that you need to be enthusiastic about it, and to be interested

14. 英語學習

瓊·渥爾樂

　　曾有許多學生問我，學習英語有什麼捷徑，就好像有什麼魔法，可以使他們一覺察就能流利地讀寫英語似的。語言和其他任何技巧一樣，必須經常地練習。你知道，假如你想成為一個鋼琴家，或想把足球踢得棒棒的，你就得每天練習，你必須先掌握基本的技巧，才能達到爐火純青的程度。學習語言也是如此：每天設法讀一點英語或說一點英語，比三天打魚，兩天曬網更有效些。

　　除此之外，幫助你取得成功的還有另外一些因素，你還可以借助一些方法，使得你的語言更為純熟。

　　研究表明，在語言學習中，動機是非常重要的，你必須有興趣，有滿腔的學習熱情。不同的人

in it. Different people will have different motives — the desire for promotion, they hope of being able to study abroad, curiosity about a very different culture, and pure intellectual enjoyment, these are only some of the possible motives. But actually wanting to learn is the most important motive of all.

Courage is an essential attribute in learning a language. It takes a lot of courage to speak a language either in front of your friends or to native speakers, but don't be afraid of making mistakes in studies. When I learnt French at school, the teacher insisted that we spoke in complete, grammatical sentences with perfect pronunciation, and as a result, when I visited France, I was afraid to say a single word in case I made a mistake. Nowadays, there are many different forms of English, each with its own constructions and can understand what is said to you, you have succeeded in communicating, which is the purpose of any language. I am not suggesting that you should not learn grammar or that you should ignore the rules of pronunciation; what I am saying is that you cannot expect to speak fluently or write well unless you are

有不同的動機──有的爲了晉升，有的希望出國
留學；有的對截然不同的文化懷有好奇心，有的則
純粹是爲了用腦的樂趣，這僅是這些可能動機中
的一部分。然而，需要學習才是最爲重要的動機。

　　勇氣是學習語言的一個基本的素質，當著你
朋友的面或在以英語爲母語的外國人面前說一門
外語是需要很大勇氣的。但不要耽心出差錯──
我們正是在錯誤中不斷學習的。我在學校學法語
時，法語老師堅持要我們說出的句子要完整，要符
合語法，發音要準確。結果，我在訪問法國時，因
爲怕出差錯，連一個法語字都不敢說。如今英語
的形式可謂多種多樣，每種形式都有自己的結構
和腔調。因此，只要你能聽懂對方說什麼，以及讓
對方明白你的意思，你的交流就算成功了。而交
流正是任何語言的目的。我這並不是說你不必學
語法，你不必重視發音規則，我要說的是：祇有不
怕犯錯誤，並從錯誤中學習提高，你才能期望說得

prepared to make mistakes and to learn by them.

Curiosity is not only a possible motivation, it is also a great help in your learning. Remember that a language is not just a grammatical system, it is the outcome of a certain culture (or in the case of English) of different cultures. It is no good learning strings of words and lists of grammatical rules unless you know as much as possible about the background of the language, so that you can understand the ideas which are being conveyed, the references which are being made, the inferences which can be drawn from then information explicitly given. So learn as much as you can about the different cultures which influence English — watch television programmers, listen to the radio, try to obtain newspapers and magazines which are written by native speakers, look at advertisements, and ,above all, read not textbooks, but novels and poems and plays. They will show you how language is really used. The English language is not an abstract system, it is a living form of expression which derives much of its meaning from the context in which it is used,

流利或寫得漂亮。

　　好奇心不僅可能成爲學習動機，而且還將大大促進你的學習。請記住，語言不只是一個語法體系，它是某一文化的產物，還是多種文化的產物（就英語來說）。僅僅學會一大堆的詞彙和一大串的語法規則是不夠的，你還必須盡可能地了解英語的背景知識，才能懂得詞語所包含的意思，其中的典故，以及從具體材料中可能得出的那些結論。因此你必須盡力了解對英語有一定影響的不同的文化——看電視節目，聽廣播，儘量弄一些原版的英語報刊雜誌看看，或看看廣告，但是，最重要的途徑是閱讀——不是讀課本，而是要讀小說、詩歌、劇本。它們會告訴你語言是怎樣眞正被使用的。英語不是一個抽象的體系，它是一個活生生的表達形式，它們的許多含義是在上下文中得以

and much of its effect from a whole network of extra-linguistic knowledge. If you live in a country where English is the native language, you acquire this knowledge naturally, just as in China you acquired your own cultural knowledge unconsciously. But, because you are unlikely to be able to visit countries where English is spoken as the native language, you have to make a conscious effort to acquire this cultural awareness and knowledge.

So far, I have been writing about the qualities which will help you, as individuals, to learn English. But what can you do in practice? Your government is laying much emphasis upon the importance of learning English, and there are many radio and television programs, as well as textbooks and tapes, which can help you. In the past, much emphasis was given to reading, less to writing, and still less to speaking and listening. But now, ideas are changing. Linguists stress the need to see all the four skills as being complementary; you cannot learn to write well unless you are also able to speak, and the so-called passive skills of reading and listening (they should not be termed passive: all commu-

體現的，它們的效果大多是在語言學之外的整個知識網中產生的。如果你是在一個以英語爲母語的國家，那你會自然而然地獲得這一知識，就如在中國，你在不知不覺中掌握了本國文化知識。但是，由於你不可能去英語國家訪問或暫住，你就必須有意識地下功夫去掌握這些國家的文化知識和獲得文化意識。

　　以上我所談的是有助於學習英語的一些個人素質。但在學習過程中你該做些什麼呢？你們的政府很強調學習英語的重要性——電臺，電視臺播放許多英語節目，還有課本，卡帶，這些都可以幫助你學習英語。在過去，英語學習更多地強調閱讀，較少注重寫作，更不注重聽與說，但現在，一些觀點正在改變。語言學家們強調指出了聽說讀寫四項互爲補充的必要性。只有說得流利，才能寫得漂亮。而所謂的被動技巧，讀與聽（它們不應當被稱作被動技巧，任何的交流，說抑或寫，都有

nication, whether spoken or written, results from interaction between addresser and addressee) are both essential to the development of the languages. You need to work at all four skills, rather than concentrating upon one.

Even so, it is perhaps easier to take oral and aural skills together, and to look for ways of developing them, and then to move on to reading and writing. When you listen to the radio and television, try to finish programs where there are native speakers, in addition to listening to the very good language — teaching courses which are available. Try recording such items as teems broadcasts, and listen to them over and over again, until you used to the speed of delivery, and have really understood them. If you are fortunate enough to have one in your city, attend English Corner — this will give you a chance to practise both speaking and listening regularly, with a sympathetic audience. Try talking to your tape recorder, or read poems and extracts from novels to it, and then listen to yourself speaking, so that you realize what mistakes you are making. Find a good friend, and spend a few minutes a day talking English to

賴於說話人和聽話人的雙向作用）也都是語言發展的重要部分。所以你必須努力掌握這四門技巧，而不要專攻其中的一門。

儘管如此，把聽和說放在一起訓練或許會更容易些。要尋求各種方法來提高這兩種技巧，然後再過渡到讀和寫。除了盡可能聽一些極好的英語課程外，你在收聽英語廣播或電視節目時，要盡量收看以英語爲母語的人主持的節目。設法把新聞這樣一些節目錄下來，一遍遍地反覆聽，直到你適應播音員的速度，並眞正聽懂爲止。如果你所在的城市有一個英語角，那你便眞是有幸。你可以參加它的活動──這會使你有機會和一群友善的人經常地練習聽和說。你還要試著和錄音機"對話"或對著它朗誦詩歌或小說片段，然後放給自己聽，這樣你就會認識到自己所犯的錯誤。找一個好朋友，每天和他一起用英語交談十幾分鐘。

each other; you will feel very foolish at first, but gradually you will start to enjoy yourself. Remember that English is a living, changing language, and that it only becomes really alive when you can actually start communicating with other people in it. Learn songs, and listen to how the original speaker uses stress and timing. Try different word games — there are many. These are a few suggestions — I am sure you will have plenty of other ideas.

Writing is less easy to practise, if you are learning on your own. Some of you may be fortunate enough to have pen-friends, and those who are studying formally will probably have classes in composition. But think about keeping a diary in English — just write a short simple entry each day about the weather or what you have done, and then gradually lengthen your entries, and make them more complex, exploring your ideas and feelings rather than just writing about facts. Try translations of short newspaper items, and ask your friends if they can understand the meaning. Word puzzles and games are extremely goodies I have mentioned, for developing vocabulary. Coping out quotations

一開始，你會覺得這樣做很荒誕，但慢慢地你就會樂在其中。請記住，英語是一門活生生的變化中的語言，因而，只有當你切實地用英語開始交際時，它們才眞正"活"了。聽英語歌曲，注意聽英美人怎樣使用重音和節奏，嘗試著做各種英語文字遊戲——這樣的遊戲種類很多。以上只是有關聽說訓練的幾條建議，我相信你們還會有許多其他的好方法。

　　靠自學練習寫作就不那麼容易了。也許有些人有幸交了一些筆友，還有些人在正規學校學習，或許在上作文課。也許你可以考慮用英文記日記——每天如流水帳似地記下天氣如何，自己做了些什麼就行。以後再逐漸加長，逐漸深化內容，這時除了記些事例，還可以闡述你的觀點，你的情感。試著翻譯一些報上的小條目，並問問你的朋友是否看得明白。我剛才已經提到，字謎和文字遊戲對積累詞彙極有幫助，摘抄一些你特別喜歡

which you particularly like gives you a sense of the structure of an English sentence — avoid proverbs as we don't often use them, but look for extracted from poems, novels and so on.

And that leads on naturally to reading. Remember, as Bacon pointed out, that there are different ways of reading. Sometimes you want to skim a passage quickly to find a particular piece of information. Sometimes you may need to follow a passage very closely, so that you have to check up on the exact meaning in context, of every word or phrase. In that case, use an English-English dictionary, rather than an English-Chinese, as this will help you increase your vocabulary and your awareness of different shades of meaning. But sometimes try reading a novel just for pleasure — don't worry about looking up every word, but try to work out meaning from the context so that you get the gist of the story. If you have already read the novel in a Chinese translation, you find it easier to follow the story in English. And don't ignore the value of the children's literature — because of its importance, some of our best writers are concentrating upon writing for children, and

的句子,可以從中品味句子的結構——不要記諺
語,因爲我們不常用到諺語。要從詩歌,小說等等
作品中摘錄。

下一步自然就談到了閱讀。請記住,恰如培
根所指出的,閱讀有各種不同的方法。有時你需
要很快地瀏覽一篇文章,以查尋某個資料。有時
爲了看透全文,你必須逐句逐句地研讀以理解它
們在上下文中的確切意義。在這種情況下,你最
好使用英英詞典,而不要使用英漢詞典,因爲英英
詞典有助於增加你的詞彙,並能使你體會到某些
細微的差別。不過你有時也要讀一讀娛樂性的小
說——這時你不必費心查閱每一個生詞,只要從
上下文中推斷詞義,能了解故事中的中心思想就
可以了。如果你已經讀了這本小說的中譯本,那
麼讀起原文來就輕鬆一些。不要忽視兒童文學的
價值——由於兒童作品的重要性,我們的一些著
名作家正全力以赴地爲兒童創作。他們的書不僅

their books are extremely well written, but at the same time easier to follow than full-length novels.

There are two different forms of writing, each at the end of spectrum, and in between, there are various modifications of them; these forms are expository and expressive. Expository writing is mainly concerned with conveying ideas and information, and its therefore usually logical and well-organized, making much use of connectives such as therefore, because, in addition, etc. , and the paragraph is used to separate different stages in the explanation of argument. Expressive writing is more personal, and aim at conveying thoughts and feelings; often it is more informal, employs figures of speech, and makes use of narrative, dialogue and imaginative description. the two extremes can be represented by a scientific textbook and a poem. The skills require by each are slightly different; in expository writing the topic sentences of each paragraph, and the connective, but in expressive writing you need to make inference and to bring more background knowledge to work; in fact you have to cooperate closely with the au-

寫得特別好,而同時又比長篇小說明白易懂。

　　寫作有兩種形式,這是同一範疇的兩個方面,在這兩個方面還有許多變體。這兩種形式叫說明式和表現式。說明式文章主要傳遞觀點和訊息,因而常常很有邏輯性,結構嚴謹,並經常地使用連詞,如,"因此、因為、還有"等等。它的段落常常是根據說明或辯論步步展開而分的。表現式文章則更具有個性,其目的在於傳遞思想情感,寫作風格也常常更為自由,可以運用修飾法,以及用記敘的、對話的或想像描繪的寫法。這兩種寫作方式的典型文章可推一部科學讀物和一篇詩歌。兩者所要求的閱讀技巧也略有不同。在說明式中你可以通過認別每段的中心論句和連詞來領會文章的結構。但在表現方式中,你必須作更多的推敲,運用更多的背景知識,事實上,你必須與作者緊密合

thor. By identifying the node of writing before starting to read the whole passage, you will be able to judge which particular skill are most required, and adapt your approach accordingly.

When you look up a word in the dictionary, find out whether there are other related words from the root; for example, if you look up the word "memory" think of other words which sound similar such as memorial, remember, memorize, memorable, and so on. If you come across a new word try to link it up with a word you are already familiar with: you know what I mean by oral English, so what about oration and oratory? "Compare" links up with comparable, comparison, incomparable, etc. And remember how many English words use prefixes and suffixes, so that, with a knowledge of these, you can build up your understanding of how words are constructed: if "tele" means at a distance, then television, telephone, telescope, telepathy all have something in common!

These are just some very basic about to improve your English; I am sure you yourselves could add many other suggestions. I hope some of them will both help and inspire you to make

作。在閱讀全文之前,先要識別寫作方式,這樣才將緊密配合。在閱讀之前,先要認別寫作方式,這樣你將能夠判斷,使用哪種最好,從而相應地調整你的閱讀方式。

當你在詞典中查一個單詞時,看看在同一個詞根上是不是還有相關的詞。例如,在查"記憶"一詞時,你就可聯想到一些類似的詞,如"紀念,記住,熟記,值得紀念的",等等。要是你遇到一個生詞,請試著把這個詞與另一個你已熟識的詞聯繫起來:你知道我說的"oralEnglish"(口語)指什麼,那麼"oration"(演說)和"oratory"(演講術)又是什麼意思呢?"Compare(比較)"和"comparable"(可比較的),"comparison"(比較),"incomparable"(不可比較)都有聯繫,等等。還要記住,有多少英語單詞使用前綴、後綴,有了這些知識,你就會對英語構詞有所了解。如果"tele"的意思是"atadistance"(有一定距離),那麼"television"(電視),"telephone"(電話),"telescope"(電望遠鏡),"telepathy"(心靈感應),就有了某種共同點!

以上所講的只是一些有關怎樣提高英語水平的很基本的方法;我肯定你們還可以補充許多建議。我希望有些方法可以幫助和激發你們新的學

fresh efforts, but remember that it is only your own desire and your willingness to practise that will really bring success. So now the rest is up to you — good luck.

習熱情，但是，請記住，只有你們自己的願望和練習的意願才真正能帶來成功。就看你們的了！——祝你們好運！

▰▰欣賞▰▰

這篇散文的主題是"怎樣提高英語水平的基本方法"。作者運用直射法、滲透法、點化法和舉例說理法等多種散文寫作技巧，剖析了提高英語水平聽說讀寫四種語言技能的基本方法，所介紹的方法可行性和有效性大，並從各種實際學習語言的經驗上總結出提高英語水平的技巧。在表現技巧上，敘議結合，議而敘，敘議渾融，使文章生出一種清新、親切、可信、可行的特殊情調。令人讀來朗暢、輕快、精警、深刻，味永情長，給人神蕩不已時又生幾分形象美和哲理中寄寓美的感受。

15. Six Keys to Quicker Learning

Patricia Skalka

A friend of mine was at a dinner party where two men she knew were discussing. The right stuff, a book about the Mercury space program. While Ted went on and on about the technical details he had picked up from the book, Dan offered only a few tentative comments. "Ted got so much more out of the reading than I did," Dan later said to my friend. "Is he much smarter than I am?"

My friend, an educator, was curious. She knew the two men had similar educational backgrounds and intelligence levels. She talked with each and discovered the answer: Ted just knew how to learn better than Dan did. Ted had made his brain more absorbent by using a few simple skills.

For years, experts had believed that an individual's ability to learn was a fixed capacity. During the last two decades, however, leading

15. 敏捷學習的六種技巧

帕翠莎·斯高克

　　在一次晚宴上，我的一個朋友看到她認識的兩個男士正在討論一本關於水星空間計劃的書，題爲《出色的計劃》。特德滔滔不絕地講述著書中的許多技術細節，而丹恩只做了少許含糊的評論。"特德從閱讀中得到的知識比我多得多。"丹恩後來對我這位朋友說："是不是他比我聰明得多?"

　　我的朋友是個教育家，這個問題使她很感興趣。她知道這兩人所受的教育和擁有的智力水平相近。她與他們一一談了話，得出這樣一個答案：特德只是更懂得運用學習技巧。憑藉幾種簡單的技巧，特德便使自己的大腦能夠吸收更多的內容。

　　很多年來，專家們一直相信個人的學習能力是一成不變的。然而，近二十年來，一些心理學權

psychologists and educators have come to think otherwise. "We have been increasing proof that human intelligence is expandable," says Jack Lochhead, director of the Cognitive Development Project at the University of Massachusetts at Amherst, "We know that with proper skills people can actually improve their learning ability."

Moreover, these skills are basic enough so that almost anyone can master them with practice. Here, gathered from the ideas of experts across the country, are six proved ways to boost your learning ability.

1. Look at the big picture first. When reading new, unfamiliar material, do not plunge directly into it. You can increase your comprehension and retention if you scan the material first. Skim subheads, photo captions and any available summaries. With reports or articles, read the first sentence of each paragraph; with books, glance at the table of contents and introduction.

   All this previewing will help anchor in your mind what you then read.

2. Slow down and talk to yourself. While speed-

威和教育家們開始改變了原有的想法。"我們已不斷證實，人的智力是可以開發的。"設在阿姆斯特的麻州大學認識發展計劃主任傑克·洛克黑德說："我們知道，憑藉正確的技巧，人確實能夠提高他們的學習能力。"

　　而且，這些技巧十分簡單，通過練習，幾乎任何人都能夠掌握。下面是我們根據全國各地專家的看法所收集的經過實踐證明能夠提高你的學習能力的六條方法：

1. 閱讀之前先瀏覽全文

　　　當你閱讀一份新的，不熟悉的材料時，不要徑直去埋頭深讀。先瀏覽全文，你的理解力和記憶力就會有所提高。瀏覽小標題，插圖說明以及其他任何概括性的文字。閱讀報道文章或論文時，要先讀每段的第一句，閱讀書籍時要粗讀目錄和內容介紹。

　　　所有這些前期工作都有利於指導你的閱讀。

2. 放慢閱讀速度，與自己對話

reading may be fine for easy material, slower reading can be much more effective for absorbing complex, challenging works. Arther Whimbey and Jack Lochhead, co-authors of the high school and college handbook Problem Solving and Comprehension, have isolated three basic differences in how good and bad learners study:

• Good learners vocalize, or voice the material, either silently or aloud. They slow down, listening to each word as they read.

• Good learners, when stymied, automatically reread until they understand the material. Poor readers by contrast, just keep going if they don't get it the first time.

• Good learners become "actively involved" with new information. They think about what they read, challenge it, make it their own.

In 1979, Whimbey introduced a slow, vocalized reading method into a five-week, pre-freshman program at Xavier University in New Orleans. Many of the 175 students using this technique jumped two grade levels in comprehension, and their college-aptitude

　　快速閱讀一些簡易材料的閱讀方法是可取的，但要吃透內容複雜，艱澀的作品，慢讀的效果會更好些。大中學生手冊《解題與理解》的作者阿瑟和傑克就閱讀能力的優劣作了分析，得出三個基本的差異。

　　優秀閱讀者對材料進行有聲閱讀，默誦或是朗誦，他們減慢速度，傾聽自己所讀的每一個詞。

　　優秀閱讀者在遇到疑難時，會自覺進行重讀，直到弄懂為止。而閱讀能力較差者恰恰相反，如果他們第一次不懂，他們會跳過去，接著往下讀。

　　優秀的閱讀者會"積極地攝入"新的訊息，他們讀有所思，邊讀邊質疑，使之消化成為自己的東西。

　　1979年惠姆貝向新奧爾州的澤維爾大學為期五週的學前預備班介紹了一種慢讀有聲閱讀方法。在175名學生中，許多人在應用了這一技巧後閱讀理解能力提高了兩級，大學能

test scores rose by as much as 14 percent.

3. Practice memory-enhancing techniques. When I was eight and couldn't spell "arithmetic", a teacher taught me a sentence that has remained locked in my mind for decades: "A rat in Tom's house may eat Tom's ice cream. " The first letters of each word spell "arithmetic. "

All such memory-enhancing techniques, called mnemonics, transform new information into more easily remembered formulations. Other first-letter mnemonics include: "Homes" (the names of the Great Lakes — Huron, Ontario, Michigan, Erie and superior); "George Eaton's old granny rode a pig home yesterday" (for spelling "geography"); and "My very educated mother just served us nine pickles" (the planet system in order Mercury, Venus, Earth, Mars, Jupiter, Saturn, Uranus, Neptune, Pluto).

Mnemonics can also work with images, the trick is to invent visual clues that will make unfamiliar material mean something to you.

力測驗分數提高了 14%。

3. 練習提高記憶技巧

　　我 8 歲時拼不出"arithmetic"（算術）這一詞，一位老師教了我一個句子，幾十年它一直牢牢地印在我的腦子裡。"AratinTom'shouse-mayeatTom'sicecream"（有只老鼠在湯姆的屋裡，它可能會吃湯姆的冰淇淋。）把這句話的每個詞的首詞相拼，就是"arithmetic"這個詞。

　　所有這些迷人的記憶技巧，又稱記憶術，它把新的訊息轉變成一種有利於記憶的公式。

　　其它的第一字母記憶法包括："Home"（家）〔美國五大湖的名字——Huron（休倫湖）；Ontario（安大略湖）；Michigan（密執安湖）；Erie（伊利湖）和 Superior（蘇必略湖）〕"George Eaton's old granny rode a pig home yesterday."（喬治的老祖母昨天騎著一頭豬回家來，用來拼"地理"一詞，"geography"），還有"My very educated mother just serve us nine pickles"（我那極有教養的母親就給了我們九塊泡菜．）（這代表了太陽系中按順序排列的九大星球--Mercury（水星），Venus（金星），Earth（地球），Mars（火星），Jupiter（木星），Saturn（土星），Uranus（天王星），Neptune（海

In studying Spanish, for example, you might learn that the word for duck is pato. Pato sounds like the English word pot. To link the two, imagine a duck waddling about with a large pot over its head. You will have a clear image that reminds you pot = pato = duck.

Once dismissed by researchers as a mere Gimmick mnemonics are now considered an effective means of boosting memory doubling or even tripling the amount of new material that test subjects can retain. "A good memory is the key to all cognitive processes," according to William G. Chase, professor of psychology at Carnedie-Mellon University in Pittsburgh". "And it is something one can all have with practice. "

Cognitive research shows that we have two kinds of memory: short-term and long-term. Short-term memory (STM) lasts for about 30 to 60 seconds. We call directory assistance for a phone number, dial the number and then forget it. Long-term memory (LTM), however, can last a lifetime. The secret to developing a good memory, says Fran-

王星）和 Pluto（冥王星）.

記憶術也可和形象聯繫使用，其訣竅是設想出一個視覺的線索，使一個陌生的材料成爲你可見的實物。

例如，在學習西班牙語時，你或許會學到鴨子這個詞在西班牙語中是 pato. Pato 這個詞聽上去像英語詞 pot，你可以把兩者聯繫起來，想像一個鴨子頭頂個水罐搖搖擺擺地走來走去。這樣你就有了一個清晰的形象，這形象會提示你，pot = pato = duck.〔水罐 = 鴨子（西班牙語）= 鴨子（英語）〕。

記憶術僅僅是一種花招的看法已經被研究者們推翻了。今天，它已被看作增強記憶的有效途徑—它可使你對測試題材中的新內容的記憶提高兩倍，甚至三倍。根據匹茲堡卡內基梅隆大學的心理學教授威廉·蔡斯所言，"良好的記憶是所有認識過程中的關鍵，"而良好記憶是我們每個人經過訓練都可以具備的。"

對認識的研究表明，人們有兩種記憶：短期記憶和長期記憶。短期記憶維持的時間是30 – 60 秒鐘。我們請接線員告訴電話號碼，然後接電話，隨即就把它忘記了。而長期記憶則可以保持終身不忘。《改善你的記憶》一書的作者弗朗西斯·貝萊樂說，培養良好記憶的秘

cis S Bellezza, author of Improve Your Memory Skills, is learning how to transfer useful information from STM to LTM and how to retrieve that information when needed.

Mnemonics can be the key that puts data into LTM and gets the information back out again. Remember, the mind and memory are like muscles — the more you use them, the stronger they get.

4. Organize facts into categories. In studies at Stanford University, students were asked to memorize 112 words. These included names of animals, items of clothing, types of transportation, and occupations. For one group, the words were divided into these four categories. For a second group, the words were listed at random. Those who studied the material in organized categories consistently outperformed the others, recalling two to three times more words.

Trying to digest new information in one lump is difficult, " says Thomas R. " Trabasso, professor of education and behavioral science at the University of Chicago. "By analyzing new material and dividing it into

訣,就是要學會怎樣把有用的訊息從短期的記憶轉變爲長期記憶,在需要時又怎樣進行提取。

　　把資料數據存入長期記憶,再把所記的東西取回來,在這一過程中記憶術是關鍵。請記住,大腦記憶猶如肌肉—你使用越多,它便越強。

4. 對資料進行分類

　　在斯坦福大學的一次研究中,學生們被要求記憶 112 個詞,包括動物的名稱,各類衣物,交通工具種類及各種職業的名稱。研究者在讓一組學生記憶時把這些詞分成四類,而讓另一組記憶時則把這些詞任意排列。結果分類記憶那一組學生的記憶效果全超過另一組學生,他們能回憶起的詞彙要比另一組學生多兩到三倍。

　　"要整塊地消化新訊息是困難的,"芝加哥大學教育與行爲科學教授托姆斯·特雷伯索說:"通過分析新材料,把它分成有意義的大塊

meaningful chunks, you make learning easier. " For example, to remember the names
of all 39 former U. S. Presidents in proper
order, cluster the leaders into groups —
those before the War of 1812, those from
1812 until the Civil War, those from the Civil War to World War I, and those after World
War I. By thus organizing complex material
into logical categories you create a permanent
storage technique.

5. Focus your attention. The next time you are
faced with new material you need to master,
ask yourself: What do I want to learn from
reading this, and how will I benefit from the
knowledge gained? " By telling ourselves
what the learning will do for us, we reduce
our resistance to studying and become better
learners, " says Rusell W. Scalpone, a psychologist and manager at A. T. kearney,
Inc. , an international management-consult-
ing firm.

Scalpone recommends four other techniques for improving concentration and focus:

• Establish a time and a place for learn-

，學起來就會容易多了。"

　　例如，要以正確的次序記憶 39 位美國前總統的名字，你可以對這些名字進行分組 – 1812 年戰爭前爲一組，1812 年到內戰爆發爲一組，內戰到第一次世界大戰爲一組，對一個複雜的材料進行邏輯分類，你便創造了一個永久性儲存的技巧。

5. 集中注意力

　　當你下次面對一份需要掌握的新材料時，先問問自己，我想從這次閱讀中得到什麼？所獲得的知識將帶給我什麼裨益？"通過告訴自己閱讀會給我們帶來什麼，我們厭學情緒就會減輕，從而成爲一個更好的閱讀者。"A·T·卡尼公司（這是一家國際經營咨詢公司）的一位經理和心理學家拉塞爾·斯凱福說。

　　斯凱爾福還就如何改善注意力推薦了其他四種技巧：

　　　·確立學習時間和地點。把電話從話機上

ing. Take the phone off the hook; close the door. By regulating your environment, you create the expectation that learning will occur.

• Guard against distractions. Don't be shy about hanging a "Do Not Disturb" sign on your door. You have a right to your time.

• Try a variety of learning methods. Diagramming, note taking, outlining, even talking into a type recorder are study techniques that can increase concentration. Use whatever study skills you are most comfortable with. Be creative.

• Monitor your progress. Being busy is not always the same as being productive. Stop occasionally and ask yourself: Am I contributing right now to my learning goal? If the answer is yes, keep working. If no, ask yourself why. If you're not making progress because of tension or fatigue, take a break — without feeling guilty. Regular breaks can improve the learning process.

6. Discover your own learning style. Educators Rita and Ken Dunn tell the story of three children who each received a bicycle for

擱開，關上門。通過對環境的調整，你就產生
了一種學習即將開始的期待心情。

　　·防止干擾。不要為在門上一塊"請勿打
擾"的牌子感到不好意思。你有權安排自己的
時間。

　　·嘗試不同的學習方法。設計圖形、記筆
記、擬提綱、甚至和錄音機對話，這些都是有助
於你集中注意力的學習技巧。使用各種你覺
得最適宜的學習技巧，要有創造性。

　　·檢查你所取得的進步。終日忙碌並不一
定意味著收獲多。偶爾放下工作，問問自己
"我現在這樣是不是對新的學習目標有益處
呢?"如果回答是肯定的，就繼續工作。如果回
答是否定的，就問問自己為什麼? 如果由於繃
得太緊感到內疚不安，常規的間歇能夠加快你
的學習進程。

6. 找到適合你自己的學習方式。教育家麗塔·鄧
　　恩和肯·鄧恩講述了一則三個孩子的故事。他
　　們在聖誕節各自收到一輛自行車。這些自行

Christmas. The bikes, purchased unassembled, had to be put together by parents. Tim's father read the directions carefully before he set to work. Mary's father laid out the pieces on the floor and handed the direction to Mary's mother. "Read this to me", he said, as he surveyed the components. George's mother instinctively began fitting pieces together, glancing at the directions only when stymied. By day's end, all three bikes were assembled, each from a different approach.

"Although they didn't realize it", says Rita Dunn, professor of education at St. John's University in New York City, "the parents had worked according to their own learning styles. " "Our approaches to unfamiliar material are as unique and specialized as we are, and a key to learning is recognizing and accommodating the style that suits us best," says ken Dunn, professor of education at Queens College in New York City.

Learning styles can vary dramatically. The Dunns have developed a Productivity Environment Preference Survey, which iden-

車買來時是零件,必須由父母們自己裝配。蒂姆的父親在進行裝配之前仔細閱讀了說明。瑪麗的父親先把零件攤在地上,把說明書給瑪麗的母親。他一邊摸著這些零件,一邊對瑪麗的母親說:"把說明讀給我聽聽"。喬治的母親則徑直裝配,只有在遇到困難時才翻看一下說明。到那傍晚,三輛自行車都裝好了,三位父母用三種不同的方法。

紐約市聖·約翰大學的教育系教授麗塔·鄧恩說,"這三位父母都是按照自己的學習風格進行工作的。""儘管他們沒有注意到這一點。"

我們對於陌生材料的態度都是獨特的,就像我們每個人都各具特點一樣,學習的關鍵在於認識和順應自己的最佳風格。"紐約市昆斯大學的教育系教授肯·鄧恩說。

學習風格可以有很大的不同。鄧恩教授夫婦作了一個"生產力環境優選"調查,這項調

tifies 21 elements that affect the way we learn. These factors include noise level, lighting, amount of supervision required, even the time of day.

What' s your style? Try some self – analysis. What, for example, is your approach to putting together an unassembled item? Do you concentrate better in the morning or in the evening? In a noisy environment or a quiet one? Make a list of the pluses and minuses you can identify. then use this list to create the learning environment best for you. Whichever style works for you, the good news is that you can expand learning capacity. And this can make your life fuller and more productive.

查鑒定出 21 種對學習方法有影響的因素。包括噪音級別、光線、監督程度、甚至一天中的某個時間。

你的風格是什麼？ 試作一下自我分析。例如，你在把零件裝配成某件東西時，習慣於採取什麼方法？ 你精力集中在何處？ 把你所能鑒別的所有正負面都列出來，然後用它來創造出一個最適合你的學習環境。

不管什麼風格，對你適合、最令人欣喜的訊息莫過於能夠提高你的學習能力，這會使你的生活更充實、更豐富。

欣賞

"學習並不等於就是摹仿某種東西，而是掌握技巧的方法。掌握工作的方法，根本不等於使自己一生都使用這種方法"（高爾基）。學習的方法是人類在不斷探索世界和改造世界的認識論和方法論。誰掌握了學習的方法，誰就可能主宰世界和改造世界。因此人類一直在追求學習方法的科學化和高效率。但任何一種學習都有它的長處和不足，並不是每一種方法都適合於所有的人。正如這篇散文的結尾所說"不管什麼風格對你適合，最令人歡喜的訊息莫過於能夠提高你的學習能力，這就會使你的生活更充實、更豐富。"這篇散文中論述的學習技巧值得一試，有它的科學價值和實際的指導意義。作者並沒有大發自己的感慨，而是旁徵博引，以大量的事例和名家的調查結果、實驗報告來論述學習的技巧和方法，每一種方法都不是憑空捏造，每一種方法都適合於某些人。

16. On Learning
Foreign Languages

M. Eastman

After spending a couple of weeks talking to Americans in Moscow, and listening through a wall to the life of the Russians. I decided to learn the language. I did not want to collect bits of second-hand information. I did not want information. I wanted the feeling of life under a proletarian dictatorship, and there was only one way to get it. I had been puttering along with my grammar and with Lhermontov and Pushkin. That was not learning anything.

I have my own system for learning foreign languages, which is based upon a profound knowledge of the human heart, and which I will here with some reservations impart to the reader. The first thing to do is to go to the capital of the country where that language is spoken, and buy a grammar, two little red dictionaries, and a railroad ticket. The railroad ticket should take

16. 論學習外語

M·伊斯曼

　　我在莫斯科待了幾個星期,跟一些美國人談了談,又隔牆窺視了一下俄羅斯人的生活,我決定學習俄語。我不想搜集零零星星的二手材料,我並不要訊息材料,我要的是在無產階級專政制度下人們生活的感受。而只有一個辦法能夠獲得這種感受。我早已花費了好多時間學習俄語語法,學習萊蒙托夫和普希金。但那是學不到什麼東西的。

　　我現在有了一套建立在對人的思想感情深刻了解基礎上的方法。我想在這裡把這種方法介紹給讀者,不過稍有保留。第一件要做的事是到說這種語言的國家首都去,再買一本語法書跟兩本紅封面的小詞典,然後再買一張火車票。這張火

you as far away from the capital as possible, clear out of the sound of your own language, and preferably to a summer resort. The reason for this is that you are going to have a good time, and you need company.

On the train, on the way to your summer resort, you have some hard work to do. It is the only work called for by my system, and it has to be done thoroughly. You have to learn the name on the language under consideration for "noun," "adjective," "adverb," "verb," "participle," "conjunction," "pronoun," and "preposition." And if you do not know in your own language just what these wonders are, you have to find out. And then you have to learn to say, "What does that mean?" and "What is the word for this?", and a few handy remarks like "Do you speak English?", "Do you speak French?", "Do you speak German?", "Do you speak Italian?", "It's too bad", and "Let's take a walk."

With that equipment you go into the dining-room of the principal hotel in your summer

車票可以讓你乘到遠離首都的地方，在那裡你完全聽不到你本族語的聲音。最佳的選擇是避暑勝地。因為你在那裡可以玩得很開心，而且有你需要的伴兒。

在火車上，在去避暑勝地的路上，你得做一些艱苦的工作。它是我的學習方法所要求的唯一的工作，而且要求你做得一絲不苟。你得學會所學語言中的有關名稱，如什麼叫"名詞"、"形容詞"、"副詞"、"分詞"、"連結詞"、"代名詞"和"前置詞"。要是你還不知道這些東西在你本族語言中是什麼意思的話，你得想辦法搞清楚。然後，你得學會說這樣的一些句子："那是什麼意思?"和"這在俄語中怎麼說?"以及這樣一些常用的話："你會說英語嗎?"，"你會說法語嗎?"，"你會說德語嗎?""你會說義大利語嗎?"，"噢，這太糟了!"，"咱們一塊兒走走好嗎?"。

你有了以上的裝備，就在避暑勝地找一家飯店，到餐廳去挑選一名老師。要是你按我上面說

resort, and pick out your teacher. You may do this quite boldly, if you have equipped yourself as I direct, for you have a power to ensnared that teacher which reaches beyond the charms of your personality. Moreover, it is advisable to have an eye to her physical beauties, for you are going to spend a good deal of time gazing on them in comparative silence.

After dinner you may go and lean up against a pillar, or the railing of a little foot-ridge in the garden, or somewhere — I need not be too specific about this — and when she comes by, you will say in your poor broken tongued and with a forlorn expression, "Mademoiselle, do you speak English?" When she says "No," you will heave a sigh and say, "Do you speak German?" At a second "No" your expression will become disconsolate, and you will say, "Do you speak French?" At a third "No" you show real consternation, and offer to speak Italian, or Bohemian, or Chinese, or what you will. If God is with you, she will decline all these offers, and you will find that she is at

的那樣裝備好了自己，你就可以放著膽子去做，因為你已經具備一種吸引你老師的力量，一種超越你性格魅力的力量。另外，我得提醒你，挑選老師時，還要注意她的外表，要漂亮一些的，因為在你倆一時無話可說而面面相覷時，你的眼睛得瞧著她許久許久呢。

　　吃過飯，你可以走到餐廳外面，靠在一根門柱上，或者花園裡小橋的欄杆上，或者其他地方——我不必說得太具體——當她經過你的時候，你得裝出滿面憂容，哀楚動人，用你剛學的那點語言，嗑嗑巴巴地對她說：“小姐，你會說英語嗎？”要是她說不會，你更嘆口氣，接著問：“你會說德語嗎？”在聽到第二聲“不會”時，你臉上的表情要變得很沮喪，緊接著說：“你會說法語嗎？”在聽到第三聲“不會”時，你要顯得驚惶失措，再問她會不會說意大利語、波希米亞語、漢語或其他你會說的任何語言。要是你運氣好，她碰巧那些語言都不會說，並且你會發現她對你的困境立刻深感不安，同時也

once seriously distressed over your plight, and in a somewhat humbled condition as to her own talents. You will find, if I am not mistaken, that you are already taking a walk with her, and you may assume that her next statement is, "Too bad you haven't a Russian dictionary," or something to that effect. At the sound of these words — no matter how bad they sound — you will produce your two little red books, and hand her the one marked "Russian-English".

Here the work, properly so called, comes to an end. She will be very curious to see what the words in your language look like, and she will examine the little red book and pretty soon point to a word, probably the word "hot", or something equally uninteresting under ordinary circumstances. Under these circumstances it acquires the charm of an incantation. It begins to open just by something less than the shadow of a hair's breadth the gate of a possible romance. You both know that that gate will be a long, long time in opening. And you both know, if you have reached years of some discretion, that

對她自己十分卑劣的語言才能感到，自慚形穢。
要是我沒有說錯的話，此時你已經跟她在一塊散
步了，而且你可以預料到她的下一句話："太糟糕
了，你沒有一本俄語詞典。"或者諸如此類的話。
在聽到這些話時——儘管聽起來不那麼悅耳——
你可以掏出你的兩本紅封面的小詞典，把標有"俄
英"的一本遞給她。

　　稱之為工作的那部分到此便告結束了。她會
非常好奇地看看你所用語言中的那些詞是什麼樣
兒。她翻閱了一下那本小紅書，很快指出一個字，
也許是那個"熱"字，或者其它在一般情況下索然
無味的字。在這種情況下，該字像咒語一般具有
一種魔力。它打開了一個浪漫故事的大門，可能
僅僅打開比邊幅絲還要細的一條縫隙。你和那位
小姐都知道要完全打開這扇門要花很多時間。你
們倆人也都知道（如果你們已經到了做事很穩重
的年齡），門一旦打開，浪漫故事也就結束了。實

when it is once wide open, the romance is gone. For there is no such thing as romance — it is only the expectation of itself.

And so, in a gentle fever of delight, you look up the word for "too" in your dictionary, and you say, "Too hot?"

It is one of the signs of our human kinship, and a blessing we never pause to appreciate, that in all languages, however the words may change, the vocal inflections have substantially the same meaning: You do not have to learn how to melodies a question in Russian, or a doubt, or a suspicion, or a declaration, or a caress. If you did, this industrious romance would probably run on the rocks in the first three minutes.

To your question, "Too hot?", she will no doubt answer rapidly and at some length, forgetting you limitations. Perhaps she will say, "Not if we could find a shady tree to sit under".

She will be a little shocked at your inability to grasp this simple proposition. A flicker of impatient contempt will cross her face. She has

際上根本不存在什麼浪漫故事————無非是一種期
望而已。

　　就這樣，你以一種欣喜的心情，在你的詞典裡
查找"太"這個字，並說："太熱了？"這是我們人的
共同特點之一，那就是在一切語言裡，不管詞彙可
能發生如何大的變化，聲調卻具有大體相同的意
思。可惜我們對這個特點從未予以足夠的注意。
你不必學習如何使俄語的問句說得悅耳動聽，也
不必學習如何表示懷疑、猜疑、陳述或愛意。要是
你認眞學了，那麼費了很大的勁建造的浪漫故事，
在最初的三分鐘裡就會觸礁了。

　　對你提的問題："太熱了？"她一定迅速作出回
答，並滔滔不絕地說個沒完，完全忘掉你只有那麼
一丁點兒俄語老底。也許她會說："要不我們找一
個有樹蔭的地方坐下。"

　　她對你連這樣簡單的提議都聽不懂感到有點
吃驚，臉上會露出一絲不耐煩、甚至輕蔑的神態。

forgotten about your magnanimous offer to speak English, French, German, Italian or Bohemian. She has forgotten that there are any such languages. She just primitively and quite naturally feels that a person who can't talk is a fool. And here you must bring forward the second part of your equipment. But use it gently. Use it sparingly, for it is possible the experience may be too bitter, and her pride not strong enough to hold her to the task.

她已經忘記了你曾經寬宏大度地提出用英語、法德語、義大利語和波希米亞語交談的建議。她忘記了天下還有這幾種語言。她本能地，也是很自然地感到不能跟別人交談的人一定是傻瓜。這時，你應該啓用你裝備中的第二部分。不過使用時，要倍加小心，不要隨便亂用，因為這是一種很痛苦的經歷。也許她的自尊心還不夠堅強到能承受住壓給她的任務。

欣賞

　　學習外語的秘訣是什麼？這是一個似乎沒有解的命題。因為任何方法都可能因人而異，任何方法都可能有它合理的一面同時又有它不合理的一面。本文試圖給予回答的也只是一個方面的問題，並不是所有問題的答案。文章的前四個自然段包括作者認為學習語言的三個基本步驟。第一步“學習語言最好到想學的語言國家去”，“那裡你完全聽不到你本族語的聲音”。第二步“你得學會所學語言中的有關名稱”，然後學會幾個簡單的日常生活中的套話。第三步是選個優秀的老師。在後面的五個自然段裡，作者運用實際的事例鼓勵學習者大膽進行語言實踐。這才是學習語言的真諦。任何好的學習語言的秘訣都離不開語言實踐，離開了語言實踐就違背了語言習得的規律和語言本身的屬性，那是不可能把語言學好的。全文皆本色文字，不經雕琢，隨意自然，從小處著手，深入淺出，化難為易。這樣易於拉近讀者與作者的距離，使讀者在不知不覺中愉快輕鬆地接受作者的觀點。文章語言光明透亮，樸實無華，顯示出自然的美。

17. How Should One Read a Book?

V. Woolf

It is simple enough to say that since books have classes — fiction, biography, poetry — we should separate them and take from each what is right that each should give us. Yet few people ask from books what books can give us. Most commonly we come to books with blurred and divided minds, asking of fiction that it shall be true, of poetry that it shall be false, of biography that it shall be flattering, of history that it shall enforce our own prejudices. If we could banish all such preconceptions when we read, that would be an admirable beginning. Don't dictate to your author; try to become him. Be his fellow — workers and accomplice. If you hang back, and reserve and criticize at first, you are preventing yourself from getting the fullest possible value from what you read. But if you open your mind as widely as possible, then signs and hints of almost imperceptible fineness from the twist and turn of the first sentence, will bring you into the presence of a human being

17. 怎樣讀書

V·沃爾夫

　　說來容易：既然書有各種各樣——小說、傳記、詩歌——那我們就應該把它們分門別類，並且各按其類來取每本書理應給予我們的內容。然而，很少人讀書時想過書本能夠提供些什麼的問題。最普遍的現象是，我們拿起書本時頭腦不清醒，目標不一致，我們要求小說敘述真人真事，要求詩歌表現虛假，要求傳記給人捧場，要求歷史證實我們自己的偏見。如果我們能在打開書本之前先驅除掉這些先入為主的看法，那將是個值得慶幸的良好開端。不要去指揮作者，要設身處地去替他設想，當他的合作者或同謀犯。如果你一開始便採取退縮矜持、有所保留或指指點點的態度，那你就在為自己設置障礙，使自己不能充分地從所閱讀的書本中獲得益處。然而，如果你沒有先入之主見，虛懷若谷，那麼，打開書本，隱晦曲折的字裡行間，難以覺察的細微跡象和暗示便會向你展示一個與眾不同的人。深入進去，沉浸其中，熟

Books

unlike any other in this, acquaint yourself with this, and soon you will find that your author is giving you, or attempting to give you, something far more definite. The thirty-two chapters of a novel — if we consider how to read a novel first — are an attempt to make something as formed and controlled as building; but words are more impalpable than bricks; reading is a longer and more complicated process than seeing. Perhaps the quickest way to understand the elements of what a novelist is doing is not to read, but to write; to make your own experience with the dangers and difficulties of words. Recall, then, some event that has left a distinct impression on you — how at the corner of the street, perhaps, you passed two people talking. A tree shook; an electric light danced; the tone of the talk was comic, but also tragic; a whole vision, an entire conception, seemed contained in that moment.

But when you attempt to reconstruct it in words, you will find that it breaks into a thousand conflicting impressions. Some must be subdued; others emphasised; in the process you will lose, probably, all grasp upon the emotion

諳這一切，你會很快發現，書的作者正在，或努力在給予你一些十分明確的東西。一部小說——如果我們先考慮一下怎樣閱讀小說的話——要有32個章節，這道理實際上跟建造有形有狀的樓房完全一樣：只不過文字不像磚塊看得見摸得著；閱讀比起觀看是一個更長更複雜的過程。也許，要懂得作者寫作過程中的細微末節，最簡便的辦法不是讀而是寫，親自動手對字句的艱難險阻進行試驗。回想一件曾經給你留下深刻印象的事情——也許在大街的拐角處有兩個人在聊天，你走過他們身邊。一棵樹搖晃起來，一道電光飛舞而過，他們聊天的口氣頗有喜劇味道，但也帶悲劇色彩，那一瞬間似乎包含了一個完整的概念。

　　然而，你動手用文字來重新構造時，你發現這一切變成了千百個互相衝突的印象。有的要淡化，有的要突出；在寫的過程裡，你可能會失去你

itself. Then turn from your blurred and littered
pages to the opening pages of some great novelist — Defoe, Jane Austen, Hardy. Now you
will be better able to appreciate their master. It
is not merely that we are in the presence of a
different person — Defoe, Jane Austen, or
Thomas Hardy — but that we are living in a different world. Here, in Robinson Crusoe, we are
trudging a plain high road; one thing happens
after another; the fact and the order of the fact
is enough. But if the open air and adventure
mean everything to Defoe they mean nothing to
Jane Austen. Hers is the drawing-room, and
people talking, and by the many mirrors of their
talk revealing their characters. And if, when we
have accustomed ourselves to the drawing-room
and its reflections, we turn to Hardy, we are
once spun around. The moors are round us and
the stars are above our heads. The other side of
the mind is now exposed — the dark side that
comes uppermost in solitude, not the light side
that shows in company. Yet different as these
worlds are, each is consistent with itself. The
maker of each is careful to observe the laws of
his own perspective and however great a strain

想捕捉的情感。這時候，放下你那寫得糊裡糊塗顛三倒四的東西，打開某些大小說家的小說讀一讀——笛福、簡‧奧斯丁、哈代。現在，你能欣賞他們的匠心功力了。我們不僅面臨一個與眾不同的人——笛福、簡‧奧爾丁或托馬斯‧哈代——還生活在一個與眾不同的世界裡。在《魯濱遜漂流記》裡我們是在一條普普通通的公路上跋涉前進；只要事實和事實的先後次序便足夠了。然而，如果說笛福著重的是野外生活和冒險行動，它們對簡‧奧斯丁來說卻毫無意義。客廳才是她的天地，還有人們的談天說地，她通過各種各樣的談話表現，談話如鏡子，反映出他們的性格。當我們習慣於這個客廳及其中閃爍多姿的映像以後又轉而去閱讀哈代，那我們又會暈頭轉向。我們周圍是沼澤，頭頂上是星星。人性的另外一面被揭示了——孤獨時得到突出表現的黑暗的一面，而不是與朋友相處時閃閃發亮的光明的一面。我們不是跟人而是跟大自然、跟每個世界的創造者都小心翼翼地遵守各自透視事物的法規，而且，不管他們給我們

they may put upon us they will never confuse us, as lesser writers so frequently do, by introducing two different kinds of reality into the same book. Thus to go from one great novelist to another — from Jane Austen to Hardy, from Peacock to Trollope, from Scott to Meredith — is to be wrenched and uprooted; to be thrown this way and then that. To read a novel fineness of perception, but of great boldness of imagination if you are going to make use of all that the novelist — the great artist — gives you.

以多大負擔，他們從來不會使我們感到迷惑，不像
有些二流作家常常在同一本書裡介紹兩種完全不
相同的現實，把讀者弄得無所適從。因此，從一位
偉大的小說家到另一位──從簡・奧斯丁到哈代，
從皮科克到特羅洛普，從司各特到梅瑞狄斯──
我們都要經受一場脫胎換骨、背井離鄉的痛苦，被
扔過來又趕過去。讀小說是一門艱難複雜的藝
術。你不僅要有高明的洞察秋毫的本事，你還要
能夠敢於進行大膽的想像，如果你想充分利用偉
大的小說家──偉大的藝術家──所給予你的一
切。

欣賞

　　讀書是人類認識世界的活動。關於讀書的方法已有
不少宏論名篇。值得一提的俯首皆是。這篇散文所說的
另外的一種讀書方法。它要求我們要讀"與作者合作"，
從作者角度去思考的書，並建議我們讀點經典著作，這正
是我們在當今強調綜合素質所要的讀書的方法。在當今
知識大爆炸的時代，不讀書不增長知識，終究會被歷史所
淘汰。這篇文章文字構思精心，謀篇週密，行文流暢，簡
潔凝鍊。結構散而不亂，緊而不嚴，感情真摯，樸素迷人。

18. Of Studies

Francis Bacon

Studies serve for delight, for ornament, and for ability. Their chief used for delight, is in privateness and retiring; for ornament, is in discourse; and for ability, is in the judgement and disposition of business. For expert men can execute, and perhaps judge of particulars, one by one; but the general counsels, and the plots and marshalling of affairs come best from those that are learned. To spend too much time in studies is sloth; to use them too much for ornament is affectation; to make judgement wholly by their rules is the humour of a scholar. They perfect nature, and are perfected by the experience, for natural abilities are like natural plants that need pruning by study; and studies themselves give forth directions too much at large, except they are bounded in by experience. Crafty men contempt studies, simple men admire them, and wise men use them; for they teach not their own use; but that is a wisdom without them, and above them, won by observa-

18. 論 學 習

弗朗西斯·培根

　　讀書可供消遣，可供裝飾，也可以增長才能。爲消遣而讀書，常見於獨處退居之時；爲裝飾而讀書，多用於高談闊論之中；爲增長才幹而讀書，主要在於對事物的判斷和處理。經驗豐富的人雖善於處理個別事物，或許也能一樁樁地做出判斷，但綜觀全局、統籌安排則唯有博學之士最能勝任。讀書費時太多是怠惰；過分的藻飾裝璜是矯情；全按書本條文而斷事是十足的學究氣。讀書使天然得以完善，又需靠後來的學習修剪整枝，而書本上的道理如不用經驗加以制約，往往是泛泛而不著邊際的。有技藝者鄙視學問，無知識者羨慕學問，唯有明知之士善用學問。然而學問本身不會教給人們它的用途：致用之道在於書外，超乎書上，只有細心觀察才能獲得。讀書不可專爲反駁作者而

tion. Read not to contradict and confuse; nor to believe and take for granted; nor to find talk and discourse; but to weigh and consider. Some books are to be tasted, others to be swallowed, and some few to be chewed and digested; that is, some books are to be read only in parts; others to reread, but not curiously; and some few to be read wholly, and with diligence and attention. Some books also may be read by deputy, and extracts made of them others; but that would be only in the less important arguments, and the meaner sort of books; else distilled books are like common distilled waters, flashy things. Reading makes a full man; conference a ready man and writing an exact man. And therefore, if a man writes little, he needs to have a great memory; if he confers little, he had need have a present wit, and if he read little, he had need have much cunning, to seem to know that he does not. Histories make men wise; poets, witty; the mathematics, subtle; natural philosophy, deep; moral, grave; logic and rhetoric, able to contend: Studies go to make a man's character. Nay, there is no impediment in the wit, but may be wrought out by

爭辯，也不可輕易相信書中所言，以爲當然如此，也不是爲了尋找談話資料，而應當權衡輕重，認眞思考。有些書淺嘗即可，另一些不妨吞咽，少數書則須咀嚼消化。這就是說，有的書祇要讀其中一部分，有的可以大致瀏覽，少數則須通讀，讀時要全神貫注，勤奮不懈。有些書也可請人代讀，取其所需作摘要，但這只限於題材不大重要和質量不高的作品。否則，提鍊過的書就像一般蒸餾過的水，變得淡而無味了。

　　讀書使人充實，討論使人機敏，筆記使人準確。因此，不常動筆的人必須具有很強的記憶力，不常討論的人必須具有隨機應變的捷才，不多讀書的人必須十分靈巧狡黠，才能假裝知道他所不知道的事物。讀歷史使人明智，讀詩歌使人聰慧，數學使人精密，哲理使人深刻，倫理學使人莊重，邏輯修辭使人善辯。總之，凡有所學，皆成性格。不僅如此，人們才智上遇到的障礙或缺陷，沒有不

fit studies: like as diseases of the body, nay have appropriate exercise. Bowling is good for the stone and reins; shooting for he lungs and breast; gentle walking for the stomach; riding for the head; and the like. So if a man's wit is wandering, let him study the mathematics; for in demonstrations, if his wit is called away never so little, he must begin again. If his wit is not apt to distinguish or find differences, let him study the schoolmen; for they are hair-splitters. If he is not apt to beat over matters, and to call up one thing to prove and illustrate another, let him study the lawyers' cases. So every effect of the mind may have a special receipt.

能通過適當的學問予以疏通或彌補的。正如人體百病,皆可藉適宜的運動來消除一樣。保齡球有利於膀胱和腎,射箭有利於胸肺,散步有益於腸胃消化,騎馬有益於頭腦靈敏,如此等等。同理,如果一個人思想散漫不集中,可讓他讀數學,因在演算時,稍不經心就會出錯,就要重新開始。缺乏辨別能力的人,可讓他研習經院哲學,因爲那些都是吹毛求疵的繁瑣學派。不善於推理或引一事闡證其他事的人,可讓他研習律師的案例。如此,頭腦上的每種缺陷,都有特效的治療妙法。

欣賞

　　這是培根論說文中最爲人熟知的不朽名篇。在培根筆下的 Studies 有多種涵義,本不限於讀書,也包括做學問(治學)、研究、求知等等,理解不同,譯法也不同。但無論怎樣譯這個題目,都不是關鍵。就本篇談論的中心來說,是如何讀書。"學以致用"的觀點在他整個論說文中佔了壓倒一切的位置,"博學多能"則是他畢生孜孜以求的目標。名篇是不朽的,無論哪個時代,這一名篇對有志之士也不失爲金玉良言,有很大的指導意義和參考價值。全文中雋語警句,俯拾即是,美不勝收。詞語句式,勻稱平衡,它所產生的和諧均衡,莊重,給人以深刻感受的美學效果。這在西方的文論中是少有的,這也正是文章的精彩絕倫之處。

19. Books

John Ruskin

The good book of the hour, then, — I do not speak of the bad ones — is simply the useful or pleasant talk of some person whom you cannot otherwise converse with, printed for you. Very useful often telling you what you need to know; very pleasant often, as a sensible friend's present talk would be. These bright accounts of travels; good-humoured and witty discussions of question; lively or pathetic story — telling in the form of novel; fact-telling, by the real agents concerned in the events of passing history; — all these books of the hour, multiplying among us as education becomes more general, are a peculiar characteristic and possession of the present age: we ought to be entirely thankful for them. And entirely ashamed of ourselves if we make no good use of them. But we make the worst possible use, if we allow them to usurp the place of true books: for, strictly speaking, they are not books at all, but merely letters or newspapers in good print. Our friend's letter

19. 讀　　書

約翰·羅斯金

　　現時的好書——我說的不是壞書——無非是
爲你們把那些無法與之交談的人所做的有益或愉
快的言談印刷了出來，這種書往往十分有益，告訴
你們需要知道的東西；往往十分令人愉快，好比一
位通情達理的朋友和你促膝談心。這些栩栩如生
的遊記，溫和而風趣的問題探討，小說形式的生動
哀婉的故事，嚴格的敍事，出自稍縱即逝的歷史事
件上的眞實人物——所有這些現時的書籍，由於
教育的逐漸普及而日益增多，成爲當今時代獨有
的特徵和財富。對此我們應該充分感激。如不好
好利用這些書籍，我們就該感到十分慚愧。如果
我們聽任它們篡奪了眞正書籍的地位，那可能就
是徹底的濫用；因爲嚴格說來，這些東西都不是
書，不過是印刷精美的信或報紙而已！今天看來，

may be delightful, or necessary, today: whether worth keeping or not, is to be considered. The newspaper may be entirely proper at breakfast time, but assuredly it is not reading for all day. So, though bound up in a volume, the long letter which gives you so pleasant an account of the inns, and roads, and weather last year at such a place, or which tells you that amusing story, or gives you the real circumstances of such and such events, however valuable for occasional reference, may not be, in the real sense of the word, a "book" at all, nor, in the real sense, to be "read". A book is essentially not a talked thing, but a written thing; and written, not with the view of mere communication, but of permanence. The book of talk is printed only because its author cannot speak to thousands of people at once; if he could, he would — the volume is mere multiply the voice merely, not to carry it merely, but to preserve it. The author has something to say which he perceives to be true and useful, or helpfully and beautiful. So far as he knows, no one has yet said it; so far as he knows, no one else can say it. He is bound to say it, clearly and melodiously if he may;

我們友人的信札令人快意，或非看不可。是不是
值得保存則該考慮一番！吃早點時，瀏覽報紙可
能完全適當，但是肯定不能成天地讀。即使裝訂
成冊──洋洋灑灑的長信，或者有聲有色地爲你
記述去年某個地方的客票、街巷、天氣，或者講述
有趣的故事，或者把某些事件的眞實情況告訴你，
雖然偶爾參考頗有價值，眞正意義來說，可能根本
不是一本“書”，從眞正意義來說，也不可供人“閱
讀”。一部書就實質而論，不是談出來的東西，而
是寫出來的東西；形諸筆墨，不是僅僅著眼於溝
通，而是旨在終古長存。談話性質的書籍之所以
印刷出來，無非因爲作者無法同時和千人萬衆說
話。假如能夠做到，他就會那麼做───一卷書無
非是他的擴音而已。可是寫書不是爲了單單擴
音，不是爲了單單傳聲，而是要把聲音保存下來。
作者言之有物，他認爲那是眞實有益的，或者優美
而有裨益。據他所知，以前無人道出；據他所知，
他人無法道出。他非說不可，可能的話，要說得清

clearly, at all events. In the sum of his life he finds this to be the thing, or group of things, manifest to him; — this the price of true knowledge, or sight, which his share of sunshine and earth has permitted him to seize. He would faint set it down for ever; engrave it on rock, if he could; saying, "This is the best of me; for the rest, I ate, and drank, and slept, loved, and hated, like another; my life was as the vapor, and is not; but this I saw and knew: this, if anything of mine, is worth your memory." That is his "writing"; it is, in his small human way, and with whatever degree of true inspiration is in him, his inscription, or scripture. That is a "Book".

Perhaps you think no books were ever so written?

But, again, I ask you, do you at all believe in honesty, or at all in kindness? Well, whatever bit of a wise man's work is honestly and benevolently done, that bit is his book, or his piece of art. It is mixed always with evil fragments — ill-done, redundant, affected work. But if you read rightly, you will easily discover the true bits, and those are the book.

清楚楚悅耳動聽；無論如何要說清楚。終其一生，
他發現就是這點東西或一些東西向他顯示出來了
——這點滴的眞知或識見，這就是他所分享的陽
光和大地讓他把捉的雪泥鴻爪。他求之不得把它
寫下來世代相傳；可能的話，把它鐫刻在岩石上：
"這是我的精華；除此以外，我和別人一樣，飲食起
居，有愛有恨；我的生命猶如一團霧靄，永遠消逝；
不過這一點我看清了明白了：如果我有什麼值得
你懷念的東西，僅此而已。"這就是他的"著述"。
人微言輕，憑藉他所具有的一點眞實的靈感，審他
的銘文，他的經書。那便是一部"書"。

　　或許你們以爲哪有書是這樣寫出來的呢？

　　不過我又要請問一聲，你究竟還相信有誠實
或有仁慈嗎？你是否認爲智者的任何一點工作，
只要是本著誠實和善意的態度做出來的，那微末
的一點東西便是他的書，或一件藝術品。其中總
是摻雜著邪惡的殘片——粗製濫造，累贅重沓，裝
腔作勢。可是如果你讀之得法，你就不難發現點
點滴滴眞實的東西，而那些東西便是全書的精華
所在。

Now books of this kind have been written in all ages by their greatest men: — by great leaders, great statesmen, and great thinkers. These are all at your choice; and life is short. Do you know, if you read this, that you cannot read that — that what you lose today you cannot gain tomorrow? Will you go and gossip with your housemaid, or your stable-boy, when you may talk with queens and kings; or flatter yourselves that it is with any worthy consciousness of your own claims to respect that you jostle with the common crowd for entree here, and audience there, when all the while this eternal court is open to you, with its society wide as the world, multitudinous as its days, the chosen, and the mighty, of every place and time? Into that you may enter always; in that you may take fellowship and rank according to your wish; from that, once entered into it, you can never be outcast but by your own fault; by your aristocracy of companionship there, your own inherent aristocracy will be assuredly tested, and the modify of the living, measured, as to all the truth and sincerity that are in them, by the place you desire to take in this company of the

　　這類書籍出自歷代最偉大的人物的手筆：偉大的領袖，偉大的政治家，偉大的思想家。這些書都可以供你選擇，然而生命卻是短暫的。你是否明白讀了這一本，就不能讀那一本——你今天失去的東西，你明天再也無法追回？當你可以同國王和皇后交談的時候，你是否願意去和你的女傭或馬夫開聊幾句？你是否自以為，你和平民百姓擠進擠出，那裡觀光，那裡聽演講，這時你便意識到自己已受人尊敬，而此時此地這座永恆的宮殿卻向你敞開著，它的社會猶如世界那般廣闊，它的歲月猶如世界那般漫長，古往今來天南地北的精英都薈萃於此，你可以隨時進入，隨心所欲地與他們為伍，一旦踏進之後，除非由於你自己的過失，否則永遠不會被驅逐出來；你和這些精神貴族相伴為伍，你生之俱來的高貴精神必將受到檢驗，你力求在活人的社會中身居高位的種種動機，其中又有多少道理和真誠，這就要根據你渴望在這些死者之中佔據的位置來衡量。

Dead.

"The place you desire", and the place you fit yourself for, I must also say; because, observe, this court of the past differs from all living aristocracy in this: — it is open to labour and to merit, but to nothing else. No wealth will bribe, no name overawe, no artifice deceive, the guardian of those Elysian gates. In the deep sense, no vile or vulgar person ever enters there. At the porteros of that silent Faubourg St Germain, there is but brief question, "Do you deserve to enter? Pass. Do you ask to be the companion of nobles? Make yourself noble, and you shall be. Do you long for the conversation of the wise? Learn to understand it, and you shall hear it. But on other terms? — no. If you will not rise to us, we cannot stoop to you. The living lord may assume courtesy, the living philosopher explain his thought to you with considerate pain; but here we neither feign nor interpret; you must rise to the level of our thoughts if you would be gladdened by them, and share our feelings, if you would recognize our presence. "

This, then, is what you have to do, and I admit that it is much. You must, in a word,

　　我還要說一句，“你所渴望的位置”，你以爲自己恰如其分的位置；記住，這座過去的宮殿不同於一切現在的貴族──它是向勞作和功績開放的，而不向其他的一切開放。天堂之門的守護者，非財富所能賄賂，非盛名所能嚇倒，非詭計所能欺騙。從深層意義來說，任何無恥或庸人俗人休想進入。在靜寂無聲的聖日爾曼市郊的門衛面前，要問一個簡短的問題：“你配不配去？請進吧。你要求成爲高貴者的伴侶嗎？你要自身高貴起來，你才能成爲高貴者的伴侶。你渴望傾聽智者的談吐嗎？先學會理解，你才會聽到。可有其他條件？──沒有。倘若你不肯上升到我們的高度，我們無法俯就你。在世的貴族可能彬彬有禮，在世的哲人可能不憚其煩地向你解說他的思想；不過在這兒，我們旣不裝模作樣，也不作解釋；如果你想欣聞我們的思想，你必須上升到它們的高度，如果你想一睹我們的風彩，你必須分享我們的感情。”

　　所以說，這就是你非得做到的，再說我也承認做到這一步就不簡單了。總括起來說，如果你想

love these people, if you are to be among them. No ambition is of any use. They scorn your ambition. You must love them, and show your love in these two following ways.

First, by a true desire to be taught by them, and to enter into their thoughts. To enter into theirs, observe; not to find your own expressed by them. If the person who wrote the book is not wiser than you, you need not read it; if he be, he will think differently from you in many respects.

Very ready we are to say of a book, "How good this is — that's exactly what I think!" But the right feeling is, "How strange that is! I never thought of that before, and yet I see it is true; or if I do not now, I hope I shall, some day." But whether thus submissively or not, at least be sure that you go to the author to get at his meaning, not to find yours. Judge it afterwards, if you think yourself qualified to do so; but ascertain it first. And be sure also, if the author is worth anything, that you will not get at his meaning all at once; his whole meaning you will not for a long time arrive in any wise. Not that he does not say what he means. and in

要置身於他們中間,你就必須熱愛這些人。任何
抱負都毫無用處。他們瞧不起你的抱負。你必須
熱愛他們,從以下兩個方面表明你的熱愛。

　　首先,要真心實意渴望得到他們的教誨,而且
進入他們的思想。為了進入他們的思想,就要善
於辨識;這並不是為了發現他們所表達的你自己
的思想。倘若寫書的人不比你聰明,那就不必去
讀他的書;倘若他比你聰明,他的想法在許多方面
就會和你有所不同。

　　我們總是脫口而出地談到一本書,"多麼好啊
——正是我所想的!"其實應有的感覺是,"那是多
麼奇怪呀! 我以前從未那樣想過,可我明白說得
有道理;假如我現在沒有想到,我希望有一天會那
樣想到。"因此不論是不是洗耳恭聽,至少應該肯
定的是,你們去找作者是為了把握他的意思,而不
是你的意思。過後再去批判,要是你認為自己已
經有資格這樣做了;不過首先是要弄清意思。而
且也應該被肯定的是,如果作者有可取之處的話,
你就不會一下子把握他的意思;——可以說,要過
很長的時間你才對他的全部意思有所領會。倒不
是他沒有說出他的意思,沒有用有力的言辭;而是

strong words too; but he cannot say it all; and
what is more strange, will not, but in a hidden
way and in parables, in order that he may be
sure you want it. I cannot quite see the reason
of this, nor analyses that cruel reticence in the
breasts of wise men which makes them always
hide their deeper thought. They do not give it
you by way of help, but of reward, and will
make themselves sure that you deserve it before
they allow you to reach it. But it is the same
with the physical type of wisdom, gold. There
seems, to you and me, no reason why the electric forces of the earth should not carry whatever
there is of gold within it at once to the mountain
tops, so that kings and people might know that
all the gold they could get was there; and without any trouble of digging, or anxiety, or
chance, or waste of time, cut it away, and coin
as much as they needed. But Nature does not
manage it so. She puts it in little fissures in the
earth, nobody knows where: you may dig long
and find none; you must dig painfully to find
any.

And it is just the same with men's best
wisdom. When you come to a good book, you

因爲他無法和盤托出；更爲奇怪的是，他不願這樣，而通過隱含的方式和寓言道出，目的是他可以確定你需要它。我不大明白其中的原因，也無從分析智者們胸懷裡那種無情緘默，它使他們總是隱藏著比較深沉的思想。他們把思想給予你不是作爲幫助，而是作爲獎賞，他們從而確信你是受之無愧的，然後才允許你獲得它。不過對待智慧的物質類型即黃金，也是同樣的道理。在你我看來，都不淸楚爲什麼。不必再怕挖掘，怕焦慮，怕冒險，怕費時間，於是半途而廢了，需要多少錢幣就去鑄造。但是造化卻不是如此對待它的。她把黃金放在大地上細小的裂縫裡，誰也不知道是在哪兒：你可能挖掘多時還是無所發現；要想有所發現你就必須苦苦地挖掘。

對待人類的優秀智慧完全是一個道理。當你接觸到一本好書時，你應該問一問自己，"我是不

must ask yourself, "Am I inclined to work as an Australian miner would? Are my pickaxes and shovels in good order, and am I in good trim myself, my sleeves well up to the elbow, and my breath good, and my temper?" And, keeping the figure a little longer, even at cost of tiresomeness, for it is a thoroughly useful one, the metal you are in search of being the author's mind or meaning, his words are as the rock which you have to crush and smelt in order to get at it. And your pickaxes are your own care, wit, and learning; your smelting furnace is your own thoughtful soul. Do not hope to get at any good author's meaning without those tools and that fire; often you will need sharpest, finest chiseling, and patientest fusing, before you can gather one grain of the metal.

是願意像澳大利亞的礦工一樣做工？我的丁字鎬和鏟子是不是完好無損，我自己的身體行不行，我的袖口捲上去了沒有，我的呼吸正常嗎，我的脾氣好不好？"而且呢，做這種事的架勢要堅持得時間長一些，即使令你感到神疲力倦，因爲它是十分有用的，而你所探尋的眞金便是作者的心靈或意思，他的文字就像岩石那樣，你非得碾碎熔鍊，才能有收獲。你的丁字鎬就是你自己的心血、機智、學問；你的熔爐就是你自己會思考的靈魂。切莫指望不用那些工具和那份磨練就能把握任何優秀作者的意思；往往你需要最猛烈、最精心的打鑿，最耐心的熔化，然後才能夠拾起一點眞金。

欣賞

　　書是訊息的載體。訊息時代書成了人們必不可少的學習工具。書要開卷有益，說起來簡單，但當我們走進書店時，被琳琅滿目的書弄得不知所措，生怕買上不好的書。的確"凡讀無益之書，皆是玩物喪志。"（王豫）讀了無用之書，敎人學壞，使人喪志。要讀好書，就得學會品味，識別和鑒別。這篇散文這一點上可以給我們幾分啓發，使我們明白幾分經書的道理。本文作者寄道理於情文，立意深刻，神形交錯，趣味橫生，意味深遠，文筆幽雅，筆路淸新。

20. Of Ambition

Francis Bacon

Ambition is like choler, which is a humour that makes men active, earnest, full of alacrity, and stirring, if it is not stopped. But if it is stopped, and cannot have his way, it becomes adust, and thereby malign and venomous. So ambitious men, if they find the way open for their rising, and still get forward, they are rather busy than dangerous; but if they are checked in their desires, they become secretly discontent and look upon men and matters with an evil eye, and are best pleased when things go backward, which is the worst property in a servant of a prince or state. Therefore it is good for princes, if they use ambitious men, to handle it so as they be still progressive and not retrograde; which because it cannot be without inconvenience, it is good not to use such nature at all. For if they rise not with their service, they will take order to make their service fall with them. But since we have said it was good not to use men of ambitious natures, except it is upon

20．論 野 心

弗朗西斯·培根

　　野心好似膽汁，要是不受阻時是一種令人積極奮發向上、行動敏捷的體液。然而一旦受阻而不能隨心所欲，它就會變成焦燥、惡毒而有害之物了。所以懷有野心的人，當他們覺得升遷有望，而且步步高升時，他們忙碌不已，倒說不上什麼危險。但當他們的慾望受到阻撓因而心懷不滿時，他們就會用一副凶煞眼光看人看事，對他人的挫折幸災樂禍。這就是一個君主國或共和國臣民最惡劣的品性。因此，君主使用有野心的人，必須善於駕馭他們，使他們感到總在前進而無後退之虞。但這種做法不可能總是順利的。所以對具有這種天性的人，還是以不用爲佳。因爲假如他們不能隨其職司步步升高時，他們肯定將設法把所承擔的工作與自身一同毀掉。前面已經說過，除非萬不得已，最好不用野心成性的人。我們還應當交

necessity, it is fit we speak in what cases they
are of necessity. Good commanders in the wars
must be taken, be they never so ambitious; for
the use of their service dispenses with the rest,
and to take a soldier without ambition is to pull
off his spurs. There is also great use of ambitious men in being screens to princes in matters
of danger and envy, for no man will take that
part, except he is like a seeled dove, that
mounts and mounts because he cannot see about
him. There is use also of ambitious men in
pulling down the greatness of any subject that
overtops; as Tiberius used Macro in the pulling
down of Sejanus. Since therefore they must be
used in such cases, there rests to speak how
they are to be bridled that they maybe less dangerous. There is less danger of them if they were
of mean birth, than if they are noble; and if
they are rather harsh of nature, than gracious
and popular; and if they are rather new raised,
than grown cunning a fortified in their greatness. It is counted by some a weakness in
princes to have favourites; but it is of all others
the best remedy against ambitious great ones.
For when the way of pleasuring and displeasing

代一下，在什麼樣的情況下，這樣的人是非用不
可。戰爭中一定要用良將，這時就不能顧及他們
有什麼野心了。他們的戰功能勝過其他一切。何
況，起用一個沒有野心的軍人就等於除掉他的踢
馬刺，那是無法供驅馳的。有野心者還有一大用
處：這就是在君王遭受危難或嫉妒時充當屏障。
因為沒有人願意扮演這種角色，除非他像一隻矇
住了眼睛的鴿子，只顧一股勁高飛，對周圍的情況
一無所見。野心家也可用來摧毀任何與君王爭雄
的臣民的權勢；比如提比洛就曾利用野心勃勃的
麥克羅去推翻篡權者西亞努斯。既然有野心的人
在上述情況下是非用不可的，我們還得說一說應
當如何駕馭這些人，以減少其危險性。一般地說，
出身微賤者比出身高貴者危險較小；天性粗暴者
比舉止優雅而深得人心者危險小；剛剛得到提拔
的人比任何一個有權勢，狡詐多謀的豪門危害小。
有些人認為君王有所寵幸是一種缺點，殊不知這
是對付權勢顯赫的野心家各種各樣辦法中最有效
的補足措施。所有賞罰都要通過寵臣，這樣就不
會有什麼人擁有過大權勢。還有一種制約野心家

lieth by the favorite, it is impossible any other should be over-great. Another means to balance them by others as proud as they do. But then there must be some middle courts the ship will roll too much. At the lest, a prince may animate and inure some meaner person to be as it were scourges to ambitious men. As for the having of them obnoxious to ruin, if they are of fearful natures, it may do well, but if they are stout and daring, it may precipitate their designs and prove dangerous. As for the pulling of them down, if the affairs require it, and that it may not be done with safety suddenly, the only way is the interchange continually of favours and disgraces, whereby they may not know what to expect, and be as it were in a wood. Of ambitions, it is less harmful, the ambition to prevail in great things, than that other, to appear in everything, for that breeds confusion, and mars business. But yet it is less danger to have an ambitious man stirring in business, than great in dependences. He that seeks to be eminent amongst able men have a great task, but that is ever good for the public. But he that plots to be the only figure amongst ciphers is the decay of

的辦法,就是選用和他們一樣傲慢的人與之抗衡。
但是爲了保持事物的穩定,還要有一些中立態度
的大臣,他們好似壓艙物,可以防止航船過於顚
簸,這樣以穩定局勢。至少,君王還可以鼓勵並提
拔一些出身和才能較差的人,使他們成爲野心家
和某種對頭。不過,要使野心家時常面臨覆滅的
可能性,必須愼重從事;如果這些人生性畏怯,這
種辦法會激發他們圖謀擧事,造成危險。至於在
事態需要的情況下,如何使他們徹底垮臺,而又不
冒猝然行動反生不測的風險,唯一的辦法就是不
停地賞罰互用,有如身在密林一樣,使他們摸不著
頭腦,弄不淸自己會有什麼樣的結果。在各種各
樣的野心中,那種意在大事上佔上風的野心比事
事都想一顯身手的野心爲害較小。因爲後者產生
混亂,妨礙正事。讓有野心的人忙於事務,比起讓
他擁有大群追隨者,其危險性是較小的。凡是想
在許多幹才中出類拔萃的人往往在面臨困難時,
無暇旁顧,而對公衆總是有好處的。至於那種圖
謀把別的人都抹成零,只想使自己成爲獨裁的野

an whole age. Homour has three things in it: the vantage ground to do good, the approach to kings and principal persons, and the raising of a man's own fortunes. He that has the best of these intentions, when he aspires, is an honest man; and that prince that can discern of these intentions in another that aspires, is a wise prince. Generally let princes and states choose such ministers as are more sensible of duty than of rising; and such as love business rather upon conscience than upon bravery; and let them discern a busy nature from a willing mind.

心家,才是一代人的毀滅者。居高位者有三利:有
行善的優越條件,易於接近王公顯要,可以增長本
人的榮華富貴。有所希冀的人們當中覺察這種良
好意願的人可算是誠實君子,堪稱是賢主。一般
地說,君王或邦國選擇大臣的時候,應當遴選那些
把責任感看得重於升遷的人,那些本著良心而非
爲了炫耀華麗而喜愛工作的大人。他們還應當把
濟世的抱負與鑽營的天性仔細區別開來。

欣賞

　　"野心"一詞有褒義,也有貶義。在這篇散文中都爲
貶義。培根把野心家的面貌、神態等描繪得入情又入理。
散文中培根極力推薦如何駕馭有野心的人的策略。但透
過散文我們也不難看出,其權術還是沒有離開"馬基雅維
利式"的權術。"馬式權術"曾因其"爲了達到目的而不擇
手段"的政治學說,在歐洲和英國有著重大的影響。對
此,英國詩人布萊克曾譏諷培根"善於向魔鬼獻策"這是
散文的第一層意思。散文第二層主要的意思是在什麼情
況下用有野心的人。他認爲:"戰爭中一定要用良將,這
時就不能顧及他們有什麼野心了。他們的戰功能勝過其
他一切。"當然這僅是玩弄權術,其結果如何恐怕無法預
測。在提到如何選拔提升對象時,培根的觀點是很有啓
發意義的。

21.Of Truth

Francis Bacon

What is truth? Said jesting Pilate, and would not stay for an answer. Certainly there is that delight in giddiness and count it bondage to fix a belief, affecting free − will in thinking as well as in acting. And though the sects of philosophers of that kind are gone, yet there remain certain discoursing wits which are of the same veins, though there is not so much blood in them as was in those of the ancients.

But it is not only the difficulty and labour which men take in finding out of truth, nor again that when it is found it imposes upon men' s thoughts, that does bring lies in favour, but a natural though corrupt love of the lie itself. One of the later school of the Grecians examines the matter and is at a stand think what should be in it , that men should love lies where neither they make for pleasure, as with poets nor for advantage, as with the merchant, but for

21. 論　真　理

弗朗西斯·培根

　　“眞理是什麼呢？”彼拉多曾取笑道，他說問題並不等於回答。的確世上有一類人以輕易改變自己的意見爲樂，認爲有了一種固定信仰就是套上了枷鎖。他們一心謀求思想和行動上都崇尙自由意志。雖然這一類形形色色的哲學家現已作古，但仍有一些心志游移的說客和他們一脈相承，儘管其聲勢血氣比起古人來已大有遜色。

　　人們之所以喜愛謊言勝於眞理，不僅因爲探索眞理是艱苦費力的，也不僅因爲求得眞理會約束人們的思想，還因爲人類對謊言本身有一種天生的愛好，雖然這種愛好帶有腐敗墮落的性質。希臘晚期哲學學派中有人研究過這個問題，他感到費解的是：謊言中究竟有什麼東西值得人們如此鍾愛呢？它既不像詩人的作品引人入勝，給人以快感，也不像商人的所爲，使人獲利，可是人們仍然爲了謊言本身而喜愛謊言啊！

the lie's sake.

But I cannot tell. This same truth is a naked and open daylight that does not show the masques and mummeries and triumphs of the world half so stately and daintily as candle-lights. Truth may perhaps come to the price of a pearl, that shows best by day; but it will not rise to the price of a diamond or carbuncle, that shows best in varied lights.

A mixture of a lie does ever add pleasure. Does any man doubt that if there were taken out of men's minds vain opinions, flattering hopes, false valuations, imaginations as one would, and the like, but it would leave the minds of a number of men poor shrunken things, full of melancholy and indisposition, and unpleasing to themselves?

One of the Fathers, in great severity, called poesy vinum daemonum because it fills the imagination and yet it is but with the shadow of a lie. But it is not the lie that passes through the mind but the lie that sinks in and settles in it, that does the hurt, such as we speak of be-

　　我也說不清是什麼緣故——或許眞理就像毫無根據遮隱的目光，在它照耀下的世間那一場場化裝舞會，滑稽劇和慶祝大典，遠不如在燭光照耀下那樣堂皇優美。眞理在世人心目中的價値好似珍珠，在陽光之下光華閃閃；但其價値怎樣也比不上鑽石和紅玉，它們能在變換不定的光影中大放異彩。

　　在眞理裡攙上一點謊言總是增添樂趣的。假如從人們心中把自鳴得意的主見，虛妄誘人的希望、虛假不實的評價、隨心所欲的想像全部取走，就會使許多人的內心變得渺小、萎縮、可憐、憂心忡忡、性情乖戾，連自己也感到厭惡自己。難道這一點還有人懷疑嗎？

　　有一位先哲曾正言厲色地把詩歌稱爲“魔鬼之酒”，因爲詩能給人以想像，而詩歌則帶有虛妄的謊言的影子。其實，眞正有害的不是那種掠過心靈的謊言，而是如前所述的那沉入心知與感情

fore. But howsoever these things are thus in men's depraved judgements and affections, yet truth, which only does judge itself, teaches that the inquiry of truth, which is the love – making or wooing of it, the knowledge of truth, which is the presence of it, and the belief of truth, which is the enjoying of it, is the sovereign good of human nature.

The first creature of God in the works of the days was the light of the sense; the last was the light of reason; and his Sabbath work ever since is the illumination of his Spirit. First he breathes light upon the face of the matter or chaos; then he breathes light into the face of man; and still he breathes and inspires light into the face of his chosen.

The poet that beautified the sect that was otherwise inferior to the rest, says yet excellently well: It is a pleasure to stand upon the shore and to see ships tossed upon the sea; a pleasure to stand in the window of a castle and to see a battle and the adventures thereof below: but no pleasure is comparable to the standing upon the

的東西，眞理有自身的尺度，她教導我們要追求眞
理，就像求愛求婚一樣；要認識眞理，一如眞理就
在我們面前；更要相信眞理，即充分享有眞理，而
這就是人性中最高的品德。

　　上帝創造世界之初，他首先創造的是感官之
光，最後創造的是理性之光。從那以後，他在安息
日的工作就是以顯靈來昭示世人。最初他在混沌
和物質上面噴射光明；而後在人的面目裡噴發光
明；從古至今仍在向他的選民吐射光明，並激發他
們追求光明。

　　有一派哲學在別的方面不如其他學派，但其
中一位詩人卻使她大放光彩。這位詩人有一段話
說得十分精妙：“站在岸上遙望大海中顛簸的航船
是一件樂事；站在堡壘的窗口觀看一場鏖戰和種
種驚險的武功也是一件樂事。但是，沒有一椿樂
事比登臨那凌駕群山的眞理高峰前沿，透過永遠

vantage ground of truth (a hill not to be com-
manded, and where the air is always clear and
serene), and to see the errors and wanderings
and mists and tempests in the vale below; so always that this prospect is with pity and not with
swelling or pride. Certainly it is heaven upon
earth to have a man's mind move in charity,
rest in providence, and turn upon the poles of
truth.

To pass from theological and philosophical
truth to the truth of civil business: it will be ac-
knowledged, even by those that practise it not
that clear and round dealing is the honour of
man's nature, and that mixture of falsehood is
like alloy in coin of gold and silver, which may
make the metal work the better, but it embases
it. For these winding and crooked courses are
the goings of the serpent, which goes basely upon the belly and not upon the feet.

There is no vice that does so cover a man
with shame as to be found false and perfidious.
And therefore Montaigne said prettily when he
inquired the reason why the work of the lie

是清新而寧靜的空氣，俯瞰下界谷坳裡的種種失誤、徘徊、迷霧和風風雨雨更引人入勝的了。"只要觀看這種景像時永存惻隱之心而無洋洋自得之意，他就永遠自得其樂。的確，一個人的心如能以仁慈爲懷抱，以天意爲歸宿，而且永遠以眞理爲軸心而旋轉，那麼他雖在人間也就與在天堂無異了。

以上說的是神學和哲學的眞理，現在再談談處世的眞理。即使那些行爲並不光明正大的人，也會承認光明正大、待人以誠是人類高貴的品性，而眞中攙假則猶如金銀幣中夾雜著其他金屬，這種合金也許更實用，但它的價值卻大大降低了。凡是彎彎曲曲而不正不直的行徑就像蛇的爬行一樣，它不是用腳走路，而是用腹部貼著地卑賤地匍匐而行的。

沒有一種惡行比被發現是虛僞和背信棄義更使人蒙羞受辱了。所以蒙田在研究謊言一詞何以如此可恥，何以成爲一種可憎的罪責時說得好："

should be such a disgrace and such an odious charge. Said he, If it is well weighed, to say that a man lies is as much to say as that he is brave towards God and a coward towards men. For a lie faces God and shrinks from man. Surely the wickedness of falsehood and breach of faith cannot possibly be so highly expressed, as in that it shall be the last peal to call the judgements of God upon the earth.

認眞思考一下吧！要是說某人說謊，就等於說他在上帝面前很大膽，而在世人面前卻很怯懦。”因爲謊言是面對上帝而躲避凡人的。曾經有個預言，說基督返回人間之日，將是大地上找不到信德之時。可見謊言是促請上帝對世世代代的人進行最後審判的鐘聲。對於虛假和背信棄義的罪惡，再不能比這一說法表達得更發人深省了。

欣賞

對於眞理的命題恐怕還沒有一致的答案。這篇散文雖以眞理爲主題，但培根筆下並沒有正面論述什麼是眞理，怎樣探求眞理等。培根從另一側面描述了人們對謊言僞說的偏愛，以一種反正的論說方法來揭示人滿爲患對眞理的疏遠和缺乏熱情。這反映出當時英國社會的某種弊端。

培根堅信眞理有自身的尺度，他以鮮明的比喻和詩意的語言，揭示了眞理的品性。一貫重視實用功利的培根，在這篇散文中似乎置身於更高的境界。他勸導人們要追求眞理，認識眞理，更要相信眞理，充分享有眞理，這是人性中最高的品德。讀罷這篇散文，我們想我們的讀者朋友不禁會想到我國屈原的一句名詩“路漫漫其修遠兮，吾將上下而求索”。

22. National Morale

Sun Yat-sen

Although we are behind the foreigners in scientific achievement, our native ability is adequate to the construction of a great material civilization, which is proved by the concrete evidence of past achievements. We invented the compass, printing, porcelain, gunpowder, and the curing of tea and weaving of silk. Foreigners have made good use of these inventions. For example, Modern Ocean transportation would be impossible if there were no compass. The fast printing machine, which turns out tens of thousands of copies per hour, had its origin in China. Foreign military greatness comes from gunpowder, which was first used by the Chinese. Furthermore, many of the latest inventions in architecture in the West have been practiced in the East for thousands of years. Those genius of our race for material inventions seems now to be lost; and so our greatness has become but the history of bygone glories.

I believe that we have many things to learn

22. 民族的天職

孫中山

　　雖然現在中國已經在科學發明上不及外國人，但是中國人的能力足以建設物質文化，過去的許多發明就是明證。中國人發明了指南針，印刷術，瓷器，火藥，茶的藥用和絲綢。外國人對這些發明大加利用。比如說，現代的航海，要是沒有發明指南針，那是不可能的。最快的印刷機，每小時可以印刷幾萬張報紙，推究他的來源，也是中國人發明的。外國軍隊的強大，也來源於火藥，火藥也是中國人發明的。還有，西方最先進的建築發明創造在東方早在幾千年前就有了。我們幾乎失去了民族發明的天才，我們昔日的偉大已成爲過去的輝煌。

　　我想我們有很多東西要學習西方，我們也能

from the West, and that we can learn them.
Many Westerners maintain that the hardest thing
to learn is aviation science; already many Chinese have become skillful aviators. If aeronau-
tics can be learned, I believe everything can be
learned by our people. Science is only three
hundred years old, and it was not highly developed until fifty years ago. Formerly coal was
used as the source of energy; now the age of
coal has given place to the age of electricity.

Recently America had a plan for national-
izing the waterpower of the country. America
has hundreds of thousands of factories. Each big
factory has to have a powerhouse which con-
sumes a tremendous amount of coal. The rail-
roads in the country are busily engaged in transporting coal, and have little time for transporting
agricultural products. As a means of economiz-
ing coal and lessening transportation, a national
central powerhouse is suggested. When such a
house is built, the entire nation will receive energy form one central station. The result will be
the elimination of lenourmous waste and the increase of efficiency. When we learn from the
West, it is evident that we should learn the latest inventions instead of repeating the different

學得到。許多西方人認爲，航天技術是難學的；可是我們中國人早就有這種技術。如果說航天技術能學得到的話，我想沒有什麼東西學不到。科學技術只有三百年的工夫，到了近五十年來，才算是十分進步。正由於這種科學的進步，所以煤可以作爲動力。如今用煤的時代以被電所替代。

　　現在美國有一個很大的計劃，要把全國的水利資源都統一起來。因爲他們全國的機器廠有幾萬家，各家工廠都有一個發動機，都要各自燒煤去生產動力。這個國家的鐵路忙於替他們運煤，更沒工夫去運農產。爲節約用煤，減少運輸，所以美國現在想做一個中央電廠，把幾萬家工廠用電力去統一。這樣可以減少浪費而提高效率。我們要學外國，很顯然，我們應當學習最新的發明創造，而不是重複不同的發展腳步。比如說，動力房，我

steps of development. In the case of the power-house, we may well learn to adopt the centralized plan of producing electricity, and need not follow the old plan of using coal to produce energy. In this way we can easily within ten years catch up with the West in material achievement.

The time is critical. We have no time to waste, and we ought to take the latest and the best that the West can offer. Our intelligence is by no means inferior to that of the Japanese. With our historical background and our natural and human resources, it should be easier for us than it was for Japan to rise to the place of a first class Power by a partial adaptation of Western civilization. We ought to be ten times stronger than Japan because our country is more than ten times bigger and richer than Japan. China is potentially equal to ten Powers. At present England, America, France, Italy, and Japan constitute the so-called "Big Five." Even with the rise of Germany and Soviet Russia, the world has only seven Powers. When China becomes strong, she can easily win first place in the Council of Nations.

Now the question is: How can we become a first class Power? Our ancestors adopted a pol-

們也可以學習採用中央電廠的方法，我們沒有必要按過去的辦法用煤去產生動力。這樣要不了十年，我們的物質生產就能趕上西方。

我們已經到了關鍵的時刻。我們沒有時間去浪費。我們應當學習西方最新最精的東西。我們的聰明才智一點也不亞於日本人。我們過去的歷史，我們的自然條件和人力資源豐富，我們通過學習西方部分文化技術，比日本要容易趕上一流的水平。我們應該比日本強十倍，因為我們的領土比日本國的十倍還大，資源豐富十倍還多。中國有著十個強國的潛力。目前，英、美、法、義和日本不過是"五大"強國，加上正在崛起的德國和蘇聯，世界之大也不過是七個強國。當中國崛起強大的時候，她將輕易而舉地成為國會中的頭一把交椅。

現在我們的問題是，我們怎樣才能成為頭號的強國。我們的祖先採取了"抑強扶弱"這是一建

icy of "helping the weak and curbing the strong": a policy of international justice resting upon a sound moral foundation. As a result, the small nations in Asia, including Annam, Burma, Korea, and Siam enjoyed peace, freedom, and independence for thousands of years. As soon as China became weak, these small nations were annexed by the Powers, and so they lost their liberty and independence. When China becomes strong again, it will be our duty to help these nations win back their freedom. This is a great responsibility! If we cannot fulfill this great responsibility, what is the use of China being strong and powerful?

Again, if China follows at the heels of the imperialistic and militaristic nations, China's ascendency to power, would not only be useless, but harmful to humanity. The only glorious and honorable path for us to pursue is to maintain in full force the old policy of "helping the weak and curbing the strong."

Gentlemen, we ought to decide at this hour what is to be the fundamental policy for which the nation is to stand, and where our hope and our greatness lie. When the days of our prosperity come, we must not forget the pain and mis-

立在健全的道德基礎上的國際公平政策。亞洲的小國,包括安南、緬甸、高麗、西阿門等幾千年前就享有和平、自由和獨立。只要中國不強大,這些小國就成爲大國的附屬國。他們也會失去自由和獨立。當中國再強大起來時,幫助這些小國重新獲得自由是我們義不容辭的職責。這是我們神聖的責任! 如果我們完全不能承擔這份神聖的責任,中國強大又有何用?

再者,如果中國走帝國主義和軍國主義同樣的路,即使中國強盛起來,不但無益,而且還有害於人類。我們唯一追求的偉大光輝的道理是全力堅持我們傳統的政策"抑強扶弱"。

先生們:此刻我們應當決定我們的立國之策,我們的希望所在,我們的偉大所在。當我們強盛的時候,我們不要忘記我們現在所蒙受的經濟和

ery which we are now suffering from the pressure of economic and political forces of the Powers. When our country becomes powerful, we should assume the responsibility of delivering those nations which suffer in the same way as we do now. This is what the Ta Hsueh means by "securing world tranquillity" (p'ing t'ien Hsia). The way to proceed is to revive our spirit of nationalism and to restore our country to its original position of a "Single Power." We should use our old moral values and our love of peace as the foundation of national reconstruction; and look forward to the day when we shall become leaders in world reconstruction upon lines of international justice and good will. This is the mission of our 400,000,000. Gentlemen, each one of you is one of the 400,000,000; and you personally should assume this responsibility. But your first step is to revive your spirit of nationalism!

來自列強政治壓力的苦難。當我們強大起來的時候，我們應當承擔解放這些小國的責任，這些小國如今像我們一樣蒙受著苦難。這就是塔薩的"保持世界安寧"的意願。要實現這一目的，只有重振我們的民族主義精神，重新把我們的國家恢復到原來的"獨立強盛"國家的地位。我們應當利用我們傳統的道德，我們熱愛和平的精神，作為我們的立國之本。我們期盼著我們在自願和國際公平政策的基礎上，在世界建設中發揮我們的主要作用。這便是我們四萬萬人的責任。諸君都是四萬萬人的一份子，都應該擔負起這個責任，我們的第一步是使我們的民族主義的精神復甦！

欣賞

這是 1924 年孫中山先生關於三民主義演說系列中的一部分。這是一篇別具色彩的演講辭。他用了許多史實確鑿證明了中國人是有創造力的，衣食住行諸方面無不早有發明。然而固步自封不進則退，他既指出應該學習外國人長處，又肯定完全能夠學到外國人先進的科學技術，並且提出了迎頭趕上的可能和必要。這是第一層意思。在對應中國重振雄風進行了一番論證後，演講辭又進而定下用固有的和平道德做基礎，去統一世界、成一個大同之治的志向，用以發揚民族主義的精神。這是第二層意思。第三層意思是中國應當依賴於傳統的"抑強扶弱"的道德觀念，以此作為我們的立國之本，決不能走帝國主義和軍國主義的老路，號召重振我們民族之精神。

23. Eight Ways to Help Your Child Excel

Patrick Welsh

As a teacher, I used to think parents should be seen and not heard at school. But now that I have three children of my own, my attitude has changed. I'm convinced that if parents take the following steps, they can make an enormous difference in what their children get out of school.

1. See that your children receive their share of the best teachers.

In every school system there are creative, caring teachers who can stimulate even the most hard to reach children. Finding them is not difficult. Ask parents who already have children in the school. Don't listen to school officials who claim all teachers are the same. They often say so because they must fill each teacher's class. When you have identified the teacher you like. Go to the counselor who makes class assignments — preferably during the summer, before school begins — and make your request. Re-

23. 讓你孩子超群的八種方法

巴特裡克·威爾士

　　身爲教師，我曾認爲父母們不僅應該給學校打電話，了解孩子的情況，還應該親自到學校去。但在我有了三個孩子以後的今天，我改變了這種看法。我深信，如果父母們能夠遵循下面這些步驟，那麼他們的孩子在學校所獲得的教益就會大大改觀。

一、設法把你的孩子安排在優秀教師所在的班級

　　　　每一個學校都有一些對工作認眞負責，而又極富創造性的老師。他們甚至能夠激發那些不開竅的孩子。要找這樣的老師並不困難，只稍問問有孩子在這所學校讀書的家長就行。不要聽信學校領導所說的，所有老師都一樣的話。他們所以經常這樣說，是因爲他必須把每個班級都排滿。當你認準了自己中意的老師後，就去找負責學生分班工作的教導員———最好在夏季，在暑期結束前———向他提出你的要

member: administrators sometimes take the expedient route, assigning children of less vocal parents to the poorer teachers.

Your youngster won't always get the most desirable teachers. If the child can't be transferred to another class, encourage him or her to focus on the subject instead of the teacher. Learning, after all, is basically up to the student.

2. Help teachers to know you and your kids.

Years ago, when teachers lived in their students neighborhoods, parents and teachers casually exchanged information after church or in the grocery. But in today's huge schools, where a teacher may have more than 120 pupils, some kids are never more than a name in a roll book. Parents can rescue their children from anonymity by getting to know teachers. Once a teacher can attach a child to a parent's face, that child becomes a flesh-and-blood individual from a real family. Contact teachers if your child has problems that may affect schoolwork. It is easy for teachers to misunderstand and give up on students who duck work or misbehave.

One mother made an appointment to talk to me about her son, a six-foot-four, 240-pound

求。請記住：行政人員有時只圖便利，把那些不聲不響父母的孩子安排到一些較差老師的班級。

你的孩子不可能總遇上最理想的老師，如果你的孩子無法換，要鼓勵他或她把精力集中在課程上，而不要集中在老師身上。學習的好壞畢竟在於學生自身。

二、幫助老師了解你的孩子

許多年前，當老師和學生們同住一個居住區時，父母和老師在做禮拜或購物時偶爾能交流情況。但是在目前這種大型學校裡，一個教師或許有一百二十多個學生，有些學生對於他來說只是點名冊上的一個名字而已。要補救這一點，做家長的應當主動去結識老師。一旦老師能夠把這個孩子與家長的面容聯繫起來，這孩子就成了一個來自真實家庭的有血有肉的一個人了。如果你的孩子遇到了影響功課的問題，你必須和老師取得聯繫。老師們常常容易誤解和嫌棄那些逃避作業或調皮搗蛋的學生。

曾有一位母親為了兒子的問題約我交談過。這孩子身高 1.95 米，體重 89.52 公斤，是

senior who sat sullenly in English class, looking as though he hated me and everything I said. As the mother talked, I saw that her son was terrified of participating in class because the other kids especially the girls — seemed to know much more about literature than he did. I had mistaken his shyness for hostility. The mother and I agreed to team up: she'd tell her son he had to push himself to talk in class, and I'd call on him more. Over the next two weeks I called on him in class and praised his responses. Soon the sullen looks evaporated, and his writing improved. He is came one of my favorite students.

The secret, I'm convinced, is that when a student sees a parent and a teacher join forces for his or her own benefit, miracles can happen.

3. Be realistic. One reason we teachers shy away from parents is that we tend to hear from them only when they are protesting a punishment the child deserved or trying to pressure us into raising a grade. I've had parents argue, "But he won't get into the college he's applied to if you give him a C!" They won't admit that the kid hasn't worked

個高年級的學生。他在英語課上總是繃著個臉、一言不發。看起來很像是他恨我，恨我所講的一切。直到這位母親找我談話時我才明白，她的兒子很害怕在班上發言，因為這個班上的孩子——特別是女孩子的文學知識似乎比他豐富得多。我把他的膽怯誤解為敵意了。我和這位母親商量好齊心協力地幫助他：她告訴兒子要在課堂上積極發言，我則多給提問的機會並表揚他。在以後的兩個星期裡，我常讓他在課堂上回答問題，並表揚他回答得好。不久，他臉上那緊繃的神色消失了，寫作也有了進步，成了我中意的學生之一。

　　我深信這其中的奧秘是：當學生看到老師和家長齊心協力要幫助他時，奇蹟便會出現！

三、要現實

　　我們做老師的不願跟家長接觸的一個原因是：我們往往只是在學生受了應得的處分、家長為此提出抗議，或家長試圖強求我們為孩子加分時，才聽得到家長的聲音。有位家長曾這樣和我爭辯："如果你給了一個 C，那他就不可能進他所報的那所大學了！"他們不願意承認孩子自己沒有下功夫，或是根本沒有能力得

or just doesn't have the ability to earn higher grades.

4. Acknowledge good educators. Most of our professional life is spent with students behind classroom doors. We get little recognition from other adults and seldom hear what effects we're having on students lives. A phone call or letter of thanks can have tremendous impact. We'll have an incentive to take special note of your child.

5. Get to know other parents. Pool information. If you suspect that a teacher is doing a poor job, for example, ask parents of others in the class whether they agree. If you have to confront a school official on a major issue, you will feel more confident with others along.

6. Shop around for guidance counselors. Most students are assigned to counselors randomly. Yet counselors can vary in quality. I've seen seniors end the year without enough credits to graduate; their counselors never checked! Others were not accepted at college because their counselors had let them apply to schools they weren't qualified to attend.

高分。

四、感謝優秀的教育者

　　我們的教書生涯多半是和學生在課堂中度過的。我們當老師的難得受到其他成人的重視，也很少聽人談起我們給學生的一生帶來了怎樣的影響。一個表示感謝的電話或一封感激信能產生極大的效應，會鼓勵我們對你的孩子倍加關注。

五、結識其他孩子的父母

　　要收集訊息。比如說，你疑心某個老師教得不好，可以問問其他孩子的父母，看看他們是否有同感。如果你為一個重要的問題不得不與學校領導交涉，有其他人和你在一起，你會更有信心些。

六、挑選指導老師

　　多數學生都被隨隨便便地分配給一些指導老師，但指導老師的素質有好有差。我曾經看到一些畢業班的學生因學分不夠而畢不了業，他們的指導老師竟從不檢查！有些學生沒有被錄取，因為他們的指導老師讓他們報了那些他們不夠格的學校。你所尋求的指導老師

Insight into young people and the ability to detect and follow up on their problems. All kinds of traits to look for in a guidance counselor.

7. Pay attention to your children. Too many parents are leaving too much up to the school and the child himself. When I look at the children of Susan and David Dawes, I realize just how much parents can do to help a child in school.

Donald Dawes now a senior at Cornell University, was our valedictorian in 1985. His brother Jim, a sophomore at the University of Pennsylvania, was our 1987 valedictorian, and Billy, the youngest, is aiming just as high. "Mom and Dad always told us that our primary job was to be students," says Donald. Where other kids work 20 or 30 hours a week to buy fancy clothes or a car, "we were expected to do one thing: study," adds Billy. The Dawes boys also had a live-in tutor — their father. In grammar school, Don remembers having difficulty with math. "I'd yell for Dad he was always there to explain something. I'd never be in engineering

應當具備這樣一些素質：善於洞察年輕人，有察覺問題徹底查明的能力。

七、注意你的孩子

　　有太多的父母把教育的責任過多地交給了學校和孩子自己。看到蘇姍和大衛·道斯的孩子們時，我意識到，父母在孩子的學校生活中也可以起很大的作用。

　　唐納德·道斯現在是康耐爾大學的四年級學生。他曾是我校 1985 年畢業的致告別辭代表。他的弟弟吉姆，賓夕法尼亞大學二年級學生，是我校 1987 年的致畢業辭代表。他最小的弟弟比利，也正朝著同樣的目標努力。"媽媽和爸爸總是對我們說，我們的主要任務就是做個學生，"唐納德說。別的學生爲買新潮時裝或汽車每週打 20 或 30 小時的工，"而我們的父母只期望我們做一件事：學習。"比利補充說。道斯家的孩子還有一個寄宿的家庭教師——那就是他們的父親。唐記得他在上中學時常常遇到數學難題，"這時，我總是呼喊爸爸，而他總會向我作些解釋。要不是爸爸的幫

today if he hadn't helped. " Both David and Susan have made time commitments that I see few parents willing to make. David turned down a job promotion that he feared would take time away from his family. Susan plans to take her first full-time job in 20 years when Billy enters college next fall. Recently I heard two students complaining that when they were small they got a great deal of attention, but now that their mothers are working, they feel their younger siblings are getting shortchanged. "My little brother is left alone a lot," said one, "and I can tell it's screwing him up. "

Our principal, John Porter, says parents' involvement seems to taper off as kids enter high school. "Parents don't realize that high-school kids need just as much attention as elementary school children — maybe more. " "The kids come home smiling, and the parents assume everything is fine. If they knew about the sex, liquor and drugs," says one boy in my honors course, "they'd drop dead. "

Parents who don't spend much time

助,我今天決不會攻讀工科。"大衛和蘇姍在孩子們身上花費了許多時間,幾乎沒有別的父母願意這樣做。大衛曾經放棄了一個工作上的晉升機會,因爲他擔心那會剝奪他用於家庭的時間。等比利在明年秋季進了大學後,蘇姍打算開始她 20 年來第一次全日制工作。最近,我聽到兩個學生抱怨說,在他們小時候,父母們十分關心他們,但現在他的母親都參加了工作,他們覺得他們的小弟妹們沒有得到應有的關心。"我的小弟弟老被一個人留在家裡,"一個說,"我敢說這會把他毀了的。"

　　我們的校長約翰·波特說,當孩子們上了中學後,父母們對孩子的關心似乎減少了。"父母們沒有認識到,一個上中學的孩子所需要的關注並不亞於一個小學生,或許需要得更多。"當孩子們笑咪咪地從學校回來,父母們便認定一切都很好。"如果他們知道性、酗酒、吸毒這些問題,"在我的優等生班中上課的一位學生說,"那他們準會嚇得昏了過去。"

　　那些沒有在孩子們身上花時間的父母到

with their children often end up looking for a quick fix to infuse their kids with knowledge. Some think a six-week course for the Scholastic. Many of these parents do little reading themselves and spend hours vegetating in front of the TV. One thing I'm certain will improve school performance: do not allow a child to have a TV in his room.

8. Celebrate your child's successes. Parents and teachers tend to focus too much on academics. Sometimes we judge children's very worth as human beings by their grades. But not all children will be academic stars. Help your child experience some form of success that engenders confidence, a goal more important than academic achievement. Last year my 17-year-old Magin, finally began to love school. Two things turned her around. One was an art award she received. The other was rowing on the junior varsity crew team and winning most of her reaches. My teacher instincts would have preferred that she get all . But fatherly love and common sense told me that the confidence she gained from her successes in drawing and rowing were infi-

頭來總想找一條捷徑填補孩子們的知識。有
人認爲六個星期的"學業能力傾向測驗"輔導
課程可以彌補幾年的失誤。這樣的家長多半
自己很少讀書，整天待在電視機前。一個準能
幫助孩子提高學習成績的做法是：不要在孩子
的房間裡安放電視。

八、慶賀你孩子的成功

　　父母和教師總是過多地關心孩子們的學
習分數。有時我們根據孩子的分數來判斷其
是否有出息。但並不是所有的孩子都能夠成
爲學術大師的。幫助孩子體驗成功的樂趣，以
此來激發他的自信心。自信心的培養比學習
成績更爲重要。去年，我 17 歲的孩子梅金終
於開始喜歡學校生活了。使她得以轉變的有
兩件事。一是她所獲得的藝術獎。二是她參
加了大學體育代表二隊的划船比賽，並從多數
中取勝。從我當教師的本能來說，我更願意她
每門功課都得 A，但是父愛和常識告訴我，她
從繪畫和划船的成功中所獲得的自信心遠比
A 重要得多。

nitely more important.

Our children will leave us all too soon. The more we participate with them now in their school years, the brighter, happier and more confident they will be when they join the world of adults.

　　我們的孩子會很快離開我們。如果我們今天更多地關心他們的學校生活，那麼他們在進入社會時也將更聰明、更愉快、更有自信。

欣賞

　　當今世界充滿競爭，在這激烈的競爭社會中，誰不願自己的兒女功成名就。“可憐天下父母心”“望子成龍”這不僅是中國人有之，外國人也有之。讀了這篇散文，我們更會覺得“子不教父之過，教不嚴師之惰，父教師嚴而學不好學問便是子之罪了。”（司馬光）的眞諦常在。作者要求父母更多地關心子女的學校生活，長長八大條建議，條條眞誠。可否是金玉良言，只好讓讀者朋友去評判。雖說沒有學究般的說理，但卻在敘事明理，理盡在其中。細細品味，你會覺得作者在促膝談心，眞誠如至；雖說沒有動人的篇章，但會讓人覺得受益無窮。

24. How to Deal with Difficult People

David D. Burns, M. D.

A business woman got into a taxi in mid-town. Because it was rush hour and she was hurrying for a train, she suggested a route. "I've been a cabby for 15 years!" the driver yelled. "You think I don't know the best way to go?"

The woman tried to explain that she hadn't meant to offend him, but the driver kept yelling. She finally realized he was too upset to be reasonable. So she did the unexpected. "You know, you're right," she told him. "It must seem dumb for me to assume you do not know the best way through the city. "

Taken aback, the driver flashed his rider a confused look in the rearview mirror, turned down the street she wanted and got her to the train on time. "He didn't say another word the rest of the ride. " She said, "until I got out and paid him. Then he thanked me. "

When you encounter people like this cab driver, there's an irresistible urge to dig in your

24. 怎樣與難處的人相處

大衛·D·伯恩斯

　　一位女商人在市中心叫了一輛出租車，由於正是上下班時間，她又急著去趕一趟火車，所以她向司機提議抄近道。"我已經當了 15 年司機了！"司機扯著大嗓門喊道。"你以爲我不知道走哪條路最好？"

　　這位婦女極力想解釋自己並非故意冒犯他，但那司機只是大喊大叫。她終於意識到，他這時已是滿肚子火，沒法和他論理。所以她採取了一個出人意料的做法，"你知道，你是對的，"她說，"我眞傻，竟以爲你不知道走哪條路穿過最好。"

　　司機驚訝不已，從後視鏡裡向乘車人迷惑不解地瞟了一眼，在她所希望的那條街停下，及時將她送上了火車。"在後來的旅程中他沉默不語，"她說，"但等我下了車，付錢給他時他謝了我。"

　　當人們遇到類似這位司機般的人時總會不可

heels. This can lead to prolonged arguments, soured friendships, lost career opportunities and brokens. As a clinical psychiatrist, I've discovered one simple but extremely unlikely principle that can prevent virtually any conflict or other difficult situation from becoming a recipe for disaster.

The key is to put yourself in the other person's shoes and look for the truth in what that person is saying. Find a way to agree. The result may surprise you. Sulkers. Steve's 14-year-old son, Adam, had been irritable for several days. When Steve asked why, Adam snapped, "Nothing's wrong! Leave me alone!" and stalked off to his room. We all know people like this. When there's problem, they may sulk or act angry and refuse to talk. So what's the solution? First, Steve needs to ask himself why Adam won't talk. Maybe the boy is worried about something that happened at school. Or he might be angry at his dad afraid to bring it up because Steve gets defensive whenever he is criticized. Steve can pursue these possibilities the next time they talk by saying, "I noticed you're upset, and I think it would help to get the problem out in the open. It may be hard be-

避免地堅持自己的觀點。這會導致更冗長的爭辯，會傷害友誼，失去工作機會，使關係破裂。作為一家診所的精神病醫師，我發現了一個極為簡單，而又非你所料的解決辦法，它可以緩解任何可能釀成的災難和衝突，或其他的一些困境。

　　關鍵在於你得設身處地，找出別人話中的在意之處。想辦法錶示同意，其結果也許會使你大吃一驚！史蒂夫14歲的兒子亞當幾天來動不動就生氣，當史蒂夫問他為什麼時，亞當就會氣惱地打斷他，"沒什麼事，別管我！"接著便大步走回自己的房間去了。我們都了解這樣的人。當他們遇到問題時，他們或是悶悶不樂，或是表現得很生氣，並拒絕交談。有什麼解決辦法呢？首先，史蒂夫必須問問自己亞當為什麼不願談話。也許這孩子在擔心學校裡發生的什麼事。也許他是在生父親的氣，但又不敢發作，因為當他指責史蒂夫時，史蒂夫都會極力辯護。在下一次談話時史蒂夫可以試試這樣一些辦法，可先發制人說，"我看你有些煩躁不安。我想還是把問題擺出來更好些。你

cause I haven't always listened very well. If
so, I feel bad because I love you and don't
want to let you down. " If Adam still refuses to
talk, Steve can take a different tack: "I'm concerned about what's going on with you, but we
can talk things over, when you're more in the
mood." This strategy allow both sides to win:
Steve doesn't have to compromise on the principle that ultimately the problem needs to be
talked out and resolved. Adam saves face by
being allowed to withdraw for a while.

　　Noisy critics. Recently, I was counseling a
businessman named Frank who tends to be over-
bearing when he's upset. Frank told me that I
was too preoccupied with money and that he
shouldn't have to pay at each of our sessions.
He wanted to be billed monthly. I felt annoyed
because it seemed Frank always had to have
things his way. I explained that I had tried
monthly billing, but it hadn't worked because
some patients didn't pay. Frank argued that he
had impeccable credit and knew much more
about credit and billing than I did. Suddenly I
realized I was missing Frank's point. "You're
right," I said. "I'm being defensive. We
should focus on the problems in your life and not

或許覺得這比較困難，因為我以前並不總是聽得很認真。如果是這樣，我感到很抱歉，因為我愛你，不想讓你失望。"如果亞當仍然不願開口，史蒂夫可以試試不同的方法："我很關心你近來的情況，不過我們可以過幾天，等你心境好一些再談。"這種方法使雙方都不失面子。史蒂夫不一定要在原則上———即問題最終需要攤開來進行解決———作出讓步，亞當也因為被允許再沉默一陣而保住了面子。

　　如何對待吹毛求疵者。最近，一個名叫費蘭克的商人到我這兒來看病，這人一生氣就變得十分專橫。弗蘭克說我只想著賺錢，還說他沒有必要按次付費，他要按月記賬。我感到極惱火，因為弗蘭克似乎總想讓別人按他的意思做。我解釋說自己曾試過按月收費的辦法，但效果不好，因為許多病人到時都不付錢。弗蘭克爭辯說他是絕對可信任的，對於信用和賬單，他知道的比我多。我突然意識到自己誤解了費蘭克的真正意思。"你說的有理，"我趕緊說，"我太只顧自己了。我們應當集中精力來解決你生活中的問題，而不要太擔心

worry so much about money. " Frank immediately softened and began talking about what was really bothering him, which were some personal problems. The next time we met, he handed me a check for 20 sessions in advance! There are times, of course, when people are unreasonably abusive and you may need to just walk away from the situation. But if the problem is one that you want solved, it's important to allow the other person to salvage some self-esteem. There's nearly always a grain of truth in the other person's point of view. If you acknowledge this, he or she will be less defensive and more likely to listen to you.

Complainers. Brad is a 32-year-old chiropractor who recently described his frustration with patient of his: "I ask Mr. Barry, 'How are you doing?' and he dumps out his whole life story — his family problems and his financial difficulties. I give him advice, but he ignores everything I tell him. "

Brad needs to recognize that habitual complainers usually don't want advice. They just want some one to listen and understand. So Brad might simply say: "Sounds like a rough week. It's no fun to have unpaid bills, people

錢的問題。"費蘭克馬上緩和下來了,開始談那些真正使他感到煩惱的事,那都是私事。等我們第二次見面時,他遞給我一張支票,預付了 20 次咨詢費。當然,確實有那麼些時候,有人會無理地出口傷人,這時你也許有必要轉身走開。但如果他鬧的正是你想解決的問題,那麼讓對方保留點自尊是很重要的。在別人的觀點中幾乎總會有那麼點兒道理,如果你承認這一點,那麼她或他就不會再堅持什麼,就會更樂於傾聽你的意見。

如何對待抱怨者。32 歲的按摩醫生佈拉德最近描述了他勸說病人的一次失敗經歷。"我問巴里,'你近來怎樣?'於是他就把他整個的人生故事都倒了出來──他的家庭問題,他的財政困境,我給他一些勸導,但他根本不屑一顧,毫不在意。"

而拉德應當認識到,喜歡抱怨的人常常是不聽勸導的。他們只需要有人傾聽和理解。所以佈拉德也許只需這樣說,"聽你說來,這一週可真夠不順心的,收到欠帳單可不是件開心的事,人們對

nagging you, and this pain besides. " The complainer will usually run out of gas and stop complaining. The secret is not to give advice. Just agreeing and validating a person's point of view will make that person feel better.

Demanding friends. Sometimes they are difficult because of the demands they place upon us. Maybe a friend puts you on the spot with a request to run an errand for him while he's out of town. If you have a crowded schedule, you may agree but end up angry and resentful. Or if you say no in the wrong way, your friend may feel hurt and unhappy. The problem is that, caught off guard, you don't know how to deal with the situation in a way that avoids bad feelings.

One method I've found helpful is "punting. " You're punting when you tell the person you need to think about the request and that you'll get back about it. Say a colleague calls and pressures me to give a lecture at his university. I've learned to say, "I'm flattered that you thought of me. Let me check my schedule, and I'll call you back. "

This gives me time to deal with any feelings of guilt if I have to say no. Suppose I de-

你嘮叨個沒完，再加上這病痛。"這時抱怨者常常會覺得沒什麼可吹的，就不再繼續抱怨了。這其中的奧秘在於：當對方抱怨時，不要加以勸導，只要順著對方的意思，表示認同和理解，對方就會覺得舒坦多了。

　　如何對待愛求人的朋友。難相處的人還不只那些愛生氣或好抱怨者。有些人之所以讓人覺得難以相處，是因為他們要求我們做這做那。也許有個朋友當場要求你，在他不在城裡時請你替他跑一次腿。如果這時你的日程表已安排得滿滿的，你或許會答應幫忙，但後來會感到很生氣或很不滿。或者，你以不恰當的方式加以回絕，這會傷了他的心，使他感到不快。問題是，事情突如其來，你不知道用什麼方法處理這種情形才不至於傷了情感。

　　我發現一個有助於處理這種情況的辦法，那就是"把球懸在那兒。"你可以告訴對方，你需要考慮一下，再給他答覆。這樣你就把球懸在那兒了。打個比方，我的一個同事打電話來，迫切要求我去他的大學作一次講座，我學會了這樣說："你來請我作講座，真使我受寵若驚，讓我看看日程安排，再打電話給你。"

　　這使我有時間處理因不得已而推辭所產生的歉疚心情。假使確定推辭這次邀請更好一些，那

cide it is better to decline; punting allows me to plan what I will say when I call back. "I appreciate being asked," I might indicate, "but I find I'm over committed right now. However, I hope you'll think of me in the future. " Responding to difficult people with patience and empathy can be tough, especially when you feel upset. But the moment you give up your need to control or be right, the other person will begin relaxing and start listening to you. The Greek philosopher Epictetus understood this when he said nearly 2000 years ago, "If someone criticizes you, agree at once. Mention that if only the other person knew you well, there would be more to criticize than that!"

Real communication results from a spirit of respect for yourself and for the other person. The benefits can be amazing.

我就會有時間考慮回電話說些什麼。"我很感激你的邀請,"我也許可以這樣說,"但我發現眼下自己已經承諾得太多了。不過我希望你下一次還能想到我。"

　　用耐心和移情法來對付難打交道的人並非易事,特別當你自己也感到煩惱時。但一旦你放棄了征服對方或堅持自己如何正確的念頭時,對方就會平靜下來,開始傾聽你的意見。希臘哲學家埃皮克提圖在近 2000 年前說下面這番話時就已經道出了這訣竅:"如果有人批評你,你要立即接受。並可以說,換了更了解我的人,或許會批評得更深刻!"

　　眞正的交往有賴於自尊和尊重他人的精神,這好處將是驚人的。

▰▰欣賞▰▰

　　現代人覺得世界上最大的網不是魚網,而是關係網。人與人相處說不清道不明。林肯說過這麼一句話:"人生最美好的東西,就是他利用別人的友誼","與人相處,友誼是美的,是人對美的渴望。""得不到友誼的人將是終身可憐的孤獨者。沒有友情的社會只是一片繁華的沙漠。"(培根)要獲得友情就必須學會與人和睦相處。這篇散文所推介的五種處世之道談不上是唯一的法寶,但卻是有效的靈丹妙藥。它強調"眞正的交往有賴於自尊和尊重他人的精神",正如"友誼首先就是相互信任"(杜·伽比)。全文以敘事弄引,以總結全文收尾,收尾充滿哲理,有點鐵成金,由平而奇,結構連環,借事明理,寓理於像的絕妙筆鋒。雖沒有學問高聲,但卻"無"理而妙。

25. Of Death

Francis Bacon

Men fear death as children fear to go in the
dark; and as that natural fear in children is in-
creased with tales, so is the other. Certainly the
contemplation of death as the wages of sin and
passage to another world is holy and religious,
but the fear of it, as a tribute due unto nature,
is weak. Yet in religious meditations there is
sometimes mixture of mortification that a man
should think with himself what the pain is if he
has but his finger's end pressed or tortured,
and thereby imagine what the pains of death are
when the whole body is corrupted and dissolved;
when many times death passed with less pain the
torture of a limb, for the most vital parts are not
the quickest of sense. And by him that spake
only as a philosopher and natural man, it was
well said: the trapping of death terrify us more
than death itself. Groans and a discolored face,
and friends weeping, and mourning garments
and obsequies and the like show death terrible.
It is worthy the observing that there is no passion in the mind of man so weak but it overpow-

25. 論　死　亡

弗朗西斯·培根

　　成人害怕死亡猶如兒童害怕走進黑暗的地方，兒童的那種天生的恐懼因聽到的傳說故事而增加，成人對於死亡的恐懼也是如此。當然，靜觀死亡，把它看作罪惡的報應和通往另一世界的門徑，是虔誠而且也迎合宗教的；但是害怕死亡，把它看作對自然的獻祭而存怯弱，則是怯弱。然而，在宗教的沉思中有時也滲有虛妄和迷信。在有些修道士的禁慾書中你可以讀到這樣的苦行錄：一個人應當試想一下要是他有一個指尖被壓或受刑，那種痛苦是什麼滋味，如全身腐敗潰爛，那痛苦就更不敢想像。實際上，即使在經歷死亡過程中，其所受的痛苦也並不比四肢受刑爲重，因爲人體中最致命的器官並不是最敏感的。世俗哲學家兼智者塞內加說得好：“伴隨死亡而來的東西，反而比死亡本身更可怕。”呻吟與痙攣，面容的變色，以及親友的哭泣，喪服和葬儀等等，都顯示出死亡的可怕。值得注意的是，在偉人的心中，無論他的

ers and masters the fear of death; and therefore
death is no such terrible enemy, when a man
has so many attendants about him that can win
the combat from him. Revenge triumphs over
death, love slights it, honour aspired to it, grief
flies to it, fear anticipates it. Bay, we read, after Otho the emperor had slain himself, pity
(which is the tenderest of affections) provoked
many to die out of mere compassion to their
sovereign, and as the truest sort of followers.
Nay, Fastidiousness and satiety: consider how
long you have been doing the same things; the
desire to die may be felt not only by the brave
man or by the wretch, but also by the man wea-
ried with ennui. A man would die, though he
were neither valiant nor miserable, only upon a
weariness to do the same thing so often over and
over. It is no less worthy to observe how little
alteration in good spirits the approaches of death
made, for they appear to be the same men till
the last instant. Augustus Caesar died in a compliment: Farewell, Livia, remember our married
life eventually. Bodily strength and vitality
failed, Tiberius, not his powers of dissimula-
tion. Vespasian in a jest, sitting upon the stool:
while I am considering, I'm becoming a god
Galba with a sentence: Strike, if it is the good

感情多麼脆弱,他們對於死亡卻毫無恐懼;所以,當一個人身邊有這麼多能戰勝死亡的"侍從"時,死亡並不是一個可怕的敵人。報復之心戰勝死亡,愛戀之心蔑視死亡,榮譽之心企求死亡,恐怖之心預期死亡;不僅如此,我們還在史書中讀到:羅馬皇帝奧托自刎後,許多人在哀憐之心(這是一種最溫柔的感情)的驅使下也紛紛自盡,他們的殉死完全是出於對其君王的同情,並且以此表明自己是那種對主最忠誠的人。此外,塞內加還加上了"苛求"和"厭煩"。他說:"想一想,你做同樣的事情已有多久了。如果老是日復一日重複做同樣的事情,不但強健的人和不幸的人會想死,而且愛挑剔的人也會想死。"一個人,雖然他既不勇敢也不可憐,但要是他對經常反覆地做同樣的事情感到厭倦,也會尋死的。同樣值得注意的是,對於心理素質很好的人來說,死亡的來臨對其情緒的影響是微乎其微的,因為他們直到生命的最後一刻看上去還是平靜如水。奧古斯都·凱撒臨終時還和藹地對皇后說:"永別了,利維亞,請你永世不要忘記我們婚後生活的那段美好時光。"提比略至死仍在弄虛作假。韋斯巴薌臨死前還坐在凳子上嬉戲地說:"我想我正在變神呢!"加爾巴臨死前則引

of the Roman people. Septimius holding forth his neck: "make haste, if anything remains for me to do and the like." Certainly the Stoics bestowed too much cost upon death, and by their great preparations made it appear more fearful. Better says he, who regards the conclusion of life as one of nature's blessings. It is as natural to die as to be born; and to a little infant, perhaps, the one is as painful as the other. He that dies in an earnest pursuit is like one that is wounded in hot blood, who for the time scarce feels the hurt; and therefore a mind fixed and bent upon somewhat that is good does avert the dolors of death. But above all, believe it the sweetest canticle is Not let (your servant to depart in peace). When a man has obtained worthy ends and expectations. Death has this also, that it opens the gate to good fame, and extinguishes envy: the same man (envies while alive) will be loved once he is dead.

頸高呼："砍吧！ 如果這有利於羅馬人民，那就砍吧！"塞普提米烏斯·塞維魯斯臨刑前也說："如果還有什麼事情需要我做的，那就乾脆利落點吧。"諸如此類的例子，不勝枚舉。 很顯然，斯多葛派在死亡問題上看得太重，對於死亡做過多的準備反而使它顯得更加可怕。尤維納爾說得比較好："他把生命的終結看成是自然的一種恩惠。"死亡與降生一樣自然，對於一個嬰兒來說，降生也許與死亡一樣痛苦。 為熱衷於追求某種事物而死去的人，猶如一個人在熱血沸騰的時候受傷一樣，刹那間是不會覺得痛楚的；所以，只要一個人專心致志於某種善事，他就不會感覺到死亡的痛苦。歸根到底地說，請你相信，在一個人達到了崇高的目的或實現了美好的願望時，最甜美的高歌就是"主啊！如今請讓你的僕人安然去世。"死亡還有這樣一點"它能打開美譽之門，泯滅嫉妒之心。一個人雖然活著的時候遭人忌恨，但"死者受人愛戴"指的正是那些生時受到嫉妒的人。

欣賞

　　培根的這篇散文以極簡鍊而遒勁的筆調，讚美了人們有力量戰勝死亡的恐懼。他引經據典，拾得那些偉人們在臨終前的肺腑之言，一躍紙上，給人留下深思，蕩漾，盡是絕妙悠然。

26.Of Anger

Francis Bacon

To seek to extinguish anger utterly is but showy attempt of the Stoics. We have better oracles: Be angry, but sin not. Let not the sun down upon your anger(Ephesans). Anger must be limited and confined, both in race and in time. We will first speak how the natural inclination and habit to be angry may be attempered and calmed. Secondly, how the particular motions of anger may be repressed, or at least refrained from doing mischief. Thirdly, how to raise anger or appease anger in another.

For the first: there is no other way but to meditate and ruminate well upon the effects of anger, how it troubles man's life. And the best time to do this is to look back upon anger when the fit is thoroughly over. Seneca says well that anger is like ruin, which breaks itself upon that it falls. The Scripture exhorts us to possess our souls in patience. Whosoever is out of patience is out of possession of his soul. Men must not turn bees, and lay down their lives in the

26. 論　惱　怒

弗朗西斯·培根

　　要想徹底杜絕發怒，這只不過是斯多噶派的
誇誇之辭。更好的神諭告誡我們：“惱怒生氣，但
別犯罪。不要悶悶終日，直到日落還不消。”對發
怒必須在程度和時間兩方面加以節制。首先，我
們談談怎樣緩解和克制發怒的天性和習慣。第
二，談談怎樣抑制發怒的特殊行為，至少要避免釀
成禍害。第三，談談怎樣會使別人發怒或使他息
怒。

　　關於第一點，沒有別的辦法，只有好好地深思
熟慮發怒的後果，它是怎樣干擾人生的。最好的
辦法就是一陣怒氣平息之後回想當時的情景。塞
內加說得好，“怒氣猶如重物下墜，把自己碎於墜
落之處”。聖經則勸導我們，“失去耐心，就失去了
靈魂。人們決不可變成蜜蜂，把他們的生命留在

wound. Anger is certainly a kind of baseness; as it appears well in the weakness of those subjects in whom it reigns: children, women, old folks, sick folds. Only men must beware that they carry their anger rather with scorn than with fear, so that they may seem rather to be will give law to himself in it.

For the second point: the causes and motives of anger are chiefly three. First, to be too sensible of hurt, for no man is angry that feels not himself hurt; and therefore tender and delicate persons must needs be often angry, they have so many things to trouble them which more robust natures have little sense of. The next is the apprehension and interpretation of the injury offered to be, in the circumstances thereof, full of contempt; for contempt is that which puts an edge upon anger, as much or more than the hurt itself. And therefore, when men are ingenious in picking out circumstances of contempt, they do kindle their anger much. Lastly, opinion of the touch of a man's reputation does multiply and sharpen anger. Wherein the remedy is, that a man should have, as Consalvo was wont to say, telam honor is a thicker web of honour.

所螫的傷口之中"。怒氣確是一種卑下的玩藝兒，因爲它總是出現在它所擺佈的臣民中的弱者之間；這些弱者就是孩子、婦女、老人、病人。人們務必注意，如免不了要生氣時，寧可使怒氣帶有輕蔑而不可帶有恐懼；這樣就顯得軟弱可欺。這樣做很簡單，只要你在這方面給自己定規矩就行了。

　關於第二點，怒氣的原因與動機主要有三。第一就是對傷害過於敏感。凡是易怒的人必會覺得自己受到了傷害；所以柔弱敏感的人必定是易怒的人；有那麼多事令他煩惱，而那些天性開朗的人卻無所謂。其次就是，一個人發現或者認爲在所受的傷害中充滿了輕蔑的成分，在這種情況下也是極易致怒的：因爲輕蔑會使憤怒火上加油，其危害超過憤怒本身。所以，當人們過於敏感地覺察出輕蔑的意味時，他們一定會燃起怒火。最後，如果一個人認爲他的名譽受到損害，這樣會加倍地激化他的怒氣。這時最好的息怒辦法，正如康薩瓦常說，一個人應該有個"結結實實的榮譽網"。

But in all refrainings of anger, it is the best remedy to win time, and to make a man's self believe that the opportunity of his revenge is not yet come, but that he foresees a time for it; and so to still himself in the meantime and reserve it.

To restrain anger from mischief, though it takes hold of a man, there are two things whereof you must have special caution. The one, of extreme bitterness of words, especially if they be stinging and personal for revilings are nothing so much; and again, that in anger a man reveal no secrets, for that makes him not fit for society. The other, that you do not peremptorily break off in any business in a fit of anger; but howsoever you show bitterness, do not act anything that is not revocable.

For raising and appeasing anger in another: it is done chiefly by choosing of times, when men are frowardest and worst disposed, to incense them. Again, by gathering (as was touched before)all that you can find out to aggravate the contempt. And the two remedies are by the contraries. The former, to take good times, when first to relate to a man an angry

但是在所有的息怒辦法中最好的莫過於贏得時間，使發怒者自己相信報復的時機尚未到來，但他可以預見那個好時機；於是他就會靜候那個復仇時機。

假如一個人怒不可支但又不想因發怒而惹禍時，有兩件事要特別注意。一是不要惡語傷人，尤其要避免帶有人身攻擊的尖刻語言；因為這不同於“一般的謾罵”那樣關係不大；另外，一個人在生氣的時候，不可把要辦的事情弄糟了；不管你怎樣表示憤怒，切不可做出無法挽回的行動來。

至於使人發怒或息怒的另一種辦法，關鍵在於掌握時機。在急燥或心情不佳的時候，一旦加劇輕蔑，人就最易被激怒。此外，就是搜集你所能發現的（如前所述）各種有關事件。兩種息怒的方法是相反的。前者首先要把握時機，因為初次印

business, for the first impression is much. Injury from the point of contempt, imputing it to
misunderstanding, fear, passion, or what you
will.

象是很重要的；後者盡可能使就傷害的說法與受人輕蔑的言論區分開來，把這種傷害歸於誤會，恐懼，感情用事或其他什麼你想說的偶然原因。

欣賞

人們對於宗敎色彩濃厚的"忍"字十分感興趣，不少人把它當做工作和爲人處世的"座右銘"，這樣做不是因爲這個斗大的字的秀美，而是因爲"忍"字可以警醒世人在盛怒之時，忍一步，就能得到海闊天空。"小不忍則亂大謀""忍得一時忿，終生無惱悶"。當然，這僅是中庸之道。培根卻從另一方面對此進行了論述。他在分析惱怒的成因，表現，現狀，性質，危害等的基礎上，進而論述了制怒的種種方法。他認爲制怒的關鍵在於掌握時間。時間一過，惱怒便消掉。因此，切不可惱怒之時，惡語傷人，更不要做出無法挽回的行動。這當然有可取的一面。但我們也不否認"憤怒是具有奇特作用的武器。人類能使用其他武器，但憤怒卻駕馭了人類。"（蒙田）這恐怕是惱怒積極的一面。這就不在話下了。

縱觀全文，因果論證，道理深刻。雖無作者的感慨，但充滿作者有力的告誡警世。願我們的讀者朋友"能忍則忍"，"該出手時就要出手"。

27. Of Vainglory

Francis Bacon

It was prettily devised of Aesop, The fly sat upon the axle-tree of the chariot to heel, and said, "What a dust do I raise!" So are there some vain persons that, whatsoever goes alone or moves upon greater means, if they have never so little hand in it, they think it is they carry that are glorious must needs be factious, for all bravery stands upon comparisons. They must needs be violent to make good their own vauther can they be secret, and therefore not effectual, but according to the French proverb, Beaucoup de bruit, peu de fruit; little fruit. Yet certainly there is use of this quality in civil affairs. Where there is an opinion and fame to be created, either of virtue or greatness, these men are good trumpeters. Again, as Tirus Livius notes in the case of Antiochus and the Aetolians: There are sometimes great effects of cross lies, as, if a man that negotiates between two princes

27. 論 虛 榮

弗朗西斯·培根

伊索在他的一則寓言中說得很妙：蒼蠅坐在戰車的輪軸上說道，"我揚起了多少塵土啊！"世上確實有些虛榮成性的人也如此。無論什麼事情，自身的作用也罷，他力也罷，只要自己在其中沾上邊就完全把功勞歸功於自己的力量。好炫耀的人一定爭強好勝，因為一切誇耀都要以比較高低為根基。這種人也必然很偏激，因為如此才能使自己的各種誇耀得意。他們不能守秘密，所以沒有什麼實際用處；正如法國的一句成語所說："聲勢大，但結果小"，然而在處理內務中這種品性確有其用。每逢人們需要造成一種大功大德的輿論的時候，這些人就是高超的吹鼓手。還有，如李維在叙述安條克三世和埃托利亞人的交往中所注意到的，有時候對有關雙方相互撒謊所產生的效果還好。例如，一個人在兩位君王之間當差，想讓他們

to draw them to join in a war against the third, does extol the forces of either of them above measure, the one to the other: and sometimes he that deals between man and man raises his own credit with both by pretending greater interest than he has in either. And I these and the like kinds, it often falls out that somewhat is produced of nothing, for lies are sufficient to breed opinion, and opinion brings substance. In boasting commanders and soldiers, vainglory is an essential point, for as iron sharpens iron, so by glory one courage sharpens another. In cases of great enterprise, upon charge and adventure, a composition of glorious natures does put life into business, and those that are of solid and sober natures have more of the ballast than of the sail. In fame of learning, the flight will be slow without some feathers of ostentation. Qui de contemnenda gloria libros scribunt, no men suum inscribunt; Socrates, Aristotoe, Galen, were men full of ostentation. Certainly vainglory helps to perpetuate a man's memory, and virtue was never so beholden to human nature, as it re

聯合起來攻擊第三方，他就對雙方都誇張另一方的力量如何如何，以此獲得在對方心目中的地位，結果也有利於提高自己在雙方心中的聲望。在諸如此類的事情中，往往都會得到無中生有的結果，這是因爲諾言足以產生實質性的意見。在將帥與軍人之中，虛榮心是一種不可或缺的要素。因爲它如同鐵塊磨鐵塊，越磨越鋒利一樣，人們的勇氣是靠著榮耀而互相"磨利"的。在要求傾家蕩產和做冒險的事情中，加入一些秉性好榮耀的人可以注入活力，而那些秉性穩重冷靜的人則似壓艙的貨物，揚不起風帆。以學問的揚名者，若沒有一些誇耀的羽毛，則名聲揚得很慢。"不看重榮耀著書立說的人也讓自己的名字出現在書的扉頁上"。蘇格拉底、亞里士多德、蓋論，都是善於誇耀的偉人。虛榮心的確有助於一個人名垂青史。德行之所以還得到了間接的報酬，那是不能不歸功於人

ceived his due at the second hand. Neither had
the fame of Cicero, Seneca, Plinius Secundus,
borne her age so well, if it had not been joined
with some vanity in themselves: like unto var-
nish, that makes ceilings not only shine but
last. But all this while, when I speak of vainglory. I mean not of that property that Tacitus
does attribute to Mucianus, *Omnium quae dix-
erat feceratque arte quadam ostentator*, for that
proceeds not of vanity, but of natural magna-
nimity and discretion, and in some persons is
not only comely, but gracious. For excusations,
concessions, modesty itself well governed, are
but arts of ostentation. And amongst those arts
there is none better than that which Plinius Secundus speaks of, which is to be liberal of
praise and commendation to others, in that
wherein a man's self has any perfection. For
says Pliny very wittily: In commending another
you do yourself right, for he that you commend
is either superior to you in that you commend,
or inferior. If he is inferior, if he is to be commended, you much more; if he is superior, if

的秉性的。西塞羅、塞內加、小普林尼的名聲若不是與這些人世間本身的某種虛榮心連在一起的話，也不會經久如新的，這種虛榮心就如同天花板上的一層油漆一樣，它使得天花板不僅光亮照人而且持久耐用。但是說了這麼久，我用"虛榮"這個字眼兒的時候，卻並不是指塔西佗歸之於穆西阿努斯的那種性質："他自己的一舉一動、一言一行顯示自己的本領。"因爲這種品質並非是出自虛榮心，而是出自天生的寬仁和謹愼的，並且這些性質在有些人那裡不但漂亮而且高雅。道歉、退讓與謙虛都不過是炫耀之術。他們毫不比小普林尼所說的那一種炫耀更好。如果在你自己所長的某些方面，別人也有一點長處，你應當不憐惜地多多稱譽讚揚他人。普林尼說得很巧妙機智："在讚揚別人的時候你其實同時是在替自己做好事。因爲你所讚揚的那人在那一方面若不是比你強就是不如你。如果他不如你，那麼他旣然值得讚揚，你自然更加值得讚揚了；如果他勝過你，那麼假如他不

he is not to be commended, you much less. Glorious men are the scorn of wise men, the admiration of fools, the idols of parasitism and the slaves of their own vaunts.

值得讚揚，你就更不值得讚揚了。"好炫耀的人是
明哲之士所輕視的，愚蠢之人所艷羨的，諂媚之徒
所奉承的，同時他們也成了誇耀自己演說者的奴
隸。

欣賞

　　俄國文學家列夫．托爾斯泰說："虛榮是一種疾病，一
種宛如天花和霍亂的惡癖。"虛榮是一種心理病症，它有
害於人純潔的心靈。一時的虛榮能毀掉一生的功名。
"虛榮是追求個人榮耀的一種慾望，它並不是根據人的品
質、業績和成就。而只是根據個人的存在就想博得別人
的欣賞、尊敬和仰慕的一種願望。所以"虛榮充其量不過
等於一個輕浮的漂亮女子。"（歌德）培根涉及論述虛榮散
文有四：《學術推進》、《論讚揚》、《論談吐》和本篇。從數
量上和散文的質量上看，培根對虛榮是非常痛恨的。他
對虛榮的形成、現象和表現等進行了細膩的具體分析。
在他看來，虛榮主要與自我炫耀有關，虛榮是人類的一個
普遍存在的弱點。無論是智者還是偉人，都是善於誇耀
的人。因此他感嘆道："虛榮心確實有助於一些人名垂青
史。"談到虛榮，培根認為，虛榮也有它積極的激勵作用的
一面。但無論虛榮的"激素"有多大，終究不可取，不可成
為虛榮和炫耀的奴隸來使自己終身受害。但願我們的讀
者朋友"主於自得，不期誠而誠；主於得名，不期僞而僞"。

28. Of Regiment of Health

Francis Bacon

There is a wisdom in this beyond the rules of physic: a man's own observation, what he finds good of, is the best physic to preserve health. But it is a safer conclusion to say, This agrees not well with me, therefore I will not continue it, than this, I find no offence of this, therefore I may use it. For strength of nature in youth passes over many excesses which are owing a man till his age. Discern of the coming on of years, and think not to do the same things still; for age will not be defied. Beware of sudden change in any great point of diet, and if necessity enforce it fit the rest to it. For it is a secret both in nature and state, that it is safer to change many things than one. Examine they customs of diet, sleep, exercise, apparel and the like, and try in anything thou shalt judge hurtful, to discontinue it by little, abandon little and little; but so as if thou do find any in-

28. 論 養 生

弗朗西斯·培根

　　養生是一種智慧,非醫學規律所能揭示。在自己觀察的基礎上,發現什麼對自己有益,什麼對自己有害,乃是最好的養生秘訣。但是,一個人在下此結論的時候,如果說:"這個對身體不合適,因此我要戒掉它"就不如說:"我覺得這個對身體沒什麼不合適,因此我可以用它"要安全得多。因爲,年輕的時候,天賦精神旺盛,身體強壯,可以使人忽略無節制而過分的行爲,而這些行爲等於記在帳上,上了年紀是要還的。所以,要留意自己年歲的增加,不要永遠想做同一件事,人的年齡是不能不顧的。就飲食而言,要注意不要發生突然變化,如果飲食改變確有必要,則別的方面也要變更,以利配合調節相宜。因爲自然界和國家都有一個秘訣,即"從多方面改變比單方面改變要穩妥得多"。考究一下自己的飲食、睡眠、運動和衣著等諸如此類的習慣,試著將其中有礙於健康的習

convenience by the change, thou come back to it again: for it is hard to distinguish that which is generally held good and wholesome from that which is good particularly and fit for thine own body. To be free-minded and cheerfully disposed at hours of meal and of sleep and of exercise, is one of the best precepts of long lasting. As for the passions and studies of the mind, avoid envy, anxious fears, anger fretting inwards, subtle and knotty inquisitions, hoys and exhilarations in excess, sadness not communicated. Entertain hopes, mirth rather than joy, variety of delights rather than surfeit of them, wonder and admiration (and therefore novelties), studies that fill the mind with splendid and illustrious objects (as histories, fables, and contemplations of nature). If you fly physic in health altogether, it will be too strange for your body when you shall need it. If you make it too familiar, it will work no extraordinary effect when sickness comes. I commend rather some diet for certain seasons than frequent use of physic, except it is grown into a custom: for

慣戒掉,恢復到原來已有的習慣上去。因爲,要把
公衆認爲有益於大家健康的行爲,與你自己認爲
有益並適合你自己身體健康的行爲區別開來,這
事是十分困難的。在吃飯、睡覺、運動的時候,心
情舒暢,精神愉快,是長壽的最有效的秘訣之一。
至於說到內心的情感和思想活動,則應該避開嫉
妒,抛棄焦慮,克服恐懼,切不可讓內心壓制著怒
氣,少執著於深奧難懂的研究,克制過度的狂歡和
興奮,憂傷不宜暗藏,享受樂趣而不縱情享樂。常
存好奇仰慕之心。應常常仔細研讀歷史、寓言和
自然之類,讓美好的事物充滿身心學問。如果你
在身體健康的時候,完全摒棄醫藥,到了你需要它
的時候,則會感覺到來時,醫藥將失去奇效。我以
爲常用藥餌,不如按不同季節換某些事物,除非服
藥已成爲一種習慣。因爲,食物能調節身體機能

those diets alter the body more, and trouble it less. Despise no new accident in your body, but ask opinion of it. In sickness, respect health principally; and in health, action. For those that put their bodies to endure inhealth may, in most sicknesses which are not very sharp, be cured only with diet and tendering. Celsus could never have spoken it as a physician, had he not been a wise man withal, when he gives it for one of the great precepts of health and lasting, that a man does vary and interchange contraries, but with an inclination to the more benign extreme: use fasting and full eating, but rather full eating; watching and sleep, but rather sleep; sitting and exercise, but rather exercise; and the like. So shall nature be cherished and yet taught masteries. Physicians are some of them so pleasing and conformable to the humour of the patient, as they press not the true cure of the disease; and some other are so regular in proceeding according to art for the disease, as they respect not sufficiently the condition of the patient. Take one of a middle tem-

，對身體也利多於弊。不要小看身體上的任何不適，不應忽視，須求醫生。在病中，主要注意健康。身體健康時，要注意運動。因爲人們在健康時身體有抵抗力。一些小病小災只需注意飲食，稍加調養就行。塞爾撒既是聖人又是醫生，否則不可能說出下面這些話來。他的養生長壽之道，最重要的一點就是，一個人應該將各種相反的習慣都替換著試一試，但應偏重於有益於人的一方。禁食與飽食，要偏重飽食；不寐與睡眠，要偏重睡眠；安坐與運動，要側重運動如此等等，都應練習。照他的方法練習，天生的體質既得滋養、又增強抗病的能力。有些醫生對於病人過於縱容遷就，以致不能儘快治療病人的疾病。有些醫生又過於嚴守治病的規則，以致忽視患者的實際病情。選擇醫生時，最好選一位能兼顧兩者的人，如果找不到這樣的人，則各請一位，兩者綜合，取長補短。在請

per; or, if it may not be found in one man, combine two of either sort; and forget not to call as well the best acquainted with your body, as the best reputed of for his faculty.

醫生的時候，固然要請德高望重之人，也別忘了請
那位最熟悉你身體健康的醫生。

欣賞

　　"久病成良醫。"培根能寫出如此優美的養生之道，恐
怕與他自幼身體欠佳是分不開的。通篇而論，這些養生
之道不是宏論，而是經驗之談，然而又富有它自身的哲
理。培根的養生之道類似中國的中醫道理。看來人與自
然的抗爭普天下都是相通的。在培根看來，養生是一種
智慧，適應自己的東西才是最好的保健品。談到飲食、運
動、休息及其他們之間的關係是，他認為精神愉快、性格
開朗，交換不同的習慣，這才是長壽的秘訣。說到用藥，
他認為不可不用。但也不可常用。依他的就醫經驗而
言，要兼顧兩種醫生，最好是了解自己健康的醫生。培根
的確多才多藝，不僅能寫出精彩的政論散文，而且還能寫
出漂亮的養生經論。在西方散文家中也是少有的。

29.Of Fortune

Francis Bacon

It cannot be denied but outward accidents conduce much to fortune: favour, opportunity, death of others , occasion fitting virtue. But chiefly the mould of a man's fortune is in his own hands. Every man is the architect of his own fortune , says the poet. And the most frequent of external causes is that the folly of one man is the fortune of another. For no man prospers so suddenly as by others' errors. Serpent must have eaten another serpent before it can become a dragon. Overt and apparent virtues bring forth praise, but there is secret and hidden virtues that bring forth fortune: certain ways of disclosing of a man's self, which have no name. The Spanish name, assured facility in speaking partly expresses them, when there are not hindrances nor restiveness in a man's nature, but that the wheels of his mind keep way with the wheels of his fortune. For so Livy (af-

29. 論　運　氣

弗朗西斯·培根

　　毋須置疑,外界的偶發事件諸如容貌、機會、他人的死亡以及與聲譽才德相適應的機遇等等,對命運的影響甚大。然而,一個人的命運掌握在自己手裡。有位詩人說:"人人都是自己命運的設計師。"影響命運的因素很多,最常見的是:一個人的愚蠢行爲便可是另一個人的幸運。因爲要想突然出人頭地,最好的捷徑莫過於利用他人的錯誤。俗話說"蛇不吃蛇難成龍"。外露而易見的德才往往贏來讚譽,但隱藏至深的德才卻都帶來幸運。這是某些難以名狀的自我表現解脫或自我表現拯救的品質。西班牙人所說的 disemboltura 倒是部分地表達其內涵;當一個人的本性裡沒有障礙,也沒有驕縱時,其心靈隨著他命運的輪子一道轉動。同樣,李維先用下面這幾句話形容了大加圖:"這

ter he had described Cato Major in these words), in this man there was such strength of body and mind that wherever he had been born it seems certain he would have made fortune his own, falls upon that, that he had versatile nature. Therefore if a man looks sharply and attentively, he shall see Fortune: for though she is blind, yet she is not invisible. The way of fortune is like the milky way in the sky, which is a meeting or knot of a number of small stars, not seen asunder but giving light together. So are there a number of little and scarce discerned virtues, or rather faculties and customs, that make men fortunate. The Italians note some of them, such as a man would little think. When they speak of one that cannot do amiss, they will throw in, into his other conditions, that he has a little of the fool. And certainly there are not two more fortunate properties than to have a little of the fool honest. Therefore extreme lovers of their country or masters were never fortunate, neither can they are for when a man places his thoughts without himself, he goes not his own

個人如此強壯、精力如此過人，無論他出生在什麼樣的家庭，看來都肯定會自行好運。"接著，李維還看到老加圖"多才多藝"。因此，一個人如果目光敏銳、留心觀察，必定會看見命運女神。命運女神雖然雙目失明，卻不是不可見。命運如同天空的銀河，由許多小星星會合或簇擁在一起形成的，分散時作爲單個的個體是不顯眼的，但聚合時卻發出了燦爛光輝。同樣一個人的品德也有許多又小又難看出，或者不如說是才能和習慣，是它們給人們帶來幸運。義大利人注意到了這一點，一般人卻很少想到。義大利人說起做事總不出差錯的人時，必定會在談論那人的種種品德時插上這樣一句話：他"有點傻氣。"確實，再沒有比他老實的了。因此，最高尚的愛國者或主的忠實僕人，從來就是不幸的，而且也不可能是幸運的。因爲一個人把自己的思慮超脫自我而置身以外的事情上，這個人也就不是按自己的意志行事了。匆匆而來的幸

way. A hasty fortune makes an enterpriser and remove (the French has it betterm entreprenant, or remuant), but the exercised fortune makes the able man. Fortune is to be honoured and it is but for her daughters, Confidence and Reputation. For those two felicity breedeth: the first within a man's self, the latter in others towards him. All wise men, to decline them to Providence and Fortune, for so they may the better assume them; and besides, it is greatness in a man to be the care of the higher powers. So Caesar said to the pilot in the tempest, "You carry Caesar and his fortune." So Sulla chose the name of Felix and not of Magnus. And it has been noted that those that ascribe openly too much to their own wisdom and policy, end infortunate. It is written that Timotheus the Athenian, after he had, in the account he gave to the state of his government, often interlaced this speech, And in this Fortune had no part, never prospered in anything he undertook afterwards. Certainly there are whose fortunes are like Homer's verses, that have a slide and easiness

運使人膽大妄為、蠢蠢欲動。法國人說得更好，他們稱這種人為"好動者"，或者"好事之徒"，但是經過磨練而來的福分卻能造就能幹的人。幸運應該受到尊重，單單為了她的兩個女兒"信心"和"榮譽"：也應該如此。因為這兩位都是幸運的孿生姊妹。信心來自於自己，榮譽卻來自於他人。聰明的人為了減少別人對自己品德才能的嫉妒，常常把自己的品德才能歸功於上天和幸運；因為這樣他們便可以較為心安理得，無所顧忌地享有這些品德才能了。再說，受到神明的護佑，正顯出了一個人的偉大。所以凱撒對能制服暴風雪中駕船的舵手說："你載的是凱撒和凱撒的運氣。"所以蘇拉選擇稱號時寧願用"幸運的"蘇拉，而不用"偉大的"蘇拉。人們還注意到那些公然把自己的成就過分地歸功於自己的聰明和精明的人，往往結局是不幸。書上記載，雅典人提莫修斯在向國家報告自己的功績時，經常在講話中夾上這麼一句話："這個嘛，與幸運無關。"後來，他無論從事什麼，都再也沒有興旺發達過。有些人的福分的確就像荷馬的詩歌比其他詩人的詩歌流暢自如得多，它總

more than the verses of other poets; as Plutarch says of Timoleon's fortune, in respect of that of Agesilaus or Epaminondas. And that this should be, no doubt it is much in a man's self.

是比別人強；就像普魯塔克把提摩利昂的幸運同
阿革西勞斯或伊帕米農達斯的幸運相比較時說的
那些話一樣。毫無疑問，這種情況之所以如此，在
很大程度上還是在於依靠自己。

▰欣賞▰

　　培根一生聰明過人，才智橫溢。雖說他在伊麗莎白
時代竭忠盡智，但仍不得志而失寵。1592 年由於他反對
女王增加國防開支的提議，引起女王本人深深的怨恨，結
果在一段時期內伊麗莎白拒絕了他的朝見。我們通過這
篇散文，可以看出培根的幾分牢騷怨氣。他說："最崇高
的愛國者或主上的忠實僕人，從來就是不幸運的，而且也
不可能幸運。"這顯然是培根對此的感慨和自嘆。在這篇
散文中，我們還可以看到培根對英國上層社會爭權奪利
和明爭暗鬥的殘酷，所以他覺得影響命運的最大的因素
莫過於自己的愚蠢，自己的愚蠢往往給別人的崛起帶來
美運。他引用了"蛇不吃蛇難成龍"這樣一句俗語，其含
義非常深刻，貼切。當今社會有，古老的社會有，東方有，
西方也有。據此，他認爲，一要隱藏自己的德才；二要多
點傻氣而少點老實氣；三要把自己的德才歸功於上帝和
幸運。難怪英美人在得到別人的讚美時，不時地說"I am
lucky."培根還認爲，一個人的命運在於自己，其哲理深刻
無比。我們應當做自己命運的主宰，而不是命運的奴隸。
我們不應當過多的埋怨和要求。"人總是人，是自己命運
的主人。"（丁尼生）讓命運之星永遠閃亮在自己的心靈。

30. Of Cunning

Francis Bacon

We take cunning for a sin better or crooked wisdom. And certainly there is great difference between a cunning man and a wise man, not only in point of honesty, but in point of ability. There is that can pack the cards, and yet cannot play well; so there are some that are good in canvasses and factions, that are otherwise weak men. Again, it is one thing to understand persons, and another thing to understand matters: for many are perfect in men's humours, that are not greatly capable of the real part of business, which is the constitution of one that has studied men more than books. Such men are fitter for plotting than for counsel, and they are good but in their own alley turn them to new men, and they have lost their aim; so as the old rule to know a fool from a wise man. Send both of them naked among strangers and then you will see (attributed to Aristipus in Diogenes Laertius, Lives of Eminent Philosophers, II. 73). And because these cunning men are like shopkeepers

30. 論 狡 猾

弗朗西斯‧培根

　　依我之見，狡猾是一種陰險或邪惡的聰明。狡猾的人和聰明人之間自然存在著很大的差異——不僅表現在誠實方面，而且表現在才能方面。有的人會做配牌，可是玩牌時並不高明；同樣地，有的人善於結黨鑽營，而在別的方面是無能之輩。再說，知人是一回事，而明理則是另外一回事。有許多人在揣摩別人的脾氣性格方面很精通，而真正辦起事情來卻並不怎麼能幹——這就是那些好琢磨而不怎麼做學問的人的特徵。這樣的人擅長於搞陰謀詐騙而不擅長出謀劃策。他們所擅長的祇是他們自己的那一套。讓他們轉而對付陌生的人，他們就難操勝券了。所以，像下面所述的那條鑒別智者和愚人的通則——"把兩人赤裸裸地派到生人面前，就能看出分曉"，對於他們來說，則是幾乎沒有什麼作用。這些狡猾的人好像小商小販

of small wares, it is not amiss to set forth their shop.

It is a point of cunning to wait upon him with whom you speak, with your eye, as the Jesuits give it in precept; for there are many wise men that have secret hearts and transparent countenances. Yet this would be done with a demure abasing of your eye sometimes, as the Jesuits also do use.

Another is that when you have anything to obtain of present great urgency, you entertain and amuse the party with whom you deal with some other discourse, that he is not too much awake to make objections. I knew a counselor and secretary that never came to Queen Elizabeth of England with bills to sign, but he would always first put her into some discourse of state, that she might the less mind the bills.

The like surprise may be moving things when the party is in haste and cannot stay to consider advisedly of that is moved.

If a man would cross a business that he doubts some other would handsomely and effectually move, let him pretend to wish it took himself up, breeds a greater appetite in him

一樣，我們不妨在這裡把他們的貨色列舉一番。

與人談話的時候目視對方是狡猾術的一種，像耶穌會徒所受訓導的要求那樣，因爲不少聰明人的隱秘心情總難免透過面部表情而有所顯現。這樣做的時候，有時又要收斂眼神，表現出謙卑恭順。耶穌會徒也是這樣做的。

當你有急事需要及時辦理的時候，要用別的交談取悅對方，使他不會過於清醒而反對你的要求，這是另一種狹義的狡猾術。據我所知，有一位負責議事和秘書工作的官員，當他請求伊麗莎白女王批準文件的時候，每一次都是先談一些有關產業等等的其他事務，借以轉移女王的注意力，使她對她要簽署的文件無心留意。

類似的出奇制勝的舉動，就是在對方處在急促情況下，無暇仔細考慮的時候提出某件事，使他作出倉猝的答覆。

假如一個人要阻撓一件可能由別人提出更有效的事情，最好由他自己提出來做，假裝深表贊同

with whom you confer, to know more.

And because it works better when anything seems to be gotten from you by question than if you offer it of yourself, you may lay a bait for a question by showing another visage and countenance than you are wont; to the end to give occasion for the party to ask what the matter is of the change. As Nehemias did: and I had not before that time been sad before the king.

In things that are tender and unpleasing, it is good to break the ice by some whose words are of less weight, and to reserve the more weighty voice to come in as by chance, so that he may be asked the question upon the other's speech. As Narcissus did, in relating to Claudius the marriage of Messalina and Silius. In things that a man would not be seen in himself, it is a point of cunning to borrow the name of the world; as to say, The world says, or, There is a speech abroad.

I knew one that, when he wrote a letter, he would put that which was most material in the postscript, as if it had been a by-matter.

I knew another that, when he came to have speech, he would pass over that theat he in-

的樣子。這種做法足以激發別人更爲濃厚的興趣，從而更想知道你要說的事情。

由於被別人問出來的話往往比自己主動說出來的話更有作用，所以，人們盡可以設置引人發問的釣餌，裝出一副和往常不同的臉色，使人感到詫異而提出問題，就像尼希米（在波斯王面前）所做的那樣：“在那以前我從來在國王面前沒有過愁苦。”

在一些難以對付和不愉快的事情上，最好是讓說話不佔份量的人先開口，然後自己裝作偶然插嘴的樣子，讓人家就剛才提到的事情發問，順著說出頗有份量的話來。例如：羅馬帝國時代的官員西撒期要向皇帝克勞底亞斯報告皇后梅沙利娜和美少年西利亞斯的結婚事件時，就是這樣做的。

在某些事情上如果某個人不願意做出頭露面的事，一種狡猾的作法就是借他人的名義，如說“人家這麼說⋯⋯”，“外面有人傳說⋯⋯”，等等。

我認識一位先生，在他寫信的時候，總是把最想託人辦的要事寫在附言裡面，似乎那只是附帶一提的事。

我還認識一位先生，在他說話的時候，總是把

tended most, and go forth, and come back a-
gain and speak of it as of a thing that he had almost forgot.

Some procure themselves to be surprised at
such times as it is like the party that they work
upon will suddenly come upon them, and to be
found with a letter in their hand, or doing somewhat which they are not accustomed; to the end
they may be questioned about those things which
of themselves they are desirous to utter.

It is a point of cunning to let fall those
words in a man's own name, which he would
have another man learn and use, and there upon
take advantage. I knew two that were competi-
tors for the secretary's place in Queen Elizabeth's time, and yet kept good terms between
themselves, and would confer one with another
upon the business; and the one of them said
that to be a secretary in the declination of a
monarchy was a ticklish thing, and that he did
not affect it. The other straight caught up those
words and discoursed with divers of his friends
that he had no reason to desire to be secretary in
the declination of a monarchy. The first man
took hold of it and found means it was told the

他最想說的事情先略過去往下說著說著再轉回來，說出最想說的事情，好像這是件他幾乎忘了的事一樣。

有些人算計對方可能出現的時刻，而在碰見對方時故作大吃一驚，並且故意拿著一封信或是做些反常的事情，目的是讓對方主動發問，這樣他就可以把難於直接吐口而出的事說出來。

還有一種狡猾術，就是自己說出某種話來，好讓別人學會和用上，然後從中漁利。我知道有兩個人，他們在伊麗莎白女王在位的時代競爭大臣的職位，然而兩人表面上相處得不錯，遇事互相商議。其中的一位說，在王權衰落的時代當大臣是件不容易的事，所以他並不想當。另一位立刻學得這句話，並且在朋友們當中談論開來。那一個人卻抓住了這句話，設法傳到女王耳邊。女王聽

Queen; who, hearing of a declination of a monarchy, took it so ill as she would never after hear of the other's suit.

There is a cunning, which we in England call the turning of the cake in the pan which is, when that which a man says to another, he lays it as if another had said it to him. And to say truth, it is not easy, when such a matter passed between two, to make it appear from which of them it first moved and began.

It is a way that some men have, to glance and dart at others by justifying themselves by negatives, as to say, This I do not; as Tigellinus did towards Burrhus, he said he did not have irreconcilable aims.

Some have in readiness so many tales and stories, as there is nothing they would insinuate but they can wrap it into a tale, which serves both to keep themselves more in guard and to make others carry it with more pleasure.

It is a good point of cunning for a man to shape the answer he would have, in his own words and propositions, for it makes the other party stick the less. It is strange how long some men will lie in wait to speak somewhat they de-

說有人散佈"衰落"的論調，大爲不悅，果然，就不提拔任用那人了。

還有一種在英國叫做"鍋裡翻餅"的狡猾，就是把自己對別人說的話反咬成別人說自己的話。確切地說，要是這種事只發生在兩人之間，而沒有第三者作證，要想弄清楚就有些人有這樣一種法子，就是用否認自己服這種事的，比如說他們會有所示意地說："我是不是這種事的"，意外之意只有對方才會服。當年梯蓋利納斯（羅馬帝國時代的奸臣）對於布拉斯大林（皇帝的老師）就是這樣服的。

有的人常常搜集許多故事。他們想要暗示的事情每每包含在他們講的故事裡面。用這種辦法即可以保護自己，又可以使別人樂於接受自己的觀點。

先用自己的話把想要得到的回答歸納勾畫一番，這不會使對方感到爲難，可以說是一種高明的狡猾。

有些人出奇地在說出眞人話以前，特別善於

sire to say, and how far about they will fetch, and how many other matters they will beat over to come near it. It is a thing of great patience, but yet of much use. A sudden, bold, and unexpected question does many times surprise man, and lay him open. Like to him, that having changed his name, and walking in Paul's, another suddenly came behind him and called him by his true name, whereat straight ways he looked back.

But these small wares and petty points of cunning are infinite, and it were a good deed to make a list of them, for that nothing does more hurt in a state than that cunning men pass for wise.

But certainly some there are that know the resorts and falls of business, that cannot sink into the main of it; like a house that has convenient stairs and entries but never a fair room. Therefore you shall see them find out pretty looses in the conclusion, but are no ways able to examine or debate matters. And yet commonly they take advantage of their in ability and would be thought wits of direction. Putting tricks upon the abusing of others, and (as we now say) put-

耐心伺機等待，善於扯得很遠，多兜圈子，這樣做
當然需要耐心，但是用處也在其中。

一個突如其來，出其不意的問題，常常能使人
大吃一驚，從而披露其心中的隱密。這就像有人
改了名字在聖德堡羅大教堂附近走，身後突然有
人喊他的名字，他必然回頭去看看那樣。

狡猾者的貨色可以說是應有盡有，不勝枚舉。
但是把它們列舉一番也是一件好事，因爲再也沒
有比狡猾冒充聰明對國家更爲有害的了。

但人間確實有那麼一些人，他們辦起事情來
只懂得手段和結局，而不能深入掌握事物的本質。
這就好比一所房子，雖有方便的樓梯和門戶，卻無
像樣的房間。他們會在得出結論時鑽空子，找突
破口，完全不能審察和探究事理，而他們卻反而用
其所短，鑽營有術，投機取巧，彷彿成了工作的決
策人。這些人靠的是欺騙他人，或者，按照我們現

ting tricks upon them, than upon soundness of their own proceedings. But Solomon says the wise man pays attentions to the steps he is taking the fool turns aside to the snares.

在的說法，是在別人身上耍花招手段，而不是堅實可靠地盡心辦事。對此，所羅門早已說過：「智者自慎其身，愚者轉而欺騙他人。」

⬛欣賞⬛

培根的這篇散文主題在於從言談、心態解剖狡猾，把狡猾的技倆分析得入木三分。他首先認定狡猾是陰險邪惡，狡猾並非真正的才幹，進而從理性和感性兩個反面揭露了狡猾者的病態心理和嘴臉。這篇散文還反映了培根對社會的見識之深，對人與人所表現出的敏銳觀察能力。在藝術表現上，本文最突出的特點是分析細膩，理氣條貫，用詞精鍊，得當，不禁使我們聯想起「言而不當，知也；默而當，亦知也」(荀子)的境界。

31.Of Adversity

Francis Bacon

It was a high speech of Seneca (after the manner of the Stoics), that the good things which belong to prosperity are to be wished, but the good things that belong to adversity are to be admired. Certainly if miracles are the command over nature, they appear most in adversity. It is yet a higher speech of his than the other (much too high for a heathen): It is true greatness to have in one the frailty of a man and the security of a god. This would have done better in poesy, where transcendencies are more allowed. And the poets indeed have been busy with it, for it is in effect the thing which is figured in that strange fiction of the ancient poets, which seems not to be without mystery; nay, and to have some approach to the state of a Christian: that Hercules, when he went to unbind Prometheus (by whom human nature is represented), sailed the length of the great ocean in an earthen pot or pitcher; lively describing Christian resolution, that sails in the frail bark of the flesh thorough the waves of the world. But to speak in a mean.

31．論　逆　境

弗朗西斯·培根

　　塞內加按斯多噶派學者發表了這樣一句高明的話：“順境帶來的美好事物值得企望，而逆境帶來的美好事物卻應當讚美。”誠然，若奇蹟是指對自然的話，那麼奇蹟大多出現在逆境之中。塞內加還說了一句話（此話出自一位多神教信仰者之口，眞是高明之至）：“集脆弱和神明的安穩與一身，這才是眞正的偉大。”這種話要是在詩歌裡，其效果會更佳。因爲詩歌可以任意選用超自然東西，而歷來詩人們也都對此表現作了孜孜不倦的追求。事實上，古代詩人們所敍述的那個超自然的故事，就表達了這句話的含意，故事本身似乎不無玄機妙意。不僅如此，故事所敍還有些類似基督徒的情形：據說赫拉克勒斯前去解救（象徵人性的）普羅米修斯的時候，是乘坐瓦盆或瓦罐駛過汪洋大海的。因此，這個故事生動地描述了基督徒的決心：“駕馭自己血肉之軀的脆弱小船，駛過人世海洋的波濤”。平心而論，順境時的美德是節制

The virtue of prosperity is temperance; the virtue of adversity is fortitude, which in morals is the more heroical virtue. Prosperity is the blessing of the Old Testament; adversity is the blessing of the New, which carries the greater benediction and the clearer revelation of God's favour. Yet even in the Old Testament, if you listen to David's harp, you shall hear as many hearse-like airs as carols; and the pencil of the Holy Ghist has labored more in describing the afflictions of Job than the felicities of Solomon. Prosperity is not without many fears and distastes, and adversity is not without comforts and hopes. We see in needleworks and embroideries, it is more pleasing to have a lively work upon a sad and solemn ground, than to have a dark and melancholy work upon a lightsome ground: judge therefore of the pleasure of the heart by the pleasure of the eye. Certainly virtue is like precious odor, most fragrant when they are incensed or crushed; for prosperity does best discover, but adversity does best discover virtue.

，逆境時的美德是堅忍，而就道德情操而言，後者是更具英雄氣概的美德。《舊約》所賜給的祝福是順境，《新約》所賜給的祝福是逆境，後者帶來更大的福祉，也更明顯地表現了上帝的恩惠。即便在《舊約》裡，人們如果諦聽大衛的琴聲，會聽到頌歌，必將聽到哀吟。而且，聖靈的筆對於約伯苦難的描寫，其著力用心之處，勝過了對所羅門幸福的敘述。順境並非沒有許多恐懼和煩惱；逆境也不是沒有種種慰藉和希望。我們觀看刺繡織品時對於背面底紋上繡出的鮮麗圖案，比對明亮背景上繡出的幽暗陰鬱圖案，感到更加賞心悅目。眼睛也如此，心靈就更可想而知了。美德確實猶如名貴香料，一旦焚燒或者碾壓，便芳香四溢；猶如順境最能顯露惡行；逆境最能顯示美德。

欣賞

　　艱苦的環境就是逆境，而在逆境中最能鍛鍊人，培養人和造就人。“逆境常使人難堪；然而即使在人群中找出一百個能忍受逆境的人，也未必找得到一個能正確對待順境的人。”(卡萊爾)培根大發感慨地認為，“順境帶來的美好事物值得企盼，但逆境帶來的美好事物也應當讚美。”“美德確實猶如名貴的香料，一旦焚燒或者碾壓，便芳香四溢；猶如順境最能顯露惡行；逆境最能顯示美德。”如此格言警句，莫不讓讀者心動神怡。

32. Of Travel

Francis Bacon

Travel in the younger sort is a part of education; in the elder, a part of experience. He that travels into a country before he has some entrance into the language, goes to school and not to travel. That young men travel under some tutor or grave servant, I allow well; so that he is such a one that has the language and has been in the country before, whereby he may be able to tell them what acquaintances they are to seek, what learning the place yields. For else young men shall go hooded, and look abroad little. It is a strange thing that in sea voyages, where there is nothing to be seen but sky and sea, men should make diaries; but in land-travel, wherein so much is to be observed, for the most part they omit it; as if chance were fitter to be regbettered than observation. Let diaries therefore be brought in use. The things to be seen and observed are: the courts of princes, specially when they give audience to ambassadors; the courts of justice, while they sit and hear causes, and so of consistories and ecclesi-

32. 論　　旅

弗朗西斯·培根

　　對年青人來說，旅遊是教育的一部分，而對長者來說，旅遊則是其經歷的一部分。一個人到他國旅遊，如果未能預先掌握一點該國的語言，則可以說是去學習而不是旅遊。年輕人在一位嚮導或一位可靠的僕從的帶領下去旅遊，我以爲是比較可取的；這位嚮導或僕從只要掌握該國語言並在以前到過那個國家就可以了，這樣他就可以告訴他在所去的國家中什麼東西值得去看，什麼人值得去結識，在那裡可以看到什麼樣的活動或風俗習慣；否則，年輕人就像雙眼被矇去旅遊，所能看到的域外情景非常少。在海上旅遊，所能見到的唯有天空和大海，人們往往記日記；而在陸上旅遊，所能看到的東西比比皆是，而旅行者在大多數情況下卻忽略了寫日記，好像偶然之所見比細細觀察到的東西更值得記錄下來似的，這實在令人驚訝。無論去何處旅遊，日記是應該記的。旅遊中應該瀏覽和考察的事物有：君王的宮廷，尤其是正在接見使節的宮廷；法庭，尤其是正在審案的法庭；此外，還有敎會會議、敎堂和寺院，以及那兒遺

astic; the churches and monasteries, with the monuments which are therein extant; the walls and fortifications of cities and towns, and so the havens and harbours; in the universities; libraries; colleges, disputations, and lectures, where any are; shipping and navies; houses and gardens of state and pleasure near great cities; houses and gardens of state and pleasure near great cities; armories; arsenals; magazines; exchanges; warehouses; exercises of horsemanship, fencing, training of soldiers, and the like; comedies, such whereunto the istter sort of persons do resort; treasuries of jewels and robes; cabinets and rarities; and, to conclude, whatsoever is memorable in the places where they go. After all which the tutors or servants ought to make diligent inquiry. As for triumphs, masques, feasts, weddings, funerals, capital executions, and such shows, men need not to be put in mind of them; yet are they not to be neglected. If you will have a young man to put his travel into a little room, and in short time to gather much, this you must do. First, as was said, he must have some entrance into the language before he goes. Then he must have such a servant or tutor as knows the country, as was likewise said. Let him carry with him also some

存至今的紀念物；城鎮的牆垣和堡壘；還有商埠與港灣，大學，圖書館、學院，辯論會和演講會（如果有的話）；航運和海軍；靠近大都市的宏偉而賞心悅耳的房屋和花園；軍械庫，兵工廠、倉庫、交易所，聖餐布盒，貨棧，馬術練習，擊劍，軍訓，以及諸如此類的事物：上流人士經常光顧的戲院；盛放珍珠袍服的寶庫；櫥櫃和珍奇之物。概而言之，他們所去的地方中那些值得留念的東西，向導或者僕從終歸對此應作出認真的調查。至於凱旋式、假面劇、宴席、婚葬禮、處決人之類的活動場面，人們不應牢記在心，不過也應該略而不計。如果你想讓一個年輕人到一個不大的地區旅行，並要在短短的時間裡得到許多情況，你就必須做到以下幾點：如上所述，首先，他在動身之前對這個地區的語言有一定的掌握。其次，他必須有一位了解該地區情況的僕從或嚮導。他還應該隨身帶上一些

card or book describing the country where he travells, which will be a good key to his inquiry. Let him keep also a diary. Let him not stay long in one city or town; more or less as the place deserves, but not long: nay, when he stays in one city or town, let him change his lodging from one end and part of the town to another, which is a great adamant of acquaintance. Let him sequester himself from the company of his countrymen, and diet in such places where there is good company of the nation where he travells. Let him upon his removes from one place to another procure recommendation to some person of quality residing in the place whither he removes, that he may use his favour in those things he desires to see or know. Thus he may abridge his travel with much profit. As for the acquaintance which is to be sought in travel, that which is most of all profitable is acquaintance with the secretaries and employed men of ambassadors, for so in travelling in one country he shall suck the experience of many. Let him also see and visit eminent persons in all kinds which are of great name abroad, that he may be able to tell how the life agrees with the fame. For quarrels, they are with care and discretion to be avoided. They are commonly for

描述他要旅遊的國家或地區的地圖或書籍,這對他的解答會起很好的引導作用。他還應當記日記。他在一個城市中不應待太長時間,具體時間視該地的價值而定,但不可過長;不僅如此,在一個城市或小鎮作停留時,他應該變換旅店,從城市的一端和一區搬遷到另一端和另一區,這是他結交熟人所必須做的一步。他應該與他的同胞分開,不要與他們待在一起,應在可以遇見旅遊國家的上層人士的地方就餐;他在從一個地方遷往另一處時,應該設法得到別人的引薦,去拜訪居住在他所遷居之處的上流人士,這樣就可借助於他去觀覽或了解他想知道的事情;這樣,他就既可縮短行期,又有很多收穫。至於在旅遊中應當去結識的那些人,當然是結識那些最有用的人,結識大使的秘書或者雇員;這樣一來他在一個國家旅行時就可獲得許多人的經驗。他還應當去拜訪各行各業的傑出人物,目的是他可以藉此了解其聲譽與其實際情況;對於爭吵應當小心謹慎地避免,這些

mistresses, healths, place, and words. And let a man beware how he keeps company with choleric and quarrelsome persons, or they will engage him into their own quarrels. When a traveller returneth home, let him not leave the countries where he has travelled altogether behind him, but maintain a corespondence by letters with those of his acquaintance which are of most worth. And let his travel appear rather in his discourse than in his apparel or gesture; and in his discourse, let him be rather advised in his answers than forwards to tell stories; and let it appear that he does not change his country manners for those of foreign parts, but only prick in some flowers of that he has learned abroad into the customs of his own country.

爭吵的原因通常在於女人、健康、地位或言詞帶刺
所致；一個人應該認識到，與急躁的、愛爭鬥好勝
的人爲伍是多麼地不好，因爲他們會使他捲入本
屬他們自身的爭鬥中去。回國後，不可把所旅遊
的國家忘得一乾二淨，而應與他所結交的最有價
值的異國朋友保持通信聯繫。他的旅遊應體現在
他與別人的談話中，而不應體現在服飾或行爲舉
止姿態上。在談話中，他應該在深思熟慮後再回
答別人的問題，而不是爭先恐後口若懸河地述說
自己的經歷；他應該讓人看到他沒有習得外國人
的習慣；而只是把他從國外學到的某些東西融入
本國習俗之中罷了。

欣賞

　　哈茲里特說：“世上最大的樂事是旅行。”之所以
“樂”，正如培根所說，旅行是教育和經歷的組成部分。是
知識的積累，是人生的閱歷。旅行即可“乘春山暖日和
風”，又可看“荷香銷晚夏，菊花入新秋”(唐．駱賓王)在培
根看來，旅行要有嚮導或僕人，有所要旅遊國家的文化，
還要記日記，結識名流，保持聯繫。我們現代人，有了現
代化的交通工具，在每每緊張的工作生活之餘，應當去領
略大千世界一番，旣調整自己又充實自己，何樂而不爲？
“春色滿園花勝錦，黃鶯只揀好枝啼。”

33. Of Discourse

Francis Bacon

Some in their discourse desire rather commendation of wit, in being able to hold all arguments, than of judgement, in discerning what is
true; as if it were a praise to know what might
be said, and not what should be thought. Some
have certain commonplaces and themes wherein
they are good, and what variety; which kind of
poverty is for the most part tedious, and when it
is once perceived, ridiculous. The honourablest
part of talk is to give the occasion, and again to
moderate and pass to somewhat else, for then a
man leads the dance. It is good, in discourse
and speech of conversation, to vary and inter-
mingle speech of the present occasion with arguments, tales with earnest; for it is a dull thing to
tire, and as we say now, to jade anything too
far. As for jest, there is certain things which
ought to be privileged from it; namely, reli-
gion, matters of state, great persons, any man'
s present business of importance, and any case
that deserves pity. Yet there is some that think

33. 論 談 吐

弗朗西斯·培根

　　有些人在談論中喜歡以能言善辯博得機智多才的美稱,而不喜歡以遠見卓識得到辨明眞理的讚美,彷彿談話方式比談話內容更值得稱道。有些人擅長於老生常談,人云亦云,缺乏新意變化,其貧乏令人生厭,一旦被人覺察出來,又顯得十分可笑。最可貴的談吐在於能夠引來話題,然後把話題轉移到其他話頭上去。能夠如此善言的人,就可以比作是社交場合中獨領風騷了。精彩的言談要富於變化,要做到即席講話時而辯論,時而夾敍夾議,既要提出問題又抒發已見。如果對一個話題大談特談,喋喋不休,就會使人厭煩。至於詼諧,有些事情可以詼諧一番。有些事情則應當避免,例如宗敎、國事、偉人、人們正在做的緊要事以及值得憐憫的事情,觸及人間痛處的事等等,是不應當任意詼諧打趣的。在有些人看來,如果說話

their wits have been asleep, except they dart out somewhat that is piquant and to the quick. That is a vein which would be bridled. Spare the whip, boy, and pull harder on the reins.

And generally, men ought to find the difference betweeen saltness and bitterness. Certainly he that has a satirical vein, as he makes others afraid of his wit, so he had need be afraid of others' memory. He that questions much shall learn much and content much, but especially if he applies his questions to the skill of the persons whom he asks; for he shall give them occasion to please themselves in speaking, and himself shall continually gather knowledge. But let his questions not be troublesome, for that is fit for a poser. And let him be sure to leave other men their turns to speak. Nay, if there is any that would reign and take up all the time, let him find means to take them off and to bring others on, as musicians use to do with those that dance too long galliards. If you dissemble sometimes your knowledge of that you are thought to know, you shall be thought another time to know that you know not. Speech of a man's self ought to be seldom and well cho-

不鋒芒畢露，好像自己不這樣就難以顯示自己的
聰明似的。這種習慣性應加以克制。古人關於騎
術所說的話說得好———"少使刺棒，勒緊繮繩"。

　　一般地說，人們都懂得酸甜苦辣。那些語言
刻薄的人，往往會使人害怕他的尖刻，也必然被人
計較。好問的人學得的東西也多，而且會博得別
人的歡心；特別是所問的內容如果合適，被問者樂
於發表簡潔的專長，因為他會給他提供發表自己
見解的機會，他自己也可從中獲得更多的知識。
不過，所提問題不要惹人生厭，提問不要好像是在
審訊人家，那就不好了。在談話時候，還應注意讓
人家有說話的機會。如果有人獨佔發言的時間，
那就最好設法把他打斷，讓別人有發言的機會，就
像舞壇的樂師們看到跳起"雙人歡樂舞"，跳起來
沒完沒了時候，所設法制止的那樣。假如有的時
候你遇事懂裝不懂，默不作聲的時候，那麼以後遇
到你真不懂的話題，人們也可能認為你是懂的。
對於關係到自身的話，以少說為佳，要講也應當出

sen. I knew one was wont to say in scorn, He
needs be a wise man, he speaks so much of
himself. And there is but one case wherein a
man may commend himself with good grace, and
that is in commending virtue in another, especially if it is such a virtue whereunto he pre-
tends. Speech of touch towards others should be
sparingly used, for discourse ought to be as a
field, without coming home to any man. I knew
two noblemen, of the west part of England,
whereof the one was given to scoff, but kept ever royal cheer in his house; the other would ask
of those that had been at the other's table, Tell
truly, was there never a flout or dry blow given?
To which the guest would answer, such and
such a thing passed. The lord would say, I
thought he would make a good dinner. Discretion of speech is more than eloquence, and to
speak agreeably to him with whom we deal is
more than to speak in good words or in good order. A good continued speech, without a good
speech of interlocution, shows slowness; and a
good reply or second speech, without a good
settled speech, shows shallowness and weakness. As we see in beasts, that those that are

言謹愼。我認識一個人，他經常用下面的話諷刺
他瞧不起的人：「他眞是個聰明人，對於自己大談
特論！」需知，稱道自己的唯一得體的方式，是通過
讚揚他人的長處適當襯托自己的長處；尤其是長
處類似的時候，這樣做更爲相宜。另外，有損於他
人的話應當少說，因爲談論應當像一片田野寬闊，
人人可在其中散心漫步，而不應當成爲一條直通
他人家門的單行道，只求合乎某一個人的意旨。
我認識兩位英國西部的貴族，其中的一位總愛貶
損別人，可又經常大辦筵席招待賓客；另一位則常
常詢問那些曾經赴他宴的客人。實話實說，「宴席
上難道沒有人受到他的嘲弄嗎？」對此客人回憶在
酒席上談論起諸如這樣那樣的事情，這位貴族就
說：「我早就料到他一定會把一桌好酒席弄糟的。」
應該懂得，謹愼的言辭勝過雄辯；對話適時的言談
比措辭優美、條理分明甚至效果更佳。滔滔不絕
的演說而不善於設問作答的言談，難免遲鈍而缺
乏生動；善於應答而不擅長長篇大論的言談，則又
會顯得淺薄無力。這就好比動物界的情況那樣，

weakest in the course are yet nimblest in the turn, as it is betwixt the greyhound and the hare. To use too many circumstances ere one comes to the matter is wearisome; to use none at all is blunt.

最不善於向前跑的動物往往是轉身最爲靈活而敏
捷的動物，如獵犬和野兔之間就有這種差別。說
話的時候，在涉及正題以前枝枝節節的話太多，就
會使人厭煩；而沒有一點枝節的話，則未免過於率
直和生硬了。

欣賞

　　莎士比亞說：“舌頭往往是敗事的禍根。不說什麼，
不做什麼，不知道什麼，也就沒有什麼可以使你受用不了
了。”舌頭是你的武器，但使用不當也會成爲你的禍因。
培根不僅精通於爲人處世的人生哲學，而且對生活的觀
察也細緻入微，他所論的談話藝術是千古經論。他推心
置腹告誡人們言談的藝術，尤以結尾最爲精彩。通篇雖
無宏論，但正是“忠言不在多言”“妙論精言，不以多爲
貴。”朋友，請記住，“聆聽能獲得智慧，談話會產生後悔。”
“會聆聽的年輕人往往受人重視和重用。
　　讀了這篇散文，我們不能不提它突出的表現手法。
好的散文離不開深厚的思想內涵，立意清新深遠，才能對
人有啓發，而散文的“意”是思想的內涵，決非乾巴巴的
“說教”。它只有融會於作者的感情分子，才能閃爍出清
澈、理智的光輝。本文“情理”有機結合，所讀之處，無不
引起共鳴，觸發思考，得到啓迪。這就是這篇散文突出的
表現藝術。

34. Of Expense

Francis Bacon

Riches are for spending; and spending for honour and good actions. Therefore extraordinary expense must be limited by the worth of the occasion, for voluntary undoing may be as well for a man's country as for the kingdom of heaven. But ordinary expense ought to be limited by a man's estate, and governed with such regard, as it is within his means, and not subject to deceit and abuse of servants, and ordered to the best show, that the bills may be less than the estimation abroad. Certainly if a man will keep but of even hand, his ordinary expenses ought to be but to the half of his receipts; and if he thinks to wax rich, but to the third part. It is no baseness for the greatest to descend and look into their own estate. Some forbear it, not upon negligence alone, but doubting to bring themselves into melancholy, in respecholy, in respects they shall find it broken. But wounds cannot be cured without searching. He that cannot look into his own estate at all, had need

34. 論　消　費

弗朗西斯·培根

　　財富是用來消費的，而消費應以榮譽和行善爲目的。因此特殊的消費由消費的價值作用來決定。爲了國家，爲了天國，人們樂意奉獻一切，但是一般的消費則應量力而行。要學會理財，量入爲出，不受僕從的欺騙和愚弄。實際支出低於自己的估計時，應當顯得慷慨大方。當然，假若一個人想使自己量入爲出，就應把日常消費控制在收入的半數之內，假如還想富裕起來，那麼他的支出只能是收入的三分之一。即使你是個偉人，檢查自己的財產並無損於你的身份。但有些人不擅長於檢查自己的財產，原因不僅是疏忽大意，也是怕因檢查而發現自己破產了，反而憂心忡忡。但是有了傷痛而沒檢查出來怎麼能治好呢？完全不會檢查自己財產的人，必須用人得當，還要經常更換

both choose well those whom he employs, and change them often; for new are more timorous and less subtle. He that can look into his estate but seldom, it is hoveth him to turn all to certainties. A man had need, if he is plentiful in some kind of expense, to be as saving again in some other. As, if he is plentiful in diet, to be saving in apparel; if he is plentiful in the hall, to be saving in the stable; and the like. For he that is plentiful in expenses of all kinds will hardly be preserved from decay. In clearing of a man's estate, he may as well hurt himself in being too sudden, as in letting it run on too long. For hasty selling is commonly as disadvantageable as interest.

；因爲新手比較膽小，計謀也少。不能常常檢查財產的人，應對自己的收支做到大體胸中有數。

　　當然，即使有資產也不能忽視一些小事。通常，與其低聲下氣以求小恩小惠，倒不如節省那些不明不白的花費。如果要負擔一筆從一開始就要注意長期支付下去的花費，務必謹慎從事，不可貿然行事。但對於一旦支出而又下不爲例的開支，不妨大方些。

欣賞

　　培根論及經濟方面的散文可以說有"論財富""論消費""論放債"三部曲。本文只是其名篇之一。這三部曲中大都涉及倫理哲學與倫理道德和財富之間的關係。培根生長在英國資本主義經濟萌芽發展時期，就當時英國經濟狀況來說，他能提出這樣的觀點是難能可貴的。在他看來財富的本能就是消費。尤其是對於個人來說，既要時常檢查自己的財富，又要能量入爲出。他提出支出應佔收入的二分之一或三分之一的比例，對於一次性消費稍可放鬆，但對於經常性消費務必謹慎從嚴，"世人用才，貴明義理"（唐彪）。說到理財，他認爲要用人得當，必要時經常性的換財務管理，這有意於財務管理。這些都是經濟管理中的經典之言。經典是永恆的。這些觀點距今幾千年，其意義還是如此。

　　散文的表現手法情感眞摯，意蘊具體，敍事夾議，雖無美麗的詞語，但剖析淋灕盡致。

35.Of Riches

Francis Bacon

I cannot call riches better than the baggage of virtue. The Roman word is better, impediments for as the baggage is to an army, so is riches to virtue. It cannot be spared nor left behind, but it hinders the march; yea, and the care of it sometime loses or disturbs the victory. Of great riches there is no real use, except it is in the distribution; the rest is but conceit. Solomon, Where much is, there are many to consume it; and what has the owner but the sight of it with his eyes? The personal fruition in any man cannot reach to feel great riches: there is a custody of them, or a power of dole and donation of them, or a fame of them; but no solid use to the owner. Do you not see what feigned prices are set upon little stones and rarities, and what works of ostentation are undertaken, because there might seem to be some use of great riches? But then you will say, they may be of use to buy men out of dangers or troubles. As Solonon says, Riches as a stronghold in the

35. 論　財　富

弗朗西斯·培根

　　在我看來，財富可以稱爲德行的行囊（bag-gage）最好不過。羅馬語中的 impedimenta 一詞（軍需輜重、行李，障礙物）則更確切一些，財富之於德行正如軍需輜重於軍隊。軍須輜重是不可能沒有的或缺的，也不能抛在後面，雖然它同時又是一種累贅，會妨礙行軍；有時由於顧慮輜重而貽誤戰機，導致戰場失利。巨大的財富除了可以用來施捨以外，並沒有什麼眞正的用處，不過是一種自我表現滿足和虛榮而已。所以，所羅門說：“財富越多，享用的人應愈多；而它的主人除了用來一飽眼福以外，又能享用多少呢？”一個人儘管有巨大的財富，其享用畢竟是有限的；他可以保管這些財富，也可以用於施捨或捐贈，或者因爲巨富而出名，但對他本人來說，這些財富並無實際的用處。君不見，有人竟然不惜錢財去買一塊漫天要價的石頭或是什麼希罕的東西嗎？君不見，有人爲了讓巨大的財富似乎能派上用場，竟攬了不少出風頭虛假頭銜嗎？也許有人會說，財富可以打通關卡，使人脫離危險或擺脫困境。所羅門曾說：“在富人的想像中，財富就像是一座堡壘。”這話倒是

imagination of the rich man. But this is excellently expressed, that it is in imagination, and not always in fact. For certainly great riches have sold more men than they have bought out. Seek not proud riches, but such as thou mayest get justly, use soberly, distribute cheerfully, and leave contentedly. Yet have no abstract nor friarly contempt of them. But distinguish, as Cicero says well of Rabirius Postumus: In his keenness to increase his wealth it was apparent that he was not seeking a prey for avarice to feed upon, but an instrument for good to work with. Hearken also to Solomon, and beware of hasty gathering of riches: He who makes haste to be rich shall not be innocent. The poets feign that when Plutus (which is riches) is sent from Jupiter, he limps and goes slowly, but when he is sent from Pluto, he runs and is swift of foot: Meaning, that riches gotten by good means and just labour pace slowly, but when they come by the death of others (as by the course of inheritance, testaments, and the like), they come tumbling upon a man. But it might be applied likewise to Pluto, taking him for the devil. For when riches come from the devil (as by fraud

說得很妙。的確,只是在想像中,財富才是如此,而事實上並不盡然,因為多財招致災禍的人往往比靠財富脫險的人還要多。對於財富的追求,不要求去追求炫耀的目的。要用正當的手段去獲取財富,合理愼重地使用財富,愉快地救濟別人或者欣慰地將財產留給別人。當然,也不要那麼超脫,像苦行僧一樣對財富採取聽其自然的態度。應當有所不同,就像西塞羅關於拉瑞亞斯·波斯丟瑪斯案情所說的話那樣,"追求財富,不是為了滿足貪慾,而是為了行善之需的工具。"還應當聽取所羅門的告誡,不要急於聚斂錢財以圖致富,"急於發財致富,"難免墜入不明不白的不義之途。

古代的詩人們託辭說,財神普盧塔斯在接受天神朱庇特的派遣時,行動遲緩,步履蹣跚;但是接受冥王普路托的派遣時,卻敏捷迅速,跑得飛快。這意味著採用善良的方法和依靠正當的勞動,財富是來得慢的;而由於別人的死亡而得來的財富(通過繼承或遺囑等等),則是突然而來的。如果把故事中的普路托當作魔鬼看待,其寓意也能成立,因為靠魔鬼得來的財富(即用欺詐、欺壓

and oppression and unjust means), they come upon speed. The ways to enrich are many, and most of them foul. Parsidimony is one of the best, and yet is not innocent, for it withholdeth men from works of liberality and charity. The improvement of the ground is the most natural obtaining of riches, for it is our great mother's blessing the earth's; but it is slow. And yet where men of great wealth do stoop to husbandry, it multiplies riches exceedingly. I knew a nobleman in England, that had the greatest audits of any man in my time: a great grazier, a great sheep-master, a great timber-man, a great collier, a great corn-master, a great lead-man, and so of iron, and a number of the like points of husbandry: so as the earth seemed a sea to him, in respect of the perpetual importation. It was truly observed by one, that himself came very hardly to a little riches, and very easily to great riches. For when a man's stock comes to that, he can expect the prime of markets, and overcome those bargains which for their greatness are few men's money, and be partner in the industries of younger men, he cannot but increase mainly. The gains of ordinary trades and

和其它不正當的手段得到的財富），往往是來得很快的。致富的門道很多，大多數難免有醜惡之嫌。其中，用吝嗇的手段聚財，還可算最好的一種；但也不能算是純潔無疵，因爲吝嗇使人不肯樂善好施。開發土地資源，是最自然的致富之路，因爲土地中的產物是我們偉大的母親——大地——的賜予。然而用這種辦法來發財，速度是很慢的。但是，倘若富有的人願意委身於開發農牧之業，就可能使其財富成倍地迅速增長。我認識一位英國的貴族，他是當今最大的富翁，因爲他是一位大草原主、大牧場主、大農場主、大林場主，也是大的煤礦主、以及許多其他類似產業的主人。對於一位貴族，土地使其財富源源不斷，就像大海一樣永不枯竭。有人認爲，發小財很難，而發大財倒很容易。因爲有錢人資源庫存可以坐待市場旺季的到來，才脫手，這樣可以左右市場，一方面做一般人無力做的買賣，另一方面又能參與較爲年輕人從事的產業活動，其財富肯定是會很快的增長起來的。

通過從事普通的貿易或就業而獲得財富，是

vocations are honest, and furthered by two things chiefly: by diligence, and by a good name for good and fair dealing. But the gains of bargains are of a more doubtful nature, when men shall wait upon others' necessity, broke by servants and instruments to draw them on, put off others cunningly that would be better chapmen, and the like practices, which are crafty adnaught. As for the chopping of bargains, when a man buys not to hold, but to sell over again, that commonly grinds double, both upon the seller and upon the buyer. Sharings do greatly enrich, if the hands be well chosen that are trusted. Usury is the certainest means of gain, though one of the worst, as that whereby a man does eat his bread. In the sweat of another man's bro and besides, does plough upon Sundays. But yet certain though it is, it has flaws, for that the scriveners and brokers do value unsound men to serve their own turn. The fortune in being the first in an invention or in a privilege does cause sometimes a wonderful overgrowth in riches, as it was with the first sugar man in the Canaries. Therefore if a man can play the true logician, to have as well judge-

天經地義的。這種財富的增進主要靠兩方面：一
是勤奮，二是通過公平交易而享有的信譽。有的
靠做生意賺來的錢卻有許許多多的可疑之處，如
乘機抬價，賄賂某人的僕從而做成生意，使別的較
爲公道的商人無從得手等等做法，都是狡詐而卑
劣的。至於那種來回殺價，貪圖便宜，從中投機倒
把而獲利的做法，則是一種雙重的榨取——即要
榨取買方和賣方。入股的生意，如果依托的對象
選擇得當，是很能致富的。放高利貸是一種最有
把握的獲利方法，雖然它是一種最壞的方法。這
種方法是靠別人的血汗來養肥自己，而且可以說
是“在安息日耕作”，有背於天理人情的。這種方
法雖說靠得住，但也有不足之處，因爲中介人會爲
信用不佳的商人誇口稱讚，從中搗鬼而謀取私利。

　　有幸依靠某種發明的優先權或專利權，有時
能夠一下子搖身變富。加那利群島的第一個糖業
專家，就是如此。因此，具有發明創造的才智、又
有判斷力的論理學家，是可以辦許多大事從而發

ment as invention, he may do great matters, especially if the times is fit. He that rests upon gains certain shall hardly grow to great riches, and he that puts all upon adventures does oftentimes break and come to poverty: it is good therefore to guard adventures with certainties that may uphold losses . Monopolies and coemption of wares for re-sale, where they are not restrained, are great means to enrich, especially if the party have intelligence what things are like to come into request, and so store himself beforehand. Riches gotten by service, though it is of the best rise, yet when they are gotten by flattery, feeding humours, and other servile conditions, they may be placed amongst the worst. As for fishing for testaments and executorships (as Tacitus says of Seneca, He seized wills and wardships as with a net. Believe not much them that seems to despise riches, for they despise them that despair of them; and none worse when they come to them. Be not penny-wise; riches have wings, and sometimes they fly away of themselves, sometimes they must be set flying to bring in more. Men leave their riches either to their kindred, or to the

財致富的；如能趕上好的時代，尤其如此。專靠固定收入的人是不易致富的；而把一切財產投入冒險事業的人又往往有可能傾家蕩產。較好的做法是保持固定的收入，作爲冒險事業的後盾，以便屆時在受到損失時能有一定的補償。取得專利，獨家經售某種貨物而不受限制，是很絕妙的致富之術；如果經營者能事先看準某項貨物將有廣大的需求而提前予以購存，就更是如此。

　　通過提供服務而取得財富，誠然是最高尚的；然而，如果這種財富是通過阿諛諂媚及其他卑躬屈節地侍奉某些平庸之輩，或以圖謀別人的遺囑和遺產監護權一類的事情而取得（如塔西陀針對塞內加所說的：“無子女者的遺囑幾乎都被他網羅走了”），則最爲卑劣。不要過於相信那些似乎對財富表示蔑視的人。他們之所以蔑視財富，是由於他們對獲得財富感到絕望；一旦他們發了財，他們的愛財之心並不亞於其他人。不要愛惜小錢。錢財是有翅膀的，有時候它自己會飛去，有時候還必須放它出去飛，以便引來更多的錢財。通常人們或是把錢財留給親屬，或是留給大家；無論留給

public, and moderate portions prosper best in both. A great state left to an heir is as a lure to all the birds of prey round about to seize on him, if he is not the istter stablished in like sacrifices without salt, and but the painted sepulchers of alms, which soon will putrefy and corrupt inwardly. Therefore measure not thine advancements by quantity, but frame them by measure: and defer not charities till death, for certainly if a man weighs it rightly, he that does so is rather liberal of another man's than of his own.

哪一方面，都以份額適量爲佳。給子女留下一份大家業未必是好事。如果子女的年齡和見識不夠成熟的話，這份家業就會像一件誘惑物，誘使各種猛禽到你子女周圍來取寵、呑噬。同樣，那種出於虛榮而贈與的捐款或基金，則好像沒有價值的祭品，不能保持長久；又好像油漆刷過的墳墓，會從內部腐敗起來。由此可見，不可從數量去衡量某人的贈與，要看目的如何和使用是否得當。也不可把用於慈善事業的捐贈推遲到去世以後，因爲，如果稍微思考，他這樣實際上是自己的錢財讓他人去慷慨，而不是他自己。

欣賞

　　本篇散文是培根經濟論說文三部曲中的第一篇，他主要從資本家初期財富積累的來源，論述了發財致富的幾大途徑，進而結合倫理道德，論述了財富的意義。蘊涵著深邃的辯證哲理，眞夠人深思。另一個方面，培根並不反對用正當手段得來的財富，充分肯定了某些生財之道和經營方式。這些觀點有不可忽視的現實意義。

國家圖書館出版品預行編目資料

散文欣賞學英語 / 何高大編著. -- 初版. --
臺北縣五股鄉：萬人，2000 [民89]
　面　；　公分

ISBN 957-8268-87-4 (平裝)

1. 英國語言 - 讀本

805.18　　　　　　　　　　　　　　89009193

散文欣賞學英語

編 著 者／何高大
發 行 者／謝長庚
出 版 者／萬人出版社有限公司
地　　址／台北縣五股工業區五權七路68號3F
電　　話／02-22980501
傳　　眞／02-22980415
郵撥帳號／01194105
２０００年八月初版
特　　價／２００元

內政部登記證局版台業字第1822號
Email:mass@mail.elite.com.tw